SOUTH VILLAGE

SOUTH VILLAGE

ROB HART

The following is a work of fiction. Names, characters, places, events and incidents are either the product of the author's imagination or used in an entirely fictitious manner. Any resemblance to actual persons, living or dead, is entirely coincidental.

Cover and jacket design by 2Faced Design
Interior designed and formatted by E.M. Tippetts Book Designs

ISBN 978-1-943818-17-4
eISBN 978-1-943818-39-6

Library of Congress Control Number: 2015951361

First trade paperback edition October 2016 by Polis Books, LLC
1201 Hudson Street, #211S
Hoboken, NJ 07030

www.PolisBooks.com

POLIS BOOKS

To Amanda

For everything

"We don't live
We just scratch on day to day
With nothing but matchbooks and sarcasm in our pockets
And all we're waiting for is for something worth waiting for."

—from KMFDM's "Dogma"

ONE

I KILLED A GUY.

The woman behind the glass partition is glaring at me like something scraped off a boot and left to rot in the sun. This makes me afraid I actually did just confess to killing someone, out loud. I pause for a moment as if the words are hanging in the air. I wonder if anyone around me is staring.

Because it's true. I did kill a guy. And some days, it buzzes in the back of my throat like I might blurt it out at any moment.

Standing in line at the store: *Debit please, and also I am a murderer.*

Waiting for the bus: *This is taking forever. Just like my eventual damnation.*

Making small talk: *Portland was lovely, except for the homicide, and then fleeing in order to protect the woman I was falling in love with.*

No one is staring. The temperature of the room hasn't changed. Maybe it's my brain messing with me. Something about being here, needling my guilt center.

"Sir."

It was an accident, and a good lawyer could probably argue it was self-defense. Though I'm sure I ruined that by burying the body off a hiking trail in the woods. And justifiable or not, I turned off a light that can't go back on.

Sometimes I wonder if people can see it, just by looking at me. Like those stereogram images—the psychedelic prints where if you stare at them long enough you see a bird or a peace sign floating in 3D. But when you look at me, instead of a bird or a peace sign, you see a dark gash across my soul. Something that oozes hatred and regret.

"Sir!"

I snap back to the gray walls, the worn green carpet. The blue-white hum of the fluorescent lights. The woman behind the glass partition is still peering at me through Coke-bottle glasses mounted to her boxy face, slate hair twisted into small ringlets. The black nametag with white lettering affixed to her lime-green blouse says: Rhonda.

"Sorry," I tell her.

"Forms," Rhonda says, gesturing toward the opening between the bottom of the glass partition and the counter. I slide the bundle of paperwork through. She flips through it, eyes scanning the boxes. "Hmm. Ashley." Rolling the name around her mouth, the way most people do when they first hear it.

"That's me," I tell her. "Modern-day boy named Sue."

"Love that song."

Rhonda smiles at me, her face suddenly smoother around the edges.

We're friends now, it seems.

"Identification, including primary and secondary," she says.

I hand over my driver's license, photocopies of my Social Security card and birth certificate, a credit card, and the Georgia library card I picked up yesterday.

The library card was the clincher. When I left New York nine months ago, I didn't change my legal address. So now that I'm applying for a passport in the state that is not my legal state of residence, I need to provide extra identification. Seems like an easy enough hoop to jump through that I wonder about the point of it.

Rhonda looks up. "Do you have proof of your upcoming trip?"

Next through the opening goes a copy of my plane ticket to Prague for two weeks from now. She looks it over and says, "Make sure you go to the bone church."

"Bone church?"

"Sedlec Ossuary in Kutná Hora. It's beautiful."

"Sure."

I repeat that in my head, try to commit it to memory. Truth is, I have zero plans on sightseeing and only a weak promise of a job, working for a company owned by the family of an old friend. The real reason I'm looking to leave the country is because of the dead guy.

It's not like the cops are hunting for me. I'm not a fugitive. But I'm living on the edge of something sharp and I've always wanted to see more of the world. If there was ever a time to do it, this is it.

I wonder if the Czech Republic extradites to the United States.

That's worth looking into, probably.

Rhonda alternates between clicking on her keyboard and slamming a stamp onto my form, seemingly at random, and with a level of force that makes it seem like she is very angry at the paper.

"I almost forgot," she says. "Photos?"

I forgot about them too, but there they are, resting under my palm. I slide them across without looking at them. I looked, briefly, after they were taken at the drug store down the block. I barely recognize my face, heavy with a bushy beard I grew out after leaving Portland. Because I thought looking different would be a good thing. Like a beard would be a cheap disguise. It certainly makes me less uncomfortable whenever I pass a cop.

Though the real truth of it is, I don't like looking at myself.

At least, it seems, I grow a pretty good beard, even though the fucking thing gets damp and itchy in the humidity.

"You should receive your passport within a few days of your trip," Rhonda says. "They usually show up in seven to eight days. Sometimes six, depends on how busy things are at processing. As for the fee, for the expediting processing and overnight delivery…"

I slide a money order for the exact amount through the opening.

She takes it, nods, and adds it to the stack. After that she gives me back my license, library card, and credit card. She forces out a tired smile. "Have a safe trip, sir. And don't forget about the bone church. Sedlec Ossuary."

"Got it. I won't."

I turn to leave. The room is mostly empty. There are a few benches and only two other people waiting. Standing by the door, arms folded, is a security guard. He wasn't there when I walked in.

Big guy, bald head gleaming in the harsh light, face like he wakes up looking for things to be angry about. We make accidental eye contact, which turns into prolonged eye contact.

At first I think it's just one of those awkward things that happens with strangers, and after a moment we'll look away and the moment will dissipate like smoke. But then I think: Does he recognize me?

Did my name come up in some computer system and the woman rang a silent alarm? Did she give him a hand signal? Is this the moment my life comes crashing down around my shoulders?

The wave hits.

Roaring in my ears, pulling me down into the dark. Filling my eyes and nose and throat, choking me. Panic prods me with a pointed finger. Oxygen stops flowing to my lungs. I will them to start back up, but they're like a dead engine. I'm tumbling in the dark, can't tell up from down.

The guard comes rushing at me.

Sorry, Dad. Sorry, Chell.

I'm dizzy, about to fold to the ground, when the guard grabs me under the arm. He pulls me up and asks, "You okay, kiddo?"

The tumbling stops. The ground stabilizes under me. I look around. At him, and Rhonda, and the people in the waiting room. Everyone staring at me. Everything is suddenly very quiet.

I nod. "Yeah. Just… tired. Sorry."

"You need a hand? Need me to call a cab for you or something?"

I shake my head at him, push away. I stumble outside, pass the elevator bank and crash through the door to the staircase, nearly fall down the three flights. When I get outside I fall to my knees and vomit. I'm not sure what I vomit up since I haven't eaten today.

It's mostly liquid.

My system sufficiently cleared out, I lean back against the brick wall. The morning heat drapes over me like a down blanket. It feels nice, and will for another minute or two, the way it does when you leave a building with robust air conditioning.

I open up my messenger bag and pull out the water bottle wrapped in duct tape. Unscrew the top, wash my mouth out with a little whiskey and spit, take a big gulp. I get a quarter of the bottle down. It's sharp and a little metallic.

After a few seconds I take another sip, feel it wrapping my synapses in gauze.

Well. That went much better than I expected.

TWO

AFTER A HALF hour of walking, it's hot like I didn't know hot could be. It gets hot in New York but not like this. Not like you're slowly being roasted alive by something that really wants to see you dead.

There's not a single cloud in the sky, the industrial edge of Atlanta washed in a brilliant blue. It's nice to look at, at least. I try to focus on that, and not on the t-shirt sodden with sweat and clinging like another layer of skin.

The gas station is packed with cars, people getting off or getting on the expressway. I keep an eye out for employees. A few people told me this is a great place to catch rides, as long as the manager doesn't see you and toss you out. I look for the cars pointed toward the southbound entrance ramp and scan faces, look for someone kindly.

My mouth still tastes like vomit so I consider going in for a pack of gum or a bottle of water, but it's going to be a long journey back and I want to get started. I sneak another swig from my hillbilly flask. The duct tape is fraying, showing peeks of the brown liquid sloshing around inside.

I survey the area and settle on an older guy, t-shirt and tan cargo shorts, tattoos sleeved down both arms. Buddy Holly glasses and a cowboy hat. He's gassing up a metallic blue car that looks like an electric razor.

His cowboy hat looks a little like my old cowboy hat and I feel a pang of loss. I really liked that hat.

I come around the side of his car and ask, "Headed south?"

He smiles like we're old friends. "Yes sir." His voice a big, booming Southern drawl.

"Looking for company?"

He frowns, probably because that sounds like a pick-up line, so I tell him, "Just looking to get a lift in the general direction of Sterling. Far south as I can get. I can spot for some gas."

The guy shrugs. "Hop on in, son. I can get you at least part of the way."

I climb into the passenger seat as he jams the handle into the pump. The gas cap makes a hard clicking sound as he tightens it. The gray interior of the car is immaculate. The car isn't new but it smells that way. The guy climbs inside and starts it up and I'm blasted by cool air. Frigid and lovely.

He extends his hand. "Bill."

I take it. His handshake is like his vise. "Johnny."

He starts the car, pulls out, and points us at I-85.

"Well Johnny, how does an able-bodied young man like

yourself end up shaking down strangers for rides at a gas station?"

Ah fuck. I was hoping he was the strong, silent type. Who the fuck is chatty *and* wears a cowboy hat? I tell him, "Had to run an errand and couldn't get a ride back. Sometimes you got to get creative."

Bill hits the on-ramp and guns the engine, sliding into traffic, weaving between cars until he's in the left lane, where his foot turns to lead. The odometer pushes up past 80 to keep up with the flow of traffic. Speed limits down here often seem like suggestions. I've got three hundred miles to cover, so this is encouraging.

"I'm headed to Savannah," he says. "I can get you as far down as I-95. How's that for you, son?"

"That's most of the trip," I tell him. "More than I could have hoped for."

He taps at the radio in the dash, flipping through until AC/DC comes on singing. He puts it on low enough so we can sustain a conversation.

"New Yorker, huh?" he asks.

"Originally, yes," I tell him.

"I can tell from the accent. It's not heavy like in those mobster movies, but it's there. Always wanted to get up to New York. Never got the chance. If I do, what's the first thing I should do?"

Turn right back around. That city is fucking poison. It took my dad. It took Chell. It damn near tried to kill me. Though truthfully, I was contributing to the effort.

"Go to Mamoun's on MacDougal. Get a shawarma. Best thing you'll ever eat."

"I have no idea what that even is, but I'll remember it."

We drive in silence for a bit. It's a comfortable silence. Brian

Johnson sings to us about the dirt-cheap rate of dirty deeds. I'm chilly, nearly shivering, like the sweat on my shirt is cooling into ice. I savor it because eventually it's going to end and I'll be back out in the heat.

"So what do you do, son?" he asks.

People call me an amateur private investigator, though I like to think of myself as a blunt instrument. Point me at a job and I get it done. Or at least, I used to. Right now, learning how to be a chef, because I'd like to have a skill that doesn't involve beating the shit out of people.

This is all too complicated. I settle on something simpler. "Still trying to figure that out."

"And you're looking for it in Sterling? Ain't nothing down there."

Being off the grid right now is kind of the point.

"Staying with some friends," I tell him.

"You don't talk a whole lot, do you?"

"Hot like it is down here, it sucks the life out of you."

"I hear that."

"So tell me," I say, hoping to get the attention off me. "What do you do, Bill?"

"I'm an animal masturbator," he says. "Simply put, I jerk off cows and horses."

I can't help but laugh at that. "Wait, what?"

He laughs, long and deep, and slaps my knee. I recoil a little bit, even though I don't mean to. He says, "Bet you never heard of that job before, huh?"

"No, I haven't. And now I wonder where that hand has been."

He points a finger at me. "Now that's not the first time I heard that one. But look, I get it. It sounds weird, right? My formal training is in veterinary tech. And whether you're doing a study on infectious diseases or some genetic testing, sometimes you need a whole lot of animal semen." He taps his thumb into his chest. "That's my time to shine."

"I take it you like your job, then?"

"I get to work outdoors. I get to work with animals. And I get to make them better. My lab is pioneering research that's going to eradicate equine combined immunodeficiency disease."

"I don't know what that is."

"It's bad news for horses is what it is, son," he says. "Look, it doesn't sound like the most glamorous job on the planet. That I will give you. But it's a job that needs to get done, and I just so happen to have the temperament for it."

"And what's the temperament for it, exactly?"

"Patience, steady hands, and the ability to laugh at yourself."

"Fair enough."

Bill seems like a nice guy, and it also seems like there's not going to be any way to get him to stop talking, so I ask, "We've got a ways to go. How about you tell me a little about how your job works?"

He smiles and starts in. "Most people aren't interested in the details."

"How could they not be? I've never met anyone who masturbated animals, legit day job or not."

"Okay okay. Well, there are three ways to do it. There are artificial vaginas, electrical stimulants, and old-fashioned hand-cranking…"

He sets off and keeps going, like a stone rolling down a hill.

It's perfect. Because really, I am curious. But also, I don't want to answer any more questions about me. So I tilt an ear at him, toss in the occasional "oh" or "interesting" where I think it might be appropriate, and watch the world barrel by outside the window.

Trees and blacktop and empty stretches of sky.

Georgia melting in the August heat.

I'M IN MUD up to my knees, and there's a slicing sound of shovel into dirt, rain pecking at the back of my neck. Something pokes my arm. I look up and Bill is smiling at me from the driver's seat.

"Fell asleep there, son," he says. "Looks like you needed a rest, so I left you to it."

We're at the single-pump gas station next to Momma's BBQ, which is right exactly where I was headed. I thought I was only getting as far down as Savannah. Bill sees the confusion on my face and says, "I wasn't in any rush. Figured I'd give you a lift the whole way. Do you need to get much further into town?"

"No, right here is perfect actually," I tell him, fumbling at my pocket. "Let me get you some gas money…"

"Think nothing of it, son," he says.

"You sure? Nothing I can give you in return? Free and clear?"

"Free and clear."

I hold his gaze for a moment but his face is flat against the expanse of his sunglasses. "Really?" I ask.

"You seem deeply suspect."

"I'm a born and bred New Yorker," I tell him. "I'm not used to people doing nice things without wanting something in return."

"Well, the world ain't such a bad place," he says. He extends his hand and we shake. "Now, you sure this spot is okay?"

"I'm headed to that restaurant right there," I tell him. "This couldn't be better."

He nods. "You get on safe, then."

"You too," I tell him.

I open the door. Pause, and consider telling him my real name. Like maybe I owe him that much. Shake it off and climb out of the blissful air conditioning, into the stifling heat, and close the door behind me.

He waves as he pulls out and onto the road. I watch him drive away, a little thrown on how to take that. He drove, what, a hundred miles out of his way? More, round-trip? That's weird. People being nice for no clear reason is weird.

I turn to the station and it's empty. Drive by fast and it might look deserted, with the way one window is boarded up and the lights inside aren't turned on. But the proprietor is there, sitting on the rocking chair in the shadow of the propped-open door. He looks like a bridge troll in overalls, and he's staring at me like he stares at everyone, with a great deal of contempt. I nod and he doesn't acknowledge me.

Momma's looks equally as empty. Given it was originally a two-story house with a wrap-around porch and a big bay window, it doesn't look much like a restaurant. The only sign it's a business is "Momma's" hand-painted in red on a white plank over the porch.

From what I hear, this place used to be nuts—they only served meat until they ran out for the day, and the only way to ensure you got some was to line up around dawn. But the housing collapse emptied out the surrounding area, and some newer restaurants opened a little further away, closer to the more affluent neighborhoods. Momma's still seems to do pretty good business, but not nearly as much as it used to.

This is also where our mail gets dropped off. Mail trucks won't come all the way down to camp, so we have to get everything sent here. In exchange we provide herbs and fresh vegetables to the owner, Luanne.

The front door is locked so I walk around the porch, footsteps echoing in the hollow underneath, follow the smell of applewood smoke and charred meat. Luanne is in the back yard, dipping a mop into a plastic bucket of thick red liquid, then leaning into a smoking rig fashioned from the remains of a massive propane tank. She drags the mop over the piles of meat inside, which snap and smoke and crackle. I skipped breakfast and didn't eat lunch and I want to stick my face inside the smoker, see where luck takes me.

She hears me approaching and drops the mop back into the bucket. She turns, smiles at me. That smile makes me think thoughts unbecoming of a gentleman. Her hands are covered in red barbecue sauce, like they're covered in blood. She runs the back of her arm across her brow to clear it of sweat. The way she stands, long limbs cocked out at odd angles, smiling like her face was built that way, skin shining like bronze in the sunlight. Fuck.

"How're you, Ash?" she asks.

"Fair to middling."

"Something I can do for you, now?" she asks, loading that question with so much subtext it's a wonder we're not both suddenly naked.

"Need a favor," I tell her. "Got a package coming within the next week or so. It's pretty important. When it arrives can you put it someplace safe?"

She nods. "Of course. I'll make sure you get it safe and sound."

"Thanks, kid," I tell her, hoping the use of the word 'kid' will deflate the sexual tension. And it does, a little. Her body unwinds. She leans down and picks up the bucket.

"That it?" she asks.

"That's it. We'll be on by in the next day or two with some baskets. You good until then?"

"Good as I can be, everything considered."

"Cheers then," I tell her. Salute, turn, and leave the yard. Feel her staring after me. Wishing I could go back. But Luanne is nice. Nice enough I don't want to risk it. She's hanging on by a thread here, trying to keep her mother's restaurant alive in what amounts to a ghost town. I tend to cut threads. Rarely is it intentional, but it's definitely becoming an unsettling pattern.

The sun has arced enough that one side of the long stretch of road is in the shade. I strip off my shirt and cram it into my belt. It's a long walk and I don't have to be worried about sunburn if I stick to the tree line. That, at least, is nice. The threatening voice of sobriety calls out to me, so I take another swig of whiskey, drain the bottle empty, and set off toward the waving lines of heat sprouting off the asphalt in the distance.

THE ROAD IS straight and uniform. Nothing to break it up, just the odd car passing by every few minutes. I lose track of how far I travel. I wish I had brought my phone. I was halfway to Atlanta before I realized I left it at camp.

Just about when I'm wondering whether I missed the turn-off, there it is, hacked through the tree line. A dirt path with a weathered wood sign at the foot, carved into it the words: SOUTH VILLAGE.

Underneath that: EST. 1973.

I follow the worn-smooth path. The canopy is so thick it takes my eyes a second to adjust to the darkness. The temperature drops a good ten degrees, too. Now I'm almost chilly.

As I walk down the path I feel two sets of eyes on me. That same set I always feel in the forest. There's not someone watching me. I know that, intellectually. But still, those eyes are there, boring into my back.

I ignore it. Wish I had more whiskey.

Concentrate on the trees. Palmettos and magnolia and cedar and holly and pine and myrtle. More trees on this walk than I've probably seen in my entire lifetime. Trees are nice. The forest is so big and so dense it feels like being inside someplace else. Nothing but the sound of my sneakers in the dirt and the occasional animal noise. The call of a bird or shrill click of an insect.

I think about Bill, too.

To take pride in your work, even if it's a little messy, that must be a very nice feeling.

A half-mile in, I hit the bridge over the stream and stop to check it. One of the visitors reported it was shaking when she drove over it, though she seemed like the nervous type. I stomp on some of the boards, hold the railing and shake. It feels solid as concrete, but then again, I'm not a car. I'll come out and take a look at it with someone who knows what they're doing, to make sure it's sound, but it doesn't seem to be in imminent danger.

Bridge cleared, it's not too much longer until I reach the Hub.

The first dome is the biggest, dark wood and covered in moss, the size of a small house. There are more behind it, no consistency to the size or order, so the domes look like giant mushrooms grown up out of the forest floor. The only pop of color, the only thing that looks artificial, are the long rows of rainbow-hued Tibetan prayer flags, crisscrossed between the domes, some of them reaching up to the canopy, haphazard the way Christmas lights are strung up around a college dorm room.

The porch in front of the Hub and the paths cutting around and behind the domes appear to be empty. There's no one in the front clearing. Which is strange. Usually this place is bustling with people doing chores, lounging, participating in workshops. There's not a single acoustic guitar playing.

There's always an acoustic guitar playing.

But all I hear now is the gentle flap of the prayer flags.

There must be an assembly somewhere. Some event I wouldn't have given a shit about if someone told me. Maybe everyone is down by the lake. It's a good day for a dip. I keep walking, past the Hub, to Eatery. Climb up the back steps and into the glorious mess of the main kitchen.

I should go back to the bus and get a clean shirt but I don't really care to, so I toss my t-shirt into the corner, pull an apron off the wall, and pull it over my head. Turn on the window fan that will keep the air moving enough so that when I turn on the ovens, I will not immediately die.

I nearly trip over Mathilda, who's poking at the floor with her beak. She doesn't look up, just clucks to acknowledge my presence, like I've annoyed her delicate chicken sensibilities.

"Fuck you too," I tell her.

It's probably not sanitary to cook in an apron with no shirt underneath while a chicken wanders around the kitchen but I'm a rebel. And anyway, not a day goes by that some goofball isn't wandering around here naked.

My stomach roars. There's a tray covered with foil on the stove. I pull the foil aside and find rows of desiccated brown twigs, glistening with oil, sprinkled with piles of rocky sea salt. Aesop roasted some mushrooms. I love when Aesop roasts mushrooms. He has to forage them; I don't know which are safe and which will kill me, but he does, and he leaves them in the oven until they turn into tiny little flavor bombs.

I grab a handful and cram them in my mouth, wipe the oil off on the apron as I chew, and wash it down with the plastic jug of whiskey I keep stashed underneath the sink, behind the cleaning supplies. That helps a little. I refill my flask and stick it into my cargo pocket.

After a few handfuls of granola, I head into the pantry to pull ingredients for the night's dinner, not even sure of what's going to be on the menu, but we're close enough that I need to get some stuff going.

What I find is an entire wall of cans, their labels torn off.

There's a shuffle from the main kitchen. Aesop is standing there, his face blanched. At least, the parts of it I can see underneath the mammoth mountain-man beard. It reaches down past his chest. He's not wearing a shirt either, and his muscular torso is riddled with tattoos. Random stuff—tribals and faces and symbols and words—all done in black and white. Some of it is intricate and professional. Some of it is muddy and uneven, a clear sign of stick-and-poke. The kind of stuff you get in prison, or after a long night of drinking and your idiot friend has a sewing needle and some printer ink. I've never asked him which.

"Can we please figure out who's recycling the labels, and tell them to do it after we use the cans, not before?" I ask him. "We're going to be eating bean and veggie and whatever the fuck else surprise for the next few weeks…"

"Ash."

"What?"

"Crusty Pete is dead."

"Ah fuck."

THREE

THE TREE REACHES out of the earth and unfurls toward the canopy like an open hand, a pale wood structure perched in the palm. The way the tree spreads up and out, it was impossible to get a ladder to the front door, so the ladder was built onto another tree twenty feet away, and the two were connected by a rope bridge.

The bridge isn't up anymore.

Everyone's here. With camp currently at capacity—the staff roster full and all the tree houses rented out—that means nearly forty people are crowded around the base of the tree. Heads downcast, still as statues.

Aesop and I approach, twigs cracking under our feet, and a few people look up, some familiar faces, most not. Some people are weeping, others are holding themselves or each other, and some are blank. A tapestry of shock and mourning. People step aside, allowing us to pass. At the center of the scrum, Tibo is crouched down so low his long dreads nearly touch the ground. He's contemplating Pete like a painting.

Pete is sprawled out on the ground, limbs askew and head kinked at an unnatural angle. He's shirtless, shoeless, wearing a pair of cargo pants cinched tight to his emaciated frame. His long red hair is spread like a burst of flame, draped across his face.

My breath catches in my chest. It's cool here in the shadows created by the trees, but the heat on the back of my neck rises. No one is staring at me, but it feels like everyone is staring at me.

This guy looks way too comfortable. Can't be his first time around a dead body.

Real dead doesn't look like dead in the movies. The skin doesn't take on a cool icy hue. The face doesn't rest in a position of serenity. The joints and muscles fall slack. Everything gone but the meat. You look at a dead body and know it's empty of something.

Pressure builds in my face like an over-filled water balloon, stretching my skin.

"Ash."

The bridge is there, lying in the dirt. It looks like the bridge Indiana Jones gets trapped on in *Temple of Doom*, stuck between Nazis and the crazy Indian death-cult. Except this bridge was twenty-five feet over the forest floor, not hundreds of feet over a croc-infested river. I've walked across the bridge. I thought it was sturdy.

"Ash." Tibo is standing next to me, his voice low. "I need you right now."

I nod at him and he turns to the assembled staffers and guests and says, "This is a tragedy, but one that must be dealt with. Could everyone please return to the Hub? We're going to call the sheriff and inform him there's been an accident."

A few people drift off, the guests and the newer staffers, the ones who didn't know Pete, but most of the crowd lingers. Ignoring Tibo, staring down at the ground, like Pete might shake off being dead and stand back up.

Tibo raises his voice. "Please, everyone. I know this is very difficult."

More departures. Tibo grabs Cannabelle as she passes. "Call the cops, okay? Ask for Ford specifically."

She nods, her eyes rimmed in red. One small hand, her fingernails caked in dirt, placed over her mouth. Not like she might throw up, more like she's trying to hold something in. She turns to me and her body looks like it's about to unwrap and fall to the ground. She wants a hug. The comfort of human contact, and anyone will do.

I step aside, let her look for someone else.

She settles on Magda, whose face is mostly hidden behind a wild bush of fuzzy gray hair, her thick body draped in a yellow sundress and yellow shawl and yellow ceramic jewelry that clacks when she moves. They fall into each other and Cannabelle glances back at me, disappointed. Tibo puts a hand on each of their shoulders.

"Okay, ladies," he says. "Head on back."

They disengage, hold hands, and walk off.

There's a sharp voice behind us. "We should start cleaning up."

Marx is standing at the edge of the clearing, tense, like he's preparing to pounce on someone. He's barefoot, wearing an old pair of jeans, the legs folded up mid-calf, and a red t-shirt, and his stupid black bowler hat.

My understanding is he and Crusty Pete were close, but he's not betraying any emotion other than anger.

Tibo takes a few steps toward him. "Why don't you head on back with the others?"

Marx puffs his chest. Tibo is wires and bone and sinew. Marx is thick and lean. The kind of body that indicates a life of working outside. I've got a big ego and I wouldn't want to fuck with him. But I kind of assume it's going to happen eventually, only because he's got a bad attitude and I'm good at inviting stupid things into my life.

"We can't leave him lying there in the dirt," Marx says.

"Yes we can," Tibo says, pushing up his thick-framed black glasses, which are sliding down his face on a sheen of nervous sweat. He's not so much looking at Marx as he's looking at some point past Marx, beyond the trees. "We can't start disturbing things. I know it's not fun, but we have to do the right thing here…"

"The right thing. Leave him lying in the dirt. Of course you wouldn't care."

"This has nothing to do with me and him," Tibo says.

Marx takes a step forward. "Does it? Maybe it does. How am I supposed to know that?"

This is the start of a familiar and very unproductive dance, so I get between them. "Marx, go back, keep everyone organized. We'll handle things here."

"What the fuck…"

"I'm not repeating myself," I tell him. "This whole thing is very unpleasant. Let's not make it even more unpleasant. In case it's not clear, yes, that is a threat."

Marx is mulling over whether a challenge is worth what's next. His eyes studying me like he's looking for a weak point. I want to tell him that no, it's not worth it, but that'd be throwing gasoline on a trash fire. I hold his jade green eyes for what seems like a moment too long, and finally he shakes his head and looks around me to Tibo. "This doesn't smell right."

Tibo still won't make eye contact with him. Marx spins around and stalks off. We watch him until he disappears, and then it's the two of us.

And Pete, lying on the ground.

"That dude is a giant walking bag of dicks," I say, nodding after Marx.

"That's a strange analogy," Tibo says. "I'd just call him an asshole."

We turn, survey the scene. The bridge. The body. Look up at the tree house.

"Can you get up there?" Tibo asks.

"Cannabelle is the resident climber. Want me to go get her?"

"I need you to go up there."

"Why?"

"Because I trust you."

I put my hands on my hips, look at Tibo. "What's going on?"

"I need to know Pete wasn't stashing any drugs," Tibo says. "Anything hard, at least. We don't have long until the sheriff gets here."

"What happened, anyway?"

"No one saw it. Sunny found him. I think the scene is pretty self-explanatory."

"Snap, fall, snap."

"It's my fault." Tibo says. He takes a big breath and sighs. "It's my fault."

"It's not your fault."

He looks at me sideways. "I'm in charge. It's my fault."

"Let's put that aside for right now."

Tibo arches an eyebrow, leans forward, and sniffs. "Little early to be drinking, isn't it?"

"Only if you lack resolve."

He rolls his eyes and hurries off, so I circle the tree, give the body a wide berth, look for a place to get a handhold. There doesn't seem to be a very good one until I get all the way around to the other side, and find a branch low enough that I can catch it and thick enough that, hopefully, it won't break under my weight.

Hopefully. One broken neck is enough.

Wait, no. One is too many.

I take a long drink from my flask, cram it back in my pocket, take a few steps and jump, grab the branch. The wood cuts into my palms and the branch dips toward me but it doesn't break, so I pull myself up and wrap my legs around it, twist myself over until I'm lying on top of it. I slide down toward the base of the tree, to where the branch is thicker, and there are enough branches around it I can get up to a standing position.

Once I'm upright it's a simple task of climbing the branches like a crooked ladder until I'm at a window of the tree house. It's not netted, thankfully, so I don't have to rip anything down. I climb onto the platform with Crusty Pete's sleeping bag, which reeks of body odor and old food.

Oh Crusty Pete and your wildly accurate nickname.

I push the sour-smelling bag aside, climb across and onto the floor. It's sparse and dim, this tree house not wired for electricity, so there's nothing to turn on. The air is thick, the breeze apparently not coming through the window or the door enough to clear it out. There's the platform, a chair, and a small table, everything roughed out from plywood by an amateur hand, unfinished and not painted. On the table there's a paper plate, two shiny black water bugs feasting on the crumbs of whatever was left.

Motherfucker. I will never get used to seeing these things. Not here. Seeing them crawl out of a sewer grate or disappear under the fridge is at least familiar. I didn't expect to find them in the woods. These are worse than New York roaches, too, because they're bigger and sometimes fly at your face.

They pay me no attention, so I crouch down, to Pete's worn and tattered duffel bag. It's full of dirty clothing and a small plastic baggie of shriveled brown shrooms, which I shove into the back pocket of my jeans. On the sleeping platform, there's a small pile of papers and books. Mostly books.

Rules for Radicals by Saul Alinsky, *1984* by George Orwell, *God and State* by Mikhail Bakunin, *A People's History of the United States* by Howard Zinn. All of them worn and beaten and standard reading for most of the folks around here. Also, an erotic novel called *The Kiss of the Rose*. Which is weird, but okay.

Underneath the books is a stack of papers, held together with a paperclip, the pages warped where they've been repeatedly soaked and dried and yellowed by age. The front page is a bad clipart image of a book of matches.

Setting Fires with Electrical Timers: An Earth Liberation Front Guide.

I flip through and it's pretty much exactly what it sounds like.

Lots of diagrams on how to commit some gnarly arson. This sets off all kinds of internal alarms. But as the son of a firefighter, it would. Even as a kid I would lecture people about the dangers of real Christmas trees and the importance of inspecting your fire extinguishers. The idea of arson is pretty fucking repellant to me.

There are two kinds of people who come through South Village: People looking for something—themselves, adventure, a story, whatever. And then there are the people who are in the tank for the hippie lifestyle. And that can run the spectrum from Woodstock to hard activism. Magda is the Woodstock type. Old-school happy fun times. Marx is the hard activism type. I've never been able to peg Crusty Pete down, because we never spoke much, but unless he's morbidly curious, this seems to be a good indication of where he lands on the scale.

There are no notes throughout the document, but the back is filled up with careful numbers in little groupings, offset by dashes. This is probably not a good thing to leave lying around. It's too thick to fold so I roll it up and jam it in my pocket with the flask.

One more quick look around. Nothing else in the open. I look back to the plate and see the two roaches, which now seem to be regarding me with some level of curiosity. Like maybe I'm edible. I kick a chair and duck in case they attack, but they scramble away and disappear.

I get down on the floor and check under the chair and the table, to make sure there's nothing taped under anything. Other than that, there aren't really any places to hide contraband. Not that it would be easy to find. The shrooms are one thing. If Pete really wanted to hide harder drugs, he probably hid them well enough that they won't be found without physically tearing this place apart.

That finished, I step onto the platform that serves as the front porch, which doesn't give me room to do much more than stand. Look down and there's Crusty Pete. He's closer to the tree house than he is the tree that held the ladder. His body is lying perpendicular to the path of the bridge so I can't tell if he was coming or going. I consider jumping down but it's too high, so I go back through the window and climb down the branches until I'm on the ground.

I walk around the tree, careful to avoid looking at Pete's body, because I don't want to look at it. I don't like the way it looks. It reminds me of what happened in Portland. The way Wilson arced through the air off my fist and cracked his neck against the bumper of his car. The way his body felt as I carried it through the woods. Woods that looked a little like these woods, and suddenly the wave hits, roaring in my ears, pulling me down into the dark...

I try to focus on something else. I go to the bridge and take a knee next to the rope. Thick, brown hemp that probably would have been period-specific for *Temple of Doom*. It shrinks when it gets wet, which is why they soak it and dry it before using new bundles. That reduces the amount it'll shrink when it rains. But I can't remember the last time it rained, and I don't even know if that would create enough tension to break it.

The rope is frayed so I twist it back together, to look down the length of it. To see if I can glean anything about how it tore. This is going to mean checking the four other rope bridges to make sure everything is sound.

Once I get it twisted back up to where it's supposed to be, twice the thickness of my thumb, I run my finger across the face of the break.

Half of it is ripped and torn and jagged.

The other half is smooth and uniform.

Like it'd been cut halfway with a sharp knife.

Just enough that maybe it'd break if someone walked across the bridge.

FOUR

TIBO LOOKS AT the rope and frowns. "Man, I don't know. I have a hard time believing someone here would do something like that."

I drop the rope to the ground and pull the apron off, stuff it in the belt of my shorts. The sun is slicing through the canopy and it's so damn hot, the air thick and wet. I know the sheriff is coming and it's probably not polite to be shirtless, but at least I'm wearing pants.

"I think it's at least worth mentioning to them," I tell Tibo.

"Disagree."

"Why?"

"Foremost, you are not a rope expert," he says, dropping into a crouch and picking it up again. "Smart money is it broke, which dovetails off my second reason, which is, do you really think anyone here is capable of murder? That's not really the vibe."

"Charles Manson was a hippie," I tell him.

"Ha, ha."

"And look, Pete wasn't beaten to death. There was no struggle. Anyone can cut a rope. It's impersonal, so nobody had to get up close. It's not like this took special skill or temperament."

"Right. But I don't think the rope was cut."

"So maybe we ought to let somebody with a forensics background look at it," I tell him.

"I have never known you to trust authority figures," Tibo says, genuinely surprised.

"Yeah, well, I used to think there was shit I could handle myself, and it turns out I can't. Maybe it's best to leave to professionals."

"I'm sorry, Ash. I really believe this was an accident. I don't mean to be unkind, but I've known you a long time now. You have a habit for building narratives. Getting too wrapped up in wanting to fight dragons."

Cheap shot, but true.

Tibo was center-stage when Chell got killed and I tore through New York like a wrecking ball, trying to find the person who did it. By the end I was convinced it was an elaborate conspiracy, but the reality was far more benign: It was a random act of violence. A drop in an overflowing bucket. One I needed to weigh down with meaning because the only way I could process my grief was to be selfish about it, and make it all about me.

"We can tell them your theory," Tibo says. "But it's going to turn into a whole thing. South Village will be crawling with investigators. Guests are going to leave. They don't come here for that. We're just laying down our roots and that'll be a big blow. This place will get a rep. Not a good one. Are you really going to do that to me?"

I start to say something, stop.

"I don't mean to be callous, but I just want you to be sure," Tibo says. He looks up and over my shoulder. "And decide quick, because they're here."

They come crunching through the underbrush, in khaki uniforms, buttoned-up and tucked-in, both of them with deep pools of sweat soaking their armpits. Sheriff Ford and Assistant Sheriff Corey.

Ford is a tree stump of a man, in both shape and complexion. His skin is tanned and ridged, age showing through everywhere but his eyes. He's in his 50s at least, maybe up in his 60s and he just eats well. His face is set in a perpetual frown. I've seen him around, but have never spoken to him.

Corey is the kind of handsome people wish for. Like he rolls out of bed with his bit of stubble and his hair all mussed, ready to break hearts. I imagine he played football for the local high school, got used to the attention, couldn't go pro, decided to take a job where people would continue to listen to what he told them.

Tibo is right. I have an incredible distrust for authority, related to the numerous times in my life I've gotten fucked over—or at least, attempted-fucked-over—by someone wearing a badge. That said, not all cops are bad. And these two seem to fall into the 'good' column, until they prove otherwise. It doesn't mean I don't get nervous when Ford looks at me and lingers on my face. Like he's trying to figure out if he recognizes me. A wanted poster, maybe?

At least I don't feel like I'm going to pee myself when I see him, which is what happened the first time he walked into camp.

"Now what have we got here, Tee-bow," Ford says, looking away from me, drawing out the name like they're old pals horsing around.

"I think that's fairly obvious," Tibo says, nodding toward Pete.

Ford extends his hand to me and we shake. His hand is huge and a little sweaty. The bones in my hand shift and creak. "Don't know if we met," he says.

"Never formally. I'm Ash." Immediately cursing myself. Why did I use my real name? Should have come up with a burner. This whole scene is wearing down too heavy on my nerves. Making me foolish.

"That short for something?"

I'm in it now. "Ashley."

Corey stifles a laugh and catches himself. Right off I can see he feels bad about it. He didn't mean for it, it just spilled out.

Ford turns and gives Corey a harsh look. "These days kids get all kinds of names. My cousin named their boy Carroll." Ford hooks his fingers into his belt and looks at the ground. "Though, the boy ain't right in the head."

"No harm, no foul," I tell them. "I got over that a long time ago."

He nods and walks around Tibo. "So, walk me through what you got."

Tibo leads them to the body, explaining when Pete was found—about an hour and a half ago—and that's pretty much it. Corey pulls a heavy-duty digital camera from his hip and takes pictures. Ford crouches to the ground and traces his fingers through the dirt.

"Lots of footprints," he says.

"When the body was found, pretty much everyone came out," Tibo says.

"Well that about fucks getting shoeprints." He walks around to the rope, bunches it up in his hand, looks at where it split. "You got any sense this was foul? Anyone have it out for this kid?"

"No," Tibo says. "I believe it was an accident, sir."

Tibo looks at me as Ford turns the rope in his hands, twisting it like I did. I look down at the ground, thinking about narratives. About this place being flooded by cops. About whether I'm sure about any of this. And the truth is: I'm not.

Ford drops the rope and nods. "That about tracks."

He probably knows more about rope than I do.

"We're going to send the coroner out," Ford says. "We'll take him, take the rope, just to have it looked at. We have to get back out on the road to get a signal. Until then, keep this area clear." Ford points up to the tree house. "Assistant Sheriff Corey, get on up there and see if anything jumps out at you."

Corey stashes the camera and looks up at the thick foliage. "Literally or figuratively?" he asks.

"Either way."

Corey furrows his brow and walks around the tree, seems to settle on the path I took up. Ford looks at me. "I didn't know this fella here, but I'm damn sorry. It's a hell of a thing."

Tibo nods. "What happens next?"

"We bag him and tag him. Look into next of kin to see if someone will identify and claim him. Do you have any information or paperwork on him you could share?"

"I don't even know his last name," Tibo says. "He went by Crusty Pete. He wasn't an employee and he paid for everything in cash. I'll look through my records but I don't think I have anything."

The corner of Ford's lip curls. "You kids and your nicknames."

"Got something, sheriff," Corey yells. He hangs out the window, holding a tiny square object in his hand. "Looks like some marry-ja-wana."

Son of a bitch. I guess I wasn't as thorough as I thought.

"Toss it on down," Ford says.

Corey fans out his fingers and the bag floats through the air, right into Ford's outstretched palm. He sticks it in his pocket. I think me and Tibo are both a little wide-eyed, because he laughs. "Little bit of weed never hurt anyone. Don't think I'm an idiot, fellas. I know y'all are smoking it out here. Most of the time I can smell it. But I know you're not selling it. At this point, if it ain't meth, I don't give a shit."

"That's very progressive, sheriff," I tell him. "But how do you know we're not selling?"

An eyebrow goes up. I was curious, but he takes it as a challenge.

"Sounds like you're from New York City," he says. "Am I correct in assuming that?"

People love to point that out down here. I don't know why. The mysticism of the big city? The cleverness over identifying an accent?

"Yes sir, you are," I say.

"Well son, I know the cops you got up there are like super-cops. I went up there with the wife a few years ago and half those fellas around Times Square look like Navy SEALS. I know you're used to a different sort. But just because we don't have the resources or training doesn't mean we don't know what we're doing."

Maybe it's just that people like putting us in our place.

"I didn't mean any offense by it," I tell him.

"Well, good," he says. "At the end of the day, let's say I know what my priorities are. And a bunch of kids getting high in the woods is not my priority."

Corey rejoins us, his face red from exertion. Ford nods to him. "Go on out to the road, give a call to the coroner. Let him know he's got a pickup. Tell 'em to send someone from forensics, too. I figure on this being an accident, but doesn't hurt to have a look around."

Ford turns back to us as Corey runs off. He looks at Tibo and tilts his head toward me. "He okay? Can we talk about something serious?"

"Me and Ash go way back," says Tibo. "I trust him more than anyone here."

Aww.

Ford nods. He looks down at Pete, one last long look, and turns, leading us out of view of the body. He says, "FBI agent visited me the other day. Asking a lot of questions about this place."

Tibo freezes. "What about?"

"I don't know, exactly. This guy came in—big motherfucker. Made Sonny Liston look like a featherweight. The questions were vague and I couldn't get a good read on it. Mostly about the type of person who comes through here. He did ask if I'd ever seen stores of gasoline or fertilizer out here. Bomb making material, you know?"

That rolled-up arson manual in my pocket suddenly feels a lot heavier.

"Does he think we're planning to blow something up?" Tibo asks.

Ford shakes his head. "There's precedent there, son. You want to live off the grid, it makes people wonder what you've got to hide."

"Do you think we have anything to hide?"

"Naw. You never cause any trouble for me. I think you're a bunch of kids want to have some fun. Nothing wrong with that. This aside," he says, nodding toward Pete, "I've never had to lose any sleep over this place. So I told that FBI agent in no uncertain terms I could vouch for you."

"Thank you," Tibo says.

"Welcome." The frown disappears off his face. "Now don't make me a liar. I will vouch for you, but if shit goes down I will not protect you. Do you understand the difference?"

"Yes sir."

The frown comes back. His version of a smile. "Good. Now I'll get in touch if forensics turn up something worth worrying about, but as for right now, I ask that you take a long hard look at the safety issues around here, make sure something like this doesn't happen again. I know tree houses look fun. Someone else falls and breaks their neck, then we're going to have issues. You got me?"

Tibo offers his hand. They shake. "Thank you."

Ford reaches over and shakes my hand. "Nice to meet you. Sorry if I dressed you down a bit back there."

"No apology necessary. I don't know when to watch my mouth."

Ford nods. "I'm going to stay here, wait for the team. Why don't y'all head back? Corey will probably have them come in down the back road. Make sure to keep everyone away from here for the time being."

"Sure thing," Tibo says.

We turn to leave and don't say anything until we're out of

earshot.

"He seems nice," I say.

"As a black man running a commune south of the Mason-Dixon, I kind of figured I'd be in for a hell of a time with the local police. He's been good to us."

"Nothing about the rope then."

"He looked at it and he didn't think anything of it," Tibo says.

"Something else." I pull out the arson manual, show him the cover.

He takes it, flips through. "Huh."

"You think it's something?"

"I don't know. It's not the first copy I've seen floating around. It's practically a historical document. Some people pick it up because they're curious."

"What do you want me to do with it?"

He hands it back. "Burn it in the campfire tonight. Stuff like this makes me nervous. It's not what we're about here."

Tibo turns toward camp and I follow. We make it through the brush and step onto a narrow wooden walkway. They're all over camp, and remind me a little of the Coney Island boardwalk, but instead of wide and straight, they're narrow and jagged, cutting through the forest like capillaries to carry people over the uneven terrain. They're fun to look at. Sometimes a random plank will be painted, or something will be carved into it. I know a lot of them, but every now and again find one I hadn't noticed before.

Our feet echo on the wood. We pass over a plank that says: *Do not hate. Meditate.*

After a minute or so of walking I ask, "What do you make of this whole FBI thing?"

"Surprised it took them so long."

"Really?"

"Ford was exactly right. Back in the 60s and 70s, when commune life got big, the FBI started embedding agents. Don't be shocked if someone shows up in the next few days in a tie-dye t-shirt talking about how many times he's seen Phish."

We step off the bridge and come up on La Biblioteca, the library dome. There are a few people outside, sitting on Adirondack chairs or sprawled out on the porch. One of the visiting Norwegian tourists is balanced precariously on the porch railing. No one's talking, but finally, there's someone strumming an acoustic guitar, and it feels like we've regained a small slice of normalcy. I don't know the name of the song but the sound of it is very sad.

"I know this is crass, but we don't have any kind of accident or liability insurance," Tibo says. "I'll put in the due diligence but I almost hope Pete doesn't have any family. I have no interest of being sued into oblivion."

"You made me sign a waiver when I got here," I tell him. "Doesn't that cover accidents?"

Tibo snaps his fingers. "Right. I forgot. Okay, I'm going to see if I can dig up his. Want to go get started on dinner? I'll probably make an address during the circle tonight."

"Sure."

Neither of us move.

"What?" Tibo asks.

"Something feels off," I tell him. "Can't shake it."

"Do you remember what happened when you got here?"

He blinks at me. I shrug.

"I asked you to be our head of security, because that seemed to fit your skillset," he says. "You refused. You told me, 'I don't do that shit anymore.' Your words exactly. Do you regret your choice?"

"No."

"Then don't act like you do. Gideon is in charge and you need to respect that. So please, for the sake of my own peace of mind, don't go running around here causing trouble. Not everything is a conspiracy."

"You told Ford you trusted me."

Tibo pauses. He gazes out through the trees. "I misspoke. I should have said I know you more than anyone else here."

We part. The sting of his words following me.

That, and the little bit of rope.

FIVE

IT'S STEAM-ROOM HUMID inside the kitchen. The battered stock pot, big enough to fit a small child—if you're into morbid systems of measurement—is bubbling on the cast iron stove. Aesop is shirtless, cutting aromatics. The pots hanging from the rack over his head sway in the breeze of the window fan. I click the button on the top of the boom box in the corner of the kitchen, hope the batteries are holding out. Kurt Cobain's voice comes blaring out. "Come As You Are." That'll do.

"What's for dinner?" Aesop asks.

"You're the boss."

Aesop points the knife at me. "You choose tonight."

"Why's that?"

Aesop puts down the knife and leans against the counter. "I know you're leaving soon, but you wanted to learn how to cook.

Fine. You need to do more than just prep."

I step around Aesop, into the cupboard, where I take a pull from my whiskey stash and pick a couple of blank cans at random. Root around in the cluttered utensil drawer for a can opener that works, passing over the three that don't. Getting people to throw shit out around here is impossible. I open four cans of beans—a mix of red kidney and black. Next up, two cans of green beans and one of baby corn. I step into the narrow hallway that leads into the storage area. The wall is covered with scraps of paper. Some of them clean sheets of computer paper, some of them receipts, some of them torn off cardboard boxes. All of them covered with recipes, from past cooks, or guests, or staffers. Family secrets and favorite dishes handed down over the years. I scan them, looking for some inspiration, and finally find it on a sticky note on the far end of the wall.

"We still got some potatoes?" I ask Aesop.

He doesn't stop chopping. "Yup."

"You said you made some good mashed potatoes out of vegan butter and almond milk, right?"

"Passable. Browned up under the broiler, they come out pretty good."

"All right. Veggie shepherd's pie. We'll throw in some tomatoes and zucchini from the garden. Plus some thyme and mushrooms. Kale salad on the side with some of that mustard vinaigrette you made last week. Given the atmosphere, I think we ought to get as close to comfort food as we can."

"Now you're thinking like a chef."

There's a sack of potatoes in the corner of the cupboard. I drag it over to the counter next to Aesop, slice it open, pile potatoes on the cutting board, and get to work. Toss the finished potatoes into a large plastic mixing bowl and the peels into the compost bucket.

"So what happened?" Aesop asks.

"Pete fell."

"Something happened. You've got a look."

"I don't know. It's weird."

Aesop pushes the chopped onions into another mixing bowl, comes back with a basket of tomatoes and sets them down on the cutting board. "What's weird?"

"This stays between you and me."

"Of course."

"I mean that."

"I know."

I put down the peeler and a half-peeled potato and peek out through the open door, make sure we're alone. "I looked at the rope. It looked like it had been cut."

"You think someone killed Pete."

"I don't know what I think."

"What did Tibo think?"

"That I'm not a rope expert. And the sheriff looked at it and it didn't seem to catch his interest. I'm wondering if maybe I'm just… I don't know. I have a habit of overthinking things."

Aesop takes tomatoes out of the basket, stacking them behind the cutting board. "It begs the question of *why* someone would kill Pete. Maybe you should start there."

"I don't have a good answer."

"What do you know about Pete?"

"Nothing, really."

Aesop takes a few cloves of garlic, lines them up on his cutting board, lays his knife over them, and slams it with the flat of his palm. The counter shakes. When he pulls the knife away the garlic is mangled. He pulls off the paper skin and dices what's left. "You do know Pete didn't want Tibo in charge anymore, right?"

"I had no idea."

Aesop doesn't take his eyes off the cutting board, his knife flying through the garlic. "You really don't know anything about that?"

"I don't pay attention to that kind of stuff."

"Get ready for a lesson in hippie politics. In communities like this, some people get all worked up about ownership creating a hierarchy, and the only fix is for the hierarchy to be eliminated. In this instance, Pete and a couple of other people here wanted Tibo to have an open deed for the land. Whoever wants to be on it could be on it. That way everything is shared and equal."

"Who else?"

Aesop stops chopping, looks up at the ceiling. "Marx, obviously. Magda and Gideon too. Maybe Job?"

"I didn't know any of that."

"Well, sit outside and talk to someone once in a while. You've been here two months and I don't think you've spoken to anyone but me and Tibo for more than five cumulative minutes. I don't take this personally, but I know you only talk to me because we work together."

Shrug. "I'm not a people person. And I talk to Sunny and Moony sometimes."

"You talk to them because they're pretty and they do porn."

"That's not true." I finish the potatoes on my board. Doesn't look like enough, so I grab a few more out of the sack. "Given this, that would sort of make Tibo the main suspect, then."

"Well, maybe yes, maybe no," Aesop says, taking a bundle of thyme off the herb basket hanging over the sink, meticulously separating the leaves into a small glass bowl. "It's not like there was this big uprising. No one was marching on his hut. There was a petition, but there's always a fucking petition. That's as far as it went."

The heat is making the back of my throat feel swollen and thick. I grab a mason jar off the rack over the sink and turn on the filtered faucet. It comes out in a weak trickle through the greywater system's filter. Even though the water is clear, it tastes like rocks.

I finish the last potato, toss it into the bowl, and dump the entire thing into the boiling water, careful not to splash. "Did you salt this?"

"No."

The salt well is empty so I go into the cupboard, get the box of kosher salt. Fill up the well, then toss in a handful. Give it a good stir and glance at the clock. Fifteen minutes ought to do. I grab a few zucchini out of the veggie basket and slice. "This kind of thing doesn't seem to rise to the level of murder."

"Definitely not. Jesus, don't you know where you are? There was talk of building a new outhouse, but the spot Job picked was too close to an active anthill. There was a two-hour discussion, after which the outhouse did not get built."

Sigh. "Maybe I am overthinking it."

"I got nothin'."

I reach down, feel the outline of the arson manual in my pocket. I consider asking about it, but Tibo asked me to get rid of it, not advertise it.

There's not much else to say and there are hungry people to feed, so we dig into the work. Once the potatoes are ready I dump them into a clean pot and go at them with the vegan butter and almond milk. I stop before I think I should. Mash potatoes too much and they get gluey. When I'm finished they're a little rough and chunky. They're not perfect. There's no substitute on this earth for milk and butter, but at least no one will starve. They'll just be slightly less happy than they could have been.

We get the casserole-ish thing into three sheet pans and into the oven to bake down for a little while, and then go after the salad. We keep it simple. Lots of kale, some dried cranberries and slivered almonds. I stop periodically to douse myself in water, or to fill up another mason jar, or to nip at my whiskey. It can get dangerous in here real quick if you don't stay hydrated. I learned that lesson during the first real heat wave I was here for, when I almost passed out face-first into a ripping hot cast iron skillet.

Once we're done with the salad I realize the tape player isn't working anymore. I slap the side of it and nothing happens. Batteries are probably dead. Or else the ancient thing, arrived here from parts unknown, finally died. I'll have to wait for the next run into town to get a package of D batteries to find out the answer.

The massive bowl of salad takes up half of the chest fridge. I am a fucking sweat monster. And I'm exhausted. It's a mix of the brutal heat and being up so early, before the sun even came up, to catch a ride up to Atlanta from a departing guest. That nap on the car ride back cut into it a little, but I need a shower and a change of clothes before dinner tonight.

Aesop seems to sense this. He nods at me. "Go ahead and get cleaned up. I'll handle the rest. Figure we'll ring the bell in an hour?"

"Perfect."

Soon as I step out of the kitchen I feel cooler. The air temperature is probably 85 to 90 degrees out here, but at least it's not standing next to a stove radiating heat like the surface of the fucking sun. I head in the general direction of home and realize I'd probably be better with a shower first. I climb onto the boardwalk path. After walking a bit, when I'm sure I'm alone, I hop off the path and take a quick piss against a tree, keeping an eye out for fire ants.

There are two shower facilities, on the remote ends of camp, before the forest drops off into uninhabitable swampland. They're both the same. A cross between a cabana and a log cabin without a roof, wooden poles sticking into the air, the inside a maze, the whole thing decorated with a mosaic of tile and broken glass. There are twists and turns offsetting the sinks and the tubs and the standing open-air showers, so multiple people can use the facilities and everyone gets a little privacy.

The dartboard out front of the cabana has a pink plastic dart sticking out of the "shower" section. The other two sections, "tub" and "sinks," are free. I stop and wait, let whoever's in there clear out.

A few minutes pass and Sunny appears, floating down the steps, stretching her arms over her head, a towel wrapped around her waist. Red hair in a long wet ponytail hanging down her back, immense breasts bare and beaded with water.

She is what The Commodores meant by a brick house.

I smile at her, keep my eyes above the neckline.

"Hi, Ash," she says, taking the dart out of "shower" and sticking it back onto the corkboard.

"Ma'am." I nod my head at her. She flashes me a smile so sharp it could cut glass, and wanders off, down the wooden pathway.

Good lord. I worked in a strip club for a little while so I know how to keep my decorum around beautiful topless women, but that doesn't mean it's easy.

I take a dart, stick it in "shower," head into the main room, where I strip down and toss my clothes onto a shelf. I grab a bottle of biodegradable soap and step onto the shower platform, which looks out over a vast stretch of empty forest. Pull the chain for the shower and a middling stream of lukewarm water pours out, brought over by the nearby lake and river system. The water and a slight breeze serve to cool me down. I soap up and rinse and stand there, look out at the sunlight cutting through the trees.

I thought Portland was green. This is green in a way I didn't know a place could be green. The air feels cleaner, like it's constantly being filtered. So far from home, too. The way it smells and the sound of it. Standing here front of this great open space, this may as well be all there is to the world.

It's kind of nice.

But things only stay nice for so long.

Maybe Tibo is right. I loved Chell too hard. She loved me but not the way I loved her. When she died I lost myself in wanting to punish the person who did it. And look what it cost me. My home. My friends. Not that they ran me out of town, but you can't do so many dumb things strung together and feel like you're still welcome.

I went to Portland, figuring I'd try a change of scenery, and made a mess there, too.

So here I am. Standing on the edge of the world, running away from one dead body, smack into another one.

"Hey."

I turn to find Gideon standing on the other end of the shower platform. The tall lanky fuck, with his stupid fucking hemp necklace and scraggly goatee. Also, he's naked.

"Can I join?" he asks.

I pivot a little to shield my bits. "Uh, no?"

"Didn't you ever do the group shower in high school? It's no big deal. You're wasting water standing there."

I grab the chain and cut the flow. "Can you give me a goddamn second?"

Gideon rolls his eyes and retreats back into the cabana. I grab a towel off the rack, give it a strong flap to make sure there's nothing alive on it, and wrap it around my waist. When I step inside he's leaned against the wall, arms crossed, like he's waiting for a train. Hips thrust forward like he wants to make me uncomfortable.

"You know, some people like a little privacy," I tell him.

"I didn't take you for a prude."

"I'm not a prude. I want to shower by myself."

He raises an eyebrow and smirks. "Typical gay panic. We all have penises, bud. It's no different than a hand or a foot. It's a part of your body and it's not something to be ashamed of."

I grab at my clothes, which are so drenched with sweat as to be repulsive, ball them up, and slip into my sneakers. As I'm leaving Gideon calls after me, "Hey, so Tibo said you were with him when the cops came."

"Yes."

"Anything worth noting?"

Sigh. I step back into the sink room. I can make Gideon out

through the gaps in the wooden poles as he reaches up and pulls the chain for the shower. "Did you talk to Tibo?" I ask.

"Yes. But I'd like to hear it from you, too."

"You know, you're a pretty shitty head of security," I tell him. "Why weren't you there?"

"Today is my writing day," Gideon says. "I was working on my manifesto."

I don't bother to stifle the laugh. "I've got to get dinner served. Let's talk later."

"Well, don't go causing any trouble."

"What the fuck is that supposed to mean?"

Gideon peeks around the wall and into the sink room, his hair plastered against his skull. "Don't think I don't know what's up."

"Why don't you tell me what the fuck you're talking about?"

"I know Tibo wanted you to take the security job. But that's my job. I'm responsible for the protection of this camp. Don't think I'm going to let you take it away from me."

"I don't want your job, asshole."

"Well, just know, I'm watching you."

I nod toward the shower. "You're wasting water."

He purses his lips and disappears behind the barrier.

Something deep in my gut wants me to walk around the divider and throw him up against the wall and ask him how tough he's willing to play this. Show him how scary real life can get. But I don't do that. Instead I leave, out into the forest.

Fucking Gideon.

Within moments I'm nearly fully dry. Something flies up under my towel and I flap it loose, keep walking. I step off the wooden walkway and into the dirt, navigate a thin trail through the brush until my bus appears out of the woods. The paint is shorn off, down to the gunmetal gray chassis. The engine block and tires missing. The few windows that are open are covered with tight layers of mosquito netting. My addition, when I moved in.

No one wants to live in the bus. I don't know why. Maybe because it's remote. So far from camp you can't hear anything. There's also something vaguely apocalyptic about it. And it was in sorry shape when I showed up. Very sorry shape. It took a few days of cleaning and dragging furniture out here to bring it up to a livable standard.

Livable for me. Because fuck this forest and all the monster bugs that dwell within. Nothing but me gets in here.

I make my way for the steps leading up to the door, and one of those roach motherfuckers is chilling on a step, glaring at me. I slam my foot down, hoping the vibration will scare it away. It starts running toward me and I hop back.

Maybe Pete got scared by a bug. He jumped. The rope snapped.

Who knows?

Pete does. That's it.

The roach breaks and runs behind the stairs and disappears. I wait until I think it's safe, climb to the top and push in hard. The accordion door opens. I get inside, drop the towel onto the driver's seat, the only thing that's still bolted down to the floor. I take a pair of shorts and a t-shirt off the bookshelf that serves as the dresser. Spray myself with some deodorant, not that it'll help much at keeping me dry, but it's nice to pretend. The dirty clothes I hang over the single bench bus seat that's pushed up against the back.

Something feels off.

I turn, look around the bus. There's not much here. A

cot, the bookshelf and seats, a small table. On the table, a few books, borrowed from the library: A nearly-fallen-apart copy of *Fahrenheit 451* by Ray Bradbury and some cookbooks. A yellow plastic flashlight. My nearly-empty plastic jug of whiskey, which reminds me I need another one of those.

Then there's the small tie folder full of personal documents, sitting on top of the bookshelf.

I'm not a neat freak, but I like to keep things tidy. Which is not hard, because I don't have a whole lot of stuff anymore. Still, this small pile of things feels off. The sleeping bag looks more pushed into the corner of the cot than normal. And the books look like they've been moved around, maybe.

The folder, though, that's what does it.

I'm right-handed. When I loop the rope back around the enclosure, I go clockwise.

But the rope is now tied counter-clockwise.

I open it up. Everything's there.

Personal documents, a couple of photos. Including the one of my dad in his bunker gear, standing outside his firehouse in Bensonhurst. I look at that for a couple of minutes before putting it back.

Speaking of. I go to my dirty shorts and dig into the cargo pocket, so I can replace the items I brought with me to the passport office, and find the arson guidebook I swiped from Crusty Pete's tree house.

Was someone in here? Were they looking for this?

I pull my cell phone out of my bag, turn it on. It's still got a bit of a charge. I take a picture of the code on the back. I turn the phone off and stick it in my pocket. The phone is mostly useless, since there's no cell signal out here, but I figure I can send it to Bombay next time I'm out by the road. He's smarter than me and might have some input. Plus I'm overdue to check in. It's been weeks since we spoke. What a sorry best friend I am.

The arson manual, I fold up and stuff into the pocket of my cargo shorts. I feel the need to keep it close. Just in case.

SIX

THE SUN IS nearly gone now, a sliver blazing orange beyond the trees. The no-see-ums are out. Like mosquitos, but more insistent. We're out of the lemon-eucalyptus spray Aesop makes and I need to remind him to make more.

Tibo is crouched low to the ground, holding a lighter to a chunk of newspaper that's been doused in cooking oil. It catches on the edge, the flame slowly crawling across, and he places it into the circle of stones on a bed of kindling. He picks up a twig and pushes the newspaper in the center so the whole thing will catch.

He stands and returns to the circle, taking hands between Cannabelle and Gideon. The entire camp is here—I think the entire camp is here—standing in one large circle around the fire sputtering and coming to life, flames licking the dead wood.

I step into the shadows, sit up on a picnic table. Tibo looks at me for a couple of moments, expecting something, like today was going to be different from every other day, but it's not. I settle into my spot, comfortably away from the circle.

A dark cloud is cast over everyone. I scan the faces I can see, that instinctual part of my brain taking over, sorting them out. There is a very good chance the person responsible for killing Pete—if he was killed—is here. Holding hands, like everyone is together in this. No one has left camp since he died, that I know of. I keep an eye out for the stereogram soul that matches mine.

Tibo clears his throat.

"Today was not a good day for us as a community..."

"Excuse me."

Tibo stops and looks over at a short Asian girl in overalls and a white tank top, her black hair in a braid that brushes her lower back. Katie, I think.

"Trigger warnings, please?" she asks, with a heavy layer of condescension.

Tibo looks at the ground and sighs. "Tonight we will be discussing death. I thought that might be obvious?"

He looks around the circle one more time, to make sure there won't be any more interruptions. Then he gives a slight nod. "Usually before dinner, we stand here and take turns sharing what we're thankful for. But this is a unique circumstance. A member of our group died today in a very unfortunate accident."

His eyes seem to flick in my direction when he says this, but I can't be sure in the failing light.

"I thought this might be a good opportunity to share our memories of Pete," Tibo says. "If you didn't know him and there's something you'd like to share, that's fine, too. Whatever you're comfortable with."

He stops and looks around, waiting for someone to speak.

TIBO. HOW TO describe Tibo.

Last I saw Tibo, before I saw him here, he was dredging the bottom of the Narrows to find several million dollars' worth of silver bars that had been lost in a shipwreck in the early 1900s. While working on this plan, he dressed like a pirate, because he thought it might help his creative process.

It was fucking lunacy. But lunacy is square in Tibo's wheelhouse. The plan worked. He found a couple of the bars, buried in the muck and mud. And he made enough money to buy this place.

He's the kind of weird that most people want to pat on the head and call "cute." Unless you're paying attention, and you realize there might be something to it. I always knew he was smart, toeing up on brilliant. But back when we were bouncing around the East Village, had someone asked me, I never would have guessed he'd be good at something like this.

The leadership role has galvanized him. That puppy-like sense of wonder is gone, replaced by a laser focus on making this place run. He talked about it for years: Finding a plot of land down south, turning it into a commune, developing a model of sustainable living. Granted, part of that was due to his belief we were approaching the apocalypse and humanity needed a place to ride that out, but motivation is motivation, no matter where you find it.

The important thing is, he's found the place where he fits in the world. The only thing I've got looming in my future is a loose plan to go to Prague and do stuff, contingent on my passport arriving in time.

My five year plan consists of two things: Be alive and not in jail.

And here's Tibo, building something. I'm proud of him. Maybe jealous, too.

This is something I would tell him if we still have conversations like that anymore.

MARX IS THE first to speak.

Of course he's the first to speak.

"Not all of you knew Pete the way I knew him," Marx says. "He was more than a person. He was a spirit leader. He was a revolutionary. He had the heart of a lion. He saw the world for what it is and dared to think differently. I can only hope to carry on Pete's good works." He glances at Tibo, clearly and deliberately. "I know not everyone agreed with him, but he was right, you know? He was right."

That doesn't sound loaded at all.

A few people in the circle nod in agreement. Marx oozes so much charisma you can almost see it, like the tentacles of an octopus, wrapping around people, pulling them toward him. If I was coming into this cold, without knowing he was a dick, I'd at least be intrigued by him.

Next up is Moony. She looks nice tonight. Yellow sheer sundress that accentuates her bony frame, dark hair in pigtails. Not smiling, which is rare for her. "Pete was… he was an interesting guy. We never spoke much, but he was kind, and I measure a person by their kindness. It's sad that he's gone."

Sunny, who's standing to Moony's left, picks up like it was a trailing sentence. "We pray for him. To Mother Earth, and to the great unknown. May the energy of his life-force travel forever amongst the stars."

People nod in acknowledgment.

Gideon says, "Excuse me, everyone. I'd like to go next."

All eyes turn toward him. A couple of them roll, mine included.

"Pete's death was a tragedy, and I hope everyone understands that." He stares at me when he says this. I am not a fan of this attention I am suddenly getting. "But I want you all to know that I'm on top of this. We're going to make sure everything is safe, and no one has to worry. Starting tomorrow we're going to begin a full accounting of all the rope bridges. We're going to check the water and electric lines, too, just to be safe."

There's crunching from the tree line, and everyone pauses. Katashi comes barreling out of the encroaching darkness. He sees the circle and winces, says, "*Sumimasen*."

Which I think means 'sorry.' It certainly sounds like it.

He steps between Sunny and Moony. They hesitate, but part and allow him to take the spot. Sunny leans forward and raises an eyebrow at Moony. Katashi, oblivious to the intrusion, sets his grip and surveys the circle. I expect he won't be contributing a memory of Pete. Growing up in New York, you get an ear for languages. I understand a little Spanish, Italian, French, Russian, and oddly, Czech. Can't speak them worth a damn, but if I hear them and the person is talking slow enough, I get the gist. Japanese, I've got nothing.

But I've been listening, paying attention to body cues. It's like a game. People carry so much of their story on their body. Katashi is the first to volunteer for a task and also content to wander alone. That makes me like him.

The ritual continues. People share memories of Pete. Nothing too deep or interesting. Nothing that blips on my radar. Happy claptrap. Some more exaltations to Mother Earth or the eternal wind or the dark matter of the universe and blah blah blah.

At the end of it, it's only me and Katashi who haven't spoken. Katashi gets a pass for not speaking English. I get a pass because no one expects me to contribute. It's not that I don't believe in what they're doing. But I never participate in the circle. If we're all going to stand around and talk about what we're thankful for, well, what part of the broken shards of my life do I have to be thankful for?

At the end Tibo lets go of Cannabelle and Gideon and walks to the center of the circle. "Let's eat. And please, if anyone needs anything, or has a concern, please come see me. I'll be here until the last person leaves."

The circle breaks apart. Me and Aesop head for the kitchen, where the trays have cooled down enough that we can haul them out to the serving table bare-handed. We set them up alongside a pile of wooden plates and metal utensils and pull back the aluminum foil.

The potatoes browned nicely, and it smells real damn good. Aesop dumps a Tupperware container of his dressing on the salad and tosses it with his hands. As he does this, he looks up at the dry erase board hanging over the food, makes sure all the ingredients are listed. A reference for those with allergies and weird eating habits.

Once the food is ready, we step away. No one would probably

be bothered if we went first, but we both like to wait until everyone has filled their plates. It's one of the reasons I think Aesop is probably a good person, even though we barely speak about anything other than cooking.

When everyone's gone up and sat down, I get my plate and take a hefty scoop of the Shepherd's pie and a bit of the salad and go to the far picnic table, at the edge of the clearing. The food is good. It'd be nice to have some meat, but I've lost a little weight since I got here, and it's weight I probably needed to lose anyway. Can't feel bad about that.

It's dark now, dinner starting way later than normal given the circumstances. The clearing is lit blue and orange. Blue by some solar-powered lights that'll last another four hours or so on the juice they sucked up today. Orange by the fire, three feet high, light dancing off the people assembled close to it.

No one here looks like a killer.

Tibo's got to be right. I'm overthinking it. That's what I do. I build narratives. I need things to make sense in my head. And apparently the only thing that makes sense is for everything to be a conspiracy. For people to be uniformly awful no matter where you go or what you do.

Maybe I bore too easily.

Maybe nothing was moved on the bus.

Maybe I closed the folder in the reverse direction without thinking about it. It was dark this morning when I closed it and I was half-asleep.

Still. I pull the pamphlet out of my pocket, look at the numbers scrawled on the back. I take a look at the fire.

The numbers could be a code.

What else would they be? The way the numbers are spaced, it certainly seems to correspond to words. I look for one that's a combination of three letters, figure if I can crack 'the' maybe I can chip away at the rest. But that doesn't work. I look for the most common number, thinking maybe it's the letter 'e' because that's the most common letter, and that doesn't seem to bear out.

I am not a code breaker, in case there was any question of that.

"Nice job tonight."

I look up and Job is standing over me, barefoot in jeans and a flannel shirt, the sleeves rolled up to his muscled biceps. His head is meticulously shaved, which contrasts with his long, thick, carefully coiffed beard. He smells a bit like shit, which I can't really blame him for. He handles the outhouses. It's a dirty job. He's the only one who seems to want to do it.

I nod at him, and he lingers. I want to tell him to leave when Cannabelle comes shuffling through the dirt toward me, suddenly assuming this is a party.

"You're welcome," I tell Job, and he walks off. Cannabelle climbs on top of the table next to me. She doesn't say anything as she balances her plate on her laps and eats.

After she demolishes half the plate she says, "Food is good tonight."

"Thanks."

"This is weird, right? This whole thing?"

"Yup."

"Is there something someone's not telling us? I feel like there's something someone's not telling us."

I look over at Cannabelle, who's looking out at the fire, chewing. Another person I've barely interacted with in my time here. And yet. She's as curious about this as I am. And maybe she senses that. I consider telling her about the rope. But I've seen how messages spread through this place. Sunny got a rash from some fire ants and the next thing people were whispering that she caught an STD and that the outhouses weren't safe and suddenly people were shitting in the woods. Our mock society falls apart with a stiff wind.

"Not sure," I tell her.

"You think maybe what happened to Pete wasn't an accident."

It's not a question.

"I don't know what I think," I tell her.

"Pete was a weird dude."

She goes back to eating. Cleans the plate, licks off the remnants of food, and places it next to her. She sits there holding a mason jar full of water between her hands, her fingers loaded with rings. She clicks them against the glass, short taps mixed with long taps.

She wants to tell me something.

"How was Pete a weird dude?" I ask.

"I see things up in the trees."

I glance up. The tops of the trees are veiled in darkness. But Cannabelle goes up empty-handed and comes down with bud and sweet leaf. Apparently there's an entire grow rig up there, something out of sight but close to the sun. I've been curious to see how it works. I'm less curious to know what it feels like to fall from up there and break my neck.

"What do you see from up in the trees?" I ask.

"I see Pete. He runs around a lot, like he's a spy on a mission."

"Where to?"

"Not sure." She takes a long sip. "I don't follow him. That

wouldn't be cool."

"You see everything here, right?"

"Just about."

"How'd he been the past few days? Anything of note?"

"He was carrying a book everywhere. Outhouse, dinner, on walks. He always had this book sticking out of his pocket."

"What book?"

"*The Monkey Wrench Gang*."

"I don't know that one."

"We have it in the library."

It's full black beyond the trees. The library lights don't get turned on at night, and I don't like fucking around with the candles in there. I don't want to be the guy who sets the place on fire.

"I'll look tomorrow," I tell her. "Thanks."

Marx crosses our field of vision. I nod toward him. "What's that asshole's deal?"

"What do you mean?"

"What's his story?"

"You don't know about his family," she says.

"What about them?"

"Died in a fire. He was a kid. Off visiting his grandparents, and his parents were at a cabin, and there was a forest fire. Turned out there was this tree-clearing operation and they did some careless thing that started it."

Huh. That casts Marx in a new light. I lost my dad to a mistake someone else made. I know what that can twist you into. Not that it's an excuse. It certainly wasn't for me.

But if anything is going to push you into a lifestyle of hard activism, that would be it. And it would be hypocritical to hold that against him. He just needs to learn to control his anger before it controls him.

"Well," I tell her. "That explains some stuff."

She nods. "Want seconds?"

"No, I'm good."

She dashes off toward the food table.

I look at the numbers on the pamphlet one last time, tear off that page, stuff it in my pocket, walk past the fire, throw the rest of the pamphlet onto the nest of flames. Watch as the corners black and curl. The older couple sitting on a log by the fire—I think their names are Ginger and Robert—are cuddled up against a log, making out like teenagers, not paying attention to me.

I wait until the pamphlet is all the way burned up before moving on. Dump my empty plate and utensils into the gray wash bin.

With dinner mostly finished, people are assembling toward the main cluster of picnic tables. Someone pulls out Monopoly and they pair off into two-person teams. Packages of loose tobacco and rolling papers come out. I feel the tug of nicotine, my brain reminding me what I'm missing.

That's one of the nice things about this place. Too hard to go out for smokes. I don't want to pay to stockpile them. And I can't smoke a rolled cigarette without wanting to puke. The first few weeks were rough, and I may or may not have thrown a chair at someone during a nic fit, but now I rarely even get the urge.

Maybe it's the fresh air. Maybe it's all the walking and the physical labor, and that feeling I sometimes get of trying to breathe through a wet sock, or in my case, a pair of shredded lungs.

That was my sacrifice. I needed something. A life without vice is a life where you have to face the things those vices otherwise would have covered up.

Anyway, I've still got my whiskey.

Aesop appears next to me. He nods toward the Monopoly setup. "You want in on the game?"

"Not tonight."

"C'mon man. You should play."

"I play Monopoly I'll end up flipping the table. That is not a game for people with anger management issues."

"Will you at least stay out with us? If ever there was a night that we all needed to be together, this is it."

"Goodnight."

He sighs, more hurt than angry. "Night."

I grab a pink flashlight from the flashlight bin and head into the woods, the sound and the light fading behind me, until I'm on a walkway far enough out that I can click off the light and the world is so dark I can't see a thing. Not my hand in front of my face, not the ground under my feet, not the trees looming over me. Not even the stars. The canopy is too thick.

Of course, as soon as I turn the light off, as soon as it's nothing but dark, I see it. Like my vision switched over to an old movie. The hole, and Wilson's body crumbled into it, rainwater pooling where his arm was pressed up against the wall of it. His glass doll eyes, staring out at nothing, and the reason for that was me.

The wave hits.

Pushing me under. Roaring in my ears, threatening to pull me down into the dark. Filling my eyes and nose and throat. I'm tumbling, can't tell up from down.

I fumble with the flashlight, try to flick the plastic button on the side to turn it on, drop it. It clatters to the ground and I fall to my knees, sweeping my hands around, trying to find it. By the time I do, I'm crying. Still not breathing, my lungs about to burst.

And then it's there, in my hands. I click it on and I'm in the woods. A hostel in the middle of Georgia. Not underwater. Not being pulled deeper. Just in the woods.

I pull my legs up and sit there for a bit until I've calmed down. Until my chest doesn't feel like it's swelling with water.

Then I get up and walk.

No monster bugs on the steps into the bus. I do a quick sweep with the flashlight when I get in, to make sure none of them broke in with plans to kill me while I was out. This is a thing that concerns me. I pull the cord that turns on the rope light running along the edges of the ceiling. The sun was good today. The solar panels soaked up enough I could squeak out a few hours of juice, not that I plan to be up long.

Underneath the bunk there are two empty plastic whiskey jugs, plus the one on the table that's half-full. I climb on top of the bunk and take a long, deep swig. It's flat and sharp and hot.

Man. Nothing says rock bottom like plastic jug whiskey.

I look around at the battered metal on the inside of the bus, at my little pile of belongings. My ridiculous suspicions and my sad, quiet evening alone. My head already swimming a little. I reach up and turn off the light so that it's pitch black. A slight breeze drifts through the netted window, along with the sound of insects and rustling leaves.

And those two sets of eyes, peeking through the window.

The silence is all-encompassing. Living in New York City, you live with the feeling of a television being on in the next room.

An electric hum you can't hear, but you can feel, even when it's quiet. Even in Portland there was a little of that. The hum never stops. I always wondered what I would learn about myself when the humming stopped and the world went silent and I couldn't hear anything but what's inside myself. The things the hum was covering.

I don't like it.

The jug of whiskey seems heavy enough that maybe I'll sleep through the night. But I'm going to need to pick up more. I take another pull and pray it's enough to drown out my dreams.

SEVEN

MY MOUTH TASTES like I've been sucking on a dirty dishrag and my skull is a size too small. I turn my head and the muscles in my neck tighten in protest.

No nightmares though. That much is a victory.

I swing my legs off the cot and kick the empty jug of whiskey. I pull on a pair of shorts and a t-shirt and put on my sneakers. On instinct I reach for my cell but remember it's at the bottom of my bag, tucked away. I'm still not used to not carrying it all the time, though I do enjoy this moment of realization I have most mornings. I don't need to carry a cell phone. That's a nice thing.

There's a half-empty bottle of water on my desk. I suck it down, put that and the three empty whiskey handles into a canvas bag, and head out. The forest is quiet in every direction and the sky is overcast, washed in dingy gray light. No sun to make a guess at what time it is.

After stopping at an outhouse and then a recycle bin to discard the jugs, I head toward the main domes, passing by the yoga clearing, where a dozen people are doing downward-facing dog on a rainbow of foam mats spread on the dusty ground. Moony is leading them, her black hair spilling over her bare shoulders. I've considered joining them. Some days I feel a tug in my lower back. Whether that's age or sleeping on an old cot, I can't be sure. Maybe I need to start some body maintenance.

Alas, today is not that day.

I pass the art space—a deck with a slanted roof held aloft by wooden columns. It looks like it should blow over with a slight breeze but somehow has been standing since this place was built. There's a clay kiln, which is currently belching white smoke, and a thick canvas the size of a bedsheet stretched taut between bamboo poles.

The canvas depicts a swirl of colors, like a wave curling up, one side of the wave a treescape, the forest reaching out and growing in on itself. The other side of the wave a starscape. They come together like they're part of the same scene, but encroaching on each other in small measures. It reminds me a little of a van Gogh. But different. Bigger. Trying to find a middle-ground between two different worlds. I look at it for a little bit, because every time I look at it I think maybe it's finished but it's still a little bit different.

Cannabelle steps onto the deck in a loose tank top and shorts, barefoot, holding a brush tipped in white, and taps at the starscape. Adding more stars to the sky. The trance breaks and I walk away, but she calls after me. "Hey Ash. C'mere for a minute?"

I climb up onto the wooden platform. "What's up?"

"Why don't you give me a hand. Pick up a brush. I've still got a few billion stars to go."

I shake my head. "Not my jam."

"You should give it a try sometime. It's therapeutic."

"What's the point of a painting that's never finished?"

"What's the point of a life that's never finished?"

I try to come up with a wiseass remark, can't, shrug, and walk away.

The picnic benches outside the main domes have an assortment of people sitting at them, reading or smoking cigarettes or eating fruit. The smell of tobacco drifts my way and it smells a little like my old life. As I'm approaching Eatery something smacks my chest and falls to the ground. I stop and look down, see it's a blue and white hacky sack.

A couple of guests are staring at me, apparently having lost control of the hacky mid-game. I pick it up and Joe, an older guy with sleeve tattoos and a slight limp, says, "Little help?"

I toss the hacky into the woods.

"Watch where you're kicking that thing," I tell him.

This results in some grumbling, which I ignore. Aesop leans out the front door of the kitchen and waves me over. Inside he's standing with a little elf of a kid. Latino, probably no more than just out of college, big wet eyes and a little stubble on his chin, like he's heard about beards and wants to know what the fun is about.

"Ash, meet Zorg."

"Zorg?" I ask.

The kid nods. "I am Zorg," he says, with a swell of body-lifting confidence.

Sigh. People like to shed their names when they get into camp.

The real world doesn't come to bear here. Mostly the nicknames are easy to remember, which is nice. This is among the more ridiculous.

Though I used to hang out with a group that included Ginny Tonic and Bombay and Good Kelli and Bad Kelli, so who the fuck am I to talk?

"I have to run and take care of something," Aesop says. "I'm supposed to show Zorg around. He's going to help me in the kitchen after you leave. Can you show him the ropes? I'll be back in a half hour, tops."

Aesop is probably lying, that motherfucker. I can see it in his eyes. He says I need to be more social and sometimes corners me with folks so maybe I'll make new friends. I want to go to the library but I'm not exactly in a rush, so I nod him off and turn to Zorg.

"Do you have any cooking experience?" I ask.

"Zorg does not."

"Look, you can call yourself Zorg and that's fine, but let's cut it with the third person just for right now, okay? I'm way too hung over for that."

He purses his lips and dips an eyebrow, like he is suddenly deeply suspect of me. "Okay. Zzz… I… do not. Do I need cooking experience?"

"No. I didn't have much. Aesop is a good teacher. Let me run you through the facilities."

I show him the cast iron stove, powered by dead wood from the forest. The electrical outlet for the occasional device we try to not use because we only have as much power as the solar panels suck up. Kitchen appliances are a hell of a drain. We can get two minutes out of the blender, tops. We run through the greywater sink and the water filter, which takes even longer than the greywater, and the whole time Zorg watches me like a lizard, his eyes wide and flat.

After the tour of the kitchen, I figure I should show him the garden. Outside we find Gideon hanging upside down from a tree, shirtless, doing sit-ups. His face is red and he's counting off very loudly, as if for our benefit, "Four… five… six…"

"Wow," Zorg says.

"That's Gideon. What you're seeing right now tells you everything you need to know about him."

As we wander down the footpath Zorg asks, "So, everyone works here?"

"Everyone works. If you're staff you have a job and you do it and you get paid a little money. If you're a guest you pay a little money for your accommodations and you pitch in on a chore."

"A lot of people come through here?"

"Most people don't stay more than a few days. That's less an indictment of the facilities and more about demand. Lots of people want to come here."

"And how does the food service work?"

"We do dinner every night. Full vegan, no exceptions. Most of it comes from our gardens, but we go into town for stuff we can't grow. Pasta and things. We don't do breakfast or lunch, that's up to everyone else. We have two chest fridges. People are welcome to use the kitchen and to store stuff. Truth is no one does anything elaborate in there. Most people wait until dinner for their big meal. Everything else is snacking."

Something shimmers in my line of vision. I stop, put my

hand out to block Zorg. I take a step forward and there's a web spun across the trees lining the path, a spider the size of a large strawberry chilling right at face-level, its abdomen a brilliant explosion of stained glass. It would be beautiful if it wasn't a giant nightmare spider. I walk around the trees, let the spider be.

"Are there a lot of those out here?" Zorg asks.

"Too many," I tell him.

We pass one of the outhouses, which is the size of a porta-potty, the outside graffitied with flowers.

"So you pee against the trees and do your other business in there?" Zorg asks.

"That's the deal," I tell him. "You cover it with sawdust. Works surprisingly well."

"Sounds scary," Zorg says.

"It is, a little. Check for bugs before you sit down. Took me two days to work up the courage the first time. Don't wait that long. It's not healthy."

We reach the garden. The canopy is cleared out here and the clouds have burned away, so the raised beds are drenched in sunlight. The temperature jumps noticeably as we step out from under the shade, enough I want to retreat. I lead him down the long rows, show him the vegetables and the herbs. The special plot we have set aside for Momma's. The chickens peck at the dirt around us. I introduce them: Diana, Leah, Consuela, Mum, Joule. Mathilda is off causing trouble somewhere.

Last stop is the goat pen.

"And that's Dana Cameron," I say, pointing to a young, fuzzy goat chewing on something. "She's mostly a pet and helps to clear land, but we do sometimes get milk for the non-vegans."

Dana looks up and makes a goat noise, goes back to chewing.

"The goat has a last name?" Zorg asks.

"I didn't name her."

"This place seems kind of old," Zorg says. "But Zz... I heard it's only been open for about a year."

"It was built back in the seventies. It used to be called Middle Earth. Apparently the founders had a thing for Tolkien. It fell off, and people have tried to reopen it a few times, but it never lasted long. Tibo is making the latest attempt. He actually had some capital to invest, so I figure he has a pretty good chance of hanging in for the long run."

"It seems nice."

"It is nice."

"But you're leaving."

He blinks his lizard eyes at me. I'm not sure why or how he's asking the question, so I choose to shrug at him. "Can you keep yourself occupied until Aesop gets back to the kitchen?"

He nods so I leave him in the garden.

THE PURPLE CURTAIN on the library dome is drawn across the entrance, so I peek in to make sure the nude book club isn't meeting. I also briefly wonder if there are so many nude activities during the colder months, or if this is a summer thing.

This is my favorite of the domes. There's a level of reverence here that doesn't exist in the other domes, which are crowded and haphazard and sometimes dirty. Here, everything is immaculate. There's one continuous shelf that starts at the floor and wraps up, running along the inside wall in a spiral to the roof, where there's a skylight that brings natural light trickling down onto the round carpet and four wingback chairs placed around an Oriental rug. Off in the corner is a cluttered desk, which is occupied by Magda, bare feet crossed, wearing a tan sundress and tan shawl and tan ceramic jewelry that clacks when she moves. She looks up at me and smiles.

"Ash," she says.

"Magda."

She places a finger to mark her place and puts the book down in front of her. "Looking for anything particular?"

"*The Monkey Wrench Gang.*"

She tilts her head. Curious.

"Cannabelle recommended it."

As if on cue, Cannabelle comes through the curtain, wearing basketball shorts and a white t-shirt, her short hair wet and pushed back on her skull like a greaser.

"Speak of the devil," I tell her.

"I wanted to come see if you got sorted," she says.

We both look at Magda, who's frowning. "Sorry, I don't think we have that one."

Cannabelle sweeps around the shelves, looking at the start of the spiral running along the floor, where the author's name would be. "I could have sworn I just saw it..."

"Maybe I should invest in an e-reader," I tell them.

"Do you know how much an e-reader costs the environment, in terms of plastic and manufacturing?" Magda asks. "Not to mention what they do to bookstores. Electronic books are putting booksellers out of business. It's a tragedy. Don't even joke about that."

Her voice is shaking a little by the end.

"I was kidding," I tell her. "Deep breath."

She shakes her head, crosses her arms.

Cannabelle's path comes around to Magda's desk. She reaches down and pulls up a book poking out from underneath a pile of magazines. "It's right here."

"Oh well..." Magda seems to stumble a little. "Someone must have returned it and it didn't get shelved yet."

Cannabelle nods and holds it over her shoulder. I cross the carpet and pluck it out of her hand, stuff it into my pocket. "I'll have it back soon."

Magda nods and I leave. Outside Cannabelle comes alongside me.

"That was a little weird," she says, her voice hushed.

"Magda isn't all there," I tell her.

"You don't sound like you believe that."

"No, I don't."

She nods. "I concur."

Cannabelle doesn't leave room for me to respond. She runs and leaps onto the branch of a thick tree hanging close to the ground and throws her legs over it. Upside down now, her shirt falling down into her face, she salutes, pulls herself up, and suddenly she's on her toes, perched on top of the branch. She leaps to another branch, and the next, higher and higher until she's gone. Off to work, leaving me alone.

I don't know what to do at this point. I could keep asking people questions but I don't know what questions to ask. If there's something untoward going on, there's no sense in tipping off the guilty parties. I already went through all of Pete's belongings, of which there were barely any.

And then it hits me.

I went through his physical belongings. I didn't go through all his stuff.

THE MAIN DOME is the one that makes me ache for home. Therefore, it is not always my favorite place to be.

It's the closest anything around here gets to 'sprawling'. It's the biggest of all of the domes by double and separated into a couple of rooms: There's an office that's used mostly for filing. There's the computer room, which is a wheezing old desktop covered with stickers that someone probably bartered for ten years ago. It still uses Internet Explorer. I'm not a computer guy and even I know that's some bullshit.

Then there's the bar/lounge. It's not exact, but in style and spirit it's a replica of Apocalypse Lounge. My favorite bar, which was being shuttered as I was leaving New York. The only place my friends and I had that felt like a beacon in a storm.

The office is dark wood and smells of cinnamon and spice. That incense smell that bothered me so much when I first got here but that I've come to appreciate. This room is the darkest, the windows covered up so the failing tube monitor is viewable. A touch of sunlight and it gets washed out.

The computer is perched between two overflowing gray filing cabinets. The seat is occupied by Alex, the little hipster girl who looks like she was plucked out of Williamsburg, wearing torn jean shorts and a Clash t-shirt with brunette bangs nearly touching her eyes. She's clacking away at the keyboard, staring at a giant block of text. I come up behind her and ask, "Can I cut in?"

She points a thin finger over her shoulder without looking up or losing stride on the keyboard. "Sign up sheet is on the wall."

I know about the sheet. I also know it's full for the rest of the afternoon.

"Bit of an emergency," I tell her.

"Got to write a love note to your slampiece?"

"I don't know what that means."

She looks at me and smiles with her cat eyes, eyeliner caked around them. "What's it worth to you?"

"I don't have much to give."

"I've heard rumors of bacon."

Great. It was only a matter of time until word got around.

At the bottom of the chest fridge, down where it's coldest, there's an old box of tempeh, which no one ever touches, because no amount of kitchen kung-fu can make it taste better than wet cardboard. There's a package of bacon inside, property of me and Aesop. We also have a special cast iron skillet for bacon only, so there's no cross-contamination.

Meat isn't technically off limits, but it will earn you a lecture. Whenever one of us feels the urge, we duck into the woods at night and fry up a few pieces.

She leans back, stretches her arms over her head. "I think we could make a deal if you could scare up some of that sweet, sweet bacon."

I lean on the desk next to her, cross my arms. "What are your terms?"

"Four pieces, extra crisp. Nearly black, but not like fully black."

"Has to be done under cover of night. I'm talking three, four in the morning."

She nods. "Night bacon. I dig it."

"So?"

She turns back to the computer, hits some keys, logs off. She gets up from the chair and sticks a pinkie out to me. "Night bacon?"

We pinkie promise. "Night bacon. We'll talk later."

Alex saunters off and I fall into the nearly-shattered office chair. I don't lean back too far because I learned that lesson already, the time I went ass-up. There's something stiff underneath me and I think maybe I sat on something, and then realize it's *The Monkey Wrench Gang*. I take it out of my back pocket, consider putting it on the desk, but slide it into one of the filing cabinets. Given that it has some value, my gut tells me this is somehow safer. If I put it anywhere else, someone will just walk off with it, either to return it to the library or read it themselves.

I'm glad Alex didn't push me too hard on this deal. Our bacon supply is running low but four strips, I can manage. And this is worth it.

Trading bacon for favors so I can solve a murder that probably isn't even really a murder. My life has gotten strange.

There's a little scratch, somewhere at the back of me. Something feels missing. Takes me a second to remember what it is: I am still sober. I pull out my hillbilly flask, dose myself with some shitty whiskey. Give it a second to settle. That evens me out.

On the log-in screen there's a long list of file folders, each with a name. I click on Pete's, which actually says "Crusty Pete," which is a little goofy. A prompt screen comes up for a password. Of course.

I log onto the general account, the one I use, and click over to my e-mail. See Bombay's name in the little chat window.

Me: Yo.

Bombay: What up bro!

Me: Need some help.

Bombay: Let me guess. Some illicit shit?

Me: You know it.

Bombay: What happened this time?

Me: Don't know. Maybe nothing. Just need to know some stuff.

Bombay: Fine. Details.

Me: I'm on a shared computer. Need to get into someone's folder. Password protected.

Bombay: OS?

Me: ?

Bombay: Operating system.

Me: Windows.

Bombay: www.teamwatch.com/download

I click on the link, get taken to a download screen. Install the program. A little window pops up with a shiny blue bar that slowly marches to the right.

Bombay: So how are things?

Me: Okay.

Bombay: Tibo good?

Me: Yeah man. He wears this leadership thing well.

Bombay: How about the hippies? Are you making friends?

Me: Loads.

Bombay: I honestly wish I was there. How funny that must be.
Me: Dude, it's fine. I'm a chef now.
Bombay: So you've given up on the other work? Wait wait wait no you haven't, because you're asking me to do some illicit shit!
Me: No comment. You been to see my ma lately?
Bombay: She's good. Misses you.
Me: That's nice. Hold up now.

The blue bar meets the end of the screen and turns from sky to French blue, marking the end of the download. Quicker than I would have expected, but the computer makes a grinding noise from the effort. I go through the steps and a screen pops up with two boxes—one marked 'address', one marked 'password', both with long strings of numbers.

Bombay: Got some numbers for me?
Me: 342840, 038113
Bombay: Okay, don't touch anything.

The screen flashes and the cursor moves around the screen without me touching it.

Bombay: lol
Bombay: Holy shit dude.

The mouse clicks on a couple of things until there's a screen full of numbers for memory and storage and speed.

Bombay: I think this is the first computer ever built.

Bombay: Okay, what do you need? You can type now.

Me: Username is Crusty Pete. Need to get in there.

Bombay: Fucking hippies man!

Me: Yup.

Bombay: Sit back, two minutes.

I watch as a black screen pops up full of white text. Typing, typing, and a long string of words spill across the screen. More commands, more words. I should pay attention. This is useful to know.

Then again, this is why I have a Bombay in my life.

Bombay: Whoever juiced this thing up didn't do too bad a job. This computer is old as fuck but still runs. Respect.

Bombay: Oh god. His password is fucking 'password'.

Bombay: What a dumbass

Me: Don't speak ill of the dead.

Bombay: Oh c'mon! You've got me hacking a dead guy's account?

Me: That sounds awful strong.

Bombay: Whatever. Call me sometime man.

Me: No cell service out here.

Bombay: Go somewhere you can get it. You still live in America, right?

Me: For now.

Bombay: ??

Me: We'll talk soon, got to work.

Bombay: Fine. Bye.

Me: <3

Oh how I miss Bombay. We met one day a long time ago when a bunch of kids were pushing him into a locker and calling him a terrorist. Being a Muslim in New York was never a cakewalk. It was a very dangerous thing after 9/11.

I made them stop. I'm not a fan of bullies. I didn't like how I got picked on for having a girl's name, I don't like other people getting picked on for anything else. Especially for things they didn't do.

It got bloody. I got suspended. By the time I came back to school, Bombay and I were inseparable. We work well as a unit, because his first response to a problem is to think through it instead of hit it. Pretty much the opposite of me.

The best kind of friend a guy could ask for. One day I hope to return the favor.

The password works and I'm in Crusty Pete's little section of the hard drive. There's not much. A folder with some pictures. Him and his unwashed friends. Another folder with some Word documents, all of them full of ranting bullshit, about the working class and income inequality. Many of the documents have the word 'manifesto' in the title. I skim a couple of them but find nothing of value.

I open my e-mail and send them to myself, just in case. Maybe there's something in there worth knowing, though I strongly doubt that. Then I check the browser's history.

News stories. A lot of them.

Activists sabotage a rail line in Mexico that will displace families and result in the removal of large swaths of trees. A fire causes $200,000 worth of damage to partially-constructed homes on previously-protected land in Canada. An agricultural center researching genetically-engineered crops is burnt down. An SUV dealership is vandalized, the cars covered in paint and lit on fire. A mink farm is raided and all the minks are released. I don't know what a mink is. A quick Google Image search shows it looks like a ferret.

There are more stories. Stuff as recent as this year, some stretching back to the early 90s. The common thread between most of them is that the Earth Liberation Front took credit, or was suspected in the attacks.

Scattered throughout are links to porn—apparently Crusty Pete had a thing for feet—but that doesn't really seem relevant to the rest of this.

As if the arson guide wasn't already ominous, this makes it downright scary.

I check the Gmail sign-in page, but his username and password aren't autosaved. That's too bad. I once asked Bombay to crack a Gmail password and he laughed at me. I'd need a keylogger, except Pete isn't here to type in his password. I can't guess at his password recovery information—phone number or favorite pet or mother's maiden name. I wouldn't even know where to start with Pete. I don't even know if Pete is his real name.

I go back to the news stories, see if there's anything I missed, and as I'm hovering over a link, there's a sound outside. Someone yelling, then the roar of an engine.

That's probably not good.

I jump out of the chair and run for the front door, into the main clearing at the foot of the road, and a black van is screeching to a halt, throwing up clouds of dust. It may as well be a spaceship. Cars never come down this far. They're supposed to stop at the lot right after the bridge.

Then a bunch of guys spill out, guns drawn, wearing bulletproof vests and ball caps. No identifying details.

One of them beelines toward me. He's big, linebacker size. He screams, "Freeze."

I put up my hands. He pushes his substantial hand into my chest, throwing me back against the outer wall of the dome. "Don't resist!"

I'm about to argue when he pulls something off his belt, holds it up, and points it at my face. A thick stream of liquid shoots into my eyes. Every nerve cell in my body lights up like a firework.

As I collapse to the ground in a crying, blubbering mess, choking on the liquid and phlegm in my throat, I feel something hard and tight clasping my hands behind my back, cutting into my skin. I think it's a zip tie.

EIGHT

MY VISION IS blurry, skin burning like I washed it with a slurry of habanero peppers. Which is probably close to exactly what that spray was. A pair of rough hands grab me under the arms and drag me across the ground. There's not much I can do but go along with it, stumbling and trying to stay upright.

I'm shoved toward the gaping maw of a black van. The person behind me pushes me inside hard, and I collide with a mass of warm bodies, skin slick with sweat, limbs writhing in confusion. It reeks of body odor.

A few more join us, bodies landing with thuds and rocking the van. I catch an elbow on the side of the head. The door slams shut. The engine starts and we're moving, bumping over the dirt pathway that leads out to the road. I twist into a sitting position. It's hard to focus but I'm crying so hard some of this shit is getting cleared out of my eyes.

After a few moments I think I have the headcount. Tibo, Marx, Aesop, Magda, Cannabelle, Katashi, and Job. Everyone's eyes red and puffy. A little bit of blood trickles from one of Job's nostrils.

At the rear of the van, by the door, is some dude with jet black hair and a face serene as a lake. He's got on a black bulletproof vest and a black baseball cap, perched on one knee, holding onto a strap in the wall of the van. There's a gun holstered on his hip.

Tibo sputters. "What is this?"

The guard says, "Don't talk."

"I'll talk all I want," Tibo says. "Who are you and where are you taking us?"

"Don't talk," the guard says, in the same tone, not looking at anyone in particular.

Marx says, "Fuck you, pig…"

The guard slams his fist across Marx's face. His head whips back, cracking on the side of the van, and he goes down. The guard's expression doesn't change. "I said don't talk."

That's enough to keep me quiet. Same for everyone else.

The ride smooths out as we hit the road. I tuck in, breathe slow, try to come to terms with the searing pain in my face, because I feel like this isn't going to get resolved any time soon.

I DON'T KNOW HOW long we've been driving when we stop. There's silence all around, and then the door opens, sunlight blasting into the back, burning my already-stinging eyes.

Men in commando gear haul us out, stand us in a row. Tibo to my left, Magda to my right. Magda is whimpering from the pain, which makes me want to do bad things to these assholes, even though a lot of them are carrying heavy artillery. Lucky for them my hands are tied together.

Though, probably more lucky for me.

Gravel crunches underfoot. A man walks in front of us, comes to a stop, looking us all up and down. Black guy, built like a fighter jet. Six feet four, arms the size of my thigh. Probably the guy who visited Ford, which makes these guys FBI, though I didn't know this was how the FBI liked to operate.

His eyes are tired and his face is covered with stubble, like he hasn't seen a bed or a mirror in days. He takes an unmarked plastic bottle out of his pocket and walks down the line, pouring it on our faces each in turn, everyone making little sounds of relief. When he gets to me, I tense up. He grabs my chin, pushes my head up, and pours the liquid in my eyes. It's cold and the burning subsides.

Once he's doused everyone he says, "Inside."

I look around. We're in a parking lot. It hasn't been used in a long time. Big heavy cracks, weeds sticking out at odd angles, the paint marking the spaces worn and faded. It's an industrial complex of some kind. Flat elevation, surrounded by buildings, concrete and metal weeping long, deep rust stains. There are fields beyond them, and then the horizon.

"C'mon, get," the man in charge says.

The prettyboy agent from inside the van puts a hand up, signaling us to follow him. He leads us across the parking lot to a long, one-story building. We step through the door and inside it smells like mildew and animals. The hallway is littered with papers, the fixtures broken, things ripped out of the walls. There's a long line of doors, many of them propped open. A female agent with tight blonde hair pulled back into a harsh ponytail gets in front of me and herds me toward a door.

"In there," she says.

I step inside and there's a card table with chairs on either side. She pushes me against the wall, pats me down. Pulls out the belongings that I have on me, which is only the flask and—much to my dismay—the piece of paper with the code on it.

"No wallet, no phone?" she asks.

"Didn't know I'd need it."

She sits me down in the chair, pulls out a small knife with a thin black blade, and cuts the zip ties. I pull my wrists forward and massage the deep red grooves they left behind.

"Get comfortable," she says, placing down the flask but taking the paper, slamming the door after her.

The room is quiet, the heavy walls cutting off sound from the outside.

So, this sucks.

No badges, no nametags. No plate on the back of the van where they herded us in. If this really is FBI, then whatever they've got planned, they don't want us to know too many identifying details.

That is not comforting.

I take stock of the room. It's small, barely bigger than the card table and the chairs. Other than that, completely empty. It doesn't even seem big enough to have been an office. Maybe a storage room. The walls are intact but most of the acoustic ceiling tiles are missing, only a few still in place, showing big gaps and wires up in the ceiling. The floor has staples and wood in the corners, so there probably used to be carpet.

There's not much to do right now but wait, so I take a long gulp of whiskey and push my chair back a little until I can rest my head against the wall. Focus on my breathing. It's not long before my head is dipping forward, waking me up every time it does.

The door opens. The giant black guy comes in and pulls the chair out, sits down. He takes the flask, sniffs it, makes a judgmental face, screws the cap back on. The corner of his mouth curls up into a smile.

"Name?" he asks, placing the paper with the numbers down, facing me.

Now, there are two ways to play this. I could answer quickly and honestly and hope it gets me out of here. Or I could make things worse. My face still hurts. This whole shock-and-awe thing doesn't sit too well for me. And making things worse is kind of my thing.

"Ask your mom," I tell him. "She was screaming it all last night."

I expect his face to twist into anger or frustration. Instead I get bored indifference. "You think you're funny."

"I am pretty funny, yeah."

He gets up, the chair scratching across the floor. He comes up to me and wraps his hand around my neck, slowly presses me against the wall until my chin tilts down over his wrist. I reach up with my free hand, try to peel his hand off, but they're like a vise. I consider gouging an eye or hitting him in the throat but I have a feeling that would not end well for me.

He squeezes. Drawing this whole thing out, to show me that what he's doing, it's not out of anger. It's because he can. Oxygen stops flowing to my lungs. It takes a second before that turns into an issue. He puts his mouth up next to my ear and I can feel his hot breath exploding on my skin.

"Here's how this is going to go," he says. "You're going to answer me, concisely and honestly. You will not lie to me. You feel me?"

I try to speak but can't, my lungs screaming.

"No one knows you're here, and you wouldn't be found for a very long time. I ask again, do you feel me?"

I nod my head and he lets go. I lean forward, take deep, greedy breaths of air. He returns to his chair and calmly sits, like none of that choking business happened.

"Now… name?"

I tell him the first name that comes to mind. "Dana. Dana Cameron."

He raises an eyebrow. "A bit on the feminine side."

Fuck, even my alias is a girl's name.

"I'm the modern day boy named Sue," I tell him, glad my favorite comeback still applies. He doesn't smile, doesn't laugh, doesn't seem to get the Johnny Cash reference. So it's a sure bet he can't be trusted.

He presses a thick finger to the paper. "Tell me about this."

"It's a scrap of paper."

"Tell me about it."

"Dude, it's a scrap of paper," I tell him, trying my best to sound sincere. "I found it on the ground and I shoved it in my pocket so that I could throw it away. Before I could pass a trash can you and your stormtroopers came in and yanked us out."

"You think I don't know a book cipher when I see one?"

That's interesting.

"I do not know what a book cipher is," I tell him, truthfully.

"What's the key?"

"I told you, I don't know what that is."

"Tell me about the Soldiers of Gaia."

"I also do not know what that is. Are they a band? They sound like a band."

He stares at me for a second, his eyes gliding over my face. He taps the paper. "You're telling me you don't know what the key is."

"I'm telling you I don't know why you're so hot on a piece of trash I found on the ground. As a representative of the federal government, shouldn't you be glad my first instinct was to ensure it was properly recycled? You are FBI, right?"

He looks up at the ceiling. "You remind me of someone I went to school with."

He says this like we're suddenly friends catching up over drinks. I don't even know how to respond to that, so I wait, to see where the fuck he's going with it.

"Guy was from New York, too," he says. "We called him Yorkie. He hated it. But we kept on doing it anyway. Do you know why we did that?"

"Because you're such a friendly guy?"

"Because he thought he was a hard motherfucker because he grew up in a town with a rep," the guy says. "But the truth is this motherfucker grew up on the Upper West Side and went to a private school. He would play like a Rottweiler but really he was this yipping little bullshit dog, no bigger than a cat. You get what I mean?"

"I stopped listening."

"It means I know you think you're a hard motherfucker. In this room, you are not. I can tell you've never heard of the Soldiers of Gaia. That I will give you. I also know you're not telling the whole truth about this paper, but that you also don't know it's a cipher. Do you know how I know that?"

"Are you a wizard?"

He smiles. "I saw it on your face. Faces give away crazy shit. Micro expressions. The way the skin moves around the mouth and the nose and the eyes. Tell you everything you need to know about a person from those little ticks. Figure out how micro expressions work and you're like a human lie detector."

I am suddenly very conscious of my face. My skin feels hot. I wonder what it's saying to him. I try to keep my skin soft and serene but he probably notices the effort. "Why not tell me what all this blabbering is about?"

He points at the wall. "There are people out there, right now, planning some bad shit. If there's anything you can tell me, anything you can share, anything you can say about activities at your funny little camp, I can make sure of two things. One, nothing touches you. Two, I don't spend the rest of my life trying to ruin yours. I need you to be honest with me, because I'll be able to tell if you're not. You feel me?"

"You want honesty?" I ask. "Here's some honesty. I don't give a fuck about any of these goofballs. I'm here for another two weeks, then I'm off to Europe. I have nothing here. No friends, no ties. Most of these people don't even like me and I'm not losing sleep over it. That place can burn the moment I fucking leave. As long as it's not a moment before, I couldn't be bothered. So, tell me, am I being honest about that?"

I feel a little guilty saying it. My feelings about South Village aside, I am loyal to Tibo, and don't want him or his dream to suffer. But we're all better off if this guy doesn't think he can use it as a way to threaten me.

He stares at me long and hard. After a few moments he gets up, pushes the chair in, picks up the paper, and walks out. The door closes behind him. I sit there for a little while, listening, waiting for him to come back.

Soldiers of Gaia.

What the fuck is that?

I don't know how long passes. Fifteen minutes, maybe? That's as long as it takes for me to get bold. I poke my head into the hallway and see Tibo looking out of one doorway, Marx out of another. Marx has a big black eye blooming on his face, which leaves me very conflicted, because I don't know who to root for in that fight.

We all share a quick look of confusion and I run to the door where they led us in, to find the van peeling out of the parking lot.

I turn and Tibo is standing beside me.

"That was unexpected," he says.

WE ASSEMBLE IN the parking lot, where we all verify that me and Marx were the only people who were physically assaulted. Which tracks, because we're the two mostly likely to say something dumb. Everyone got quizzed about the Soldiers of Gaia. Nobody knows why. Or at least, pretends to not know why. No one brings up the book cipher, but Marx keeps glancing at me. There's something about that.

A few people had the wherewithal to demand a name or a badge number, but none of the agents would give anything up. All we know is what the big motherfucker told Tibo: To call him Tim. No last name.

So, Tim is an asshole. The next time I see him I'm probably going to take a swing at him. He may be a mountain of muscle, but stuff like that has never stopped me before. At very least I'll make him hurt a little before he pummels me into dust.

Marx and Job are whispering to each other, both of them agitated. Magda is weeping and Cannabelle wraps her arms around the older woman, holds her tight. Katashi looks terribly confused and Aesop pats him on the shoulder, nods, tries to comfort him.

Tibo is the only one with a working cell phone, but it's not getting any reception, so he walks off to look for some. He doesn't invite me but I follow after. I have no sense of how far we are from South Village, or how we're even going to get back.

Once we're out of earshot I ask him, "Any idea what the fuck is happening?"

He turns, surprised to see me. "I'm not sure yet."

"Have you heard of the Soldiers of Gaia?"

"I told Tim I didn't." He looks at his cell and frowns. "That's not exactly true. You found that Earth Liberation Front manual in Crusty Pete's tree house. You do know what they are, correct?"

"Eco-terrorists. They burn down Humvee dealerships and construction sites, stuff like that."

"I've only heard rumors. But supposedly the Soldiers of Gaia is an offshoot. They think burning stuff down isn't extreme enough. They want to take things to the 'next level', whatever the hell that means."

"Do you think any of that is going on at South Village?"

Tibo pauses. "If anyone was involved I'd think it was Marx. It seems to be up his alley. But even that feels like a little much. I can't know everything, but I'd like to think I'd notice some kind of radical terrorist organization was taking root."

We turn onto a long stretch of road, flat and blue sky stretching out and away from us. There's nothing to go by. We pick a direction and walk, Tibo checking the face of his cell and sighing.

"Weird this is hitting around the same time as Pete dying," I tell him.

"Yes."

"What do we do about it? This whole thing doesn't strike me as exactly legal."

"It's not. That's what you call a black site interrogation."

"Black site?"

Tibo stops, puts his hands on his hips. "It's when the authorities want to question people but don't want to do it through the proper channels. And lest you think I should be fitted for a tin-foil hat, there's precedent. Just recently, out in Chicago, narco cops were holding people at an old department store. They called it a narcotics headquarters, but the reality is, it was a black site. No lawyers, no phone calls, and advanced interrogation. Which is the nice way of saying light torture. Look it up." His voice rises and his face twists. "Should be a huge scandal. No one gives a shit because it was brothers and sisters on the receiving end."

"So where does this leave us?"

Tibo looks up in the sky. "We could find the FBI in the yellow pages. Tell whoever answers that we think a bunch of people who may or may not be FBI pulled us out to an abandoned factory site so they could curb-stomp our civil liberties. When they ask for names and badge numbers we can tell them we have no idea. What do you think of that plan?"

"That's a shit plan."

"Exactly. Meanwhile, Tim made it pretty clear that if he gets even a whiff that there's something going down at South Village, he'll have it destroyed. He told me by the time he was done there'd be nothing but empty forest."

We keep walking. A pickup truck crests the horizon and barrels down the road in our direction. Me and Tibo put our hands into the air, try to get the truck to stop. It doesn't, flying past us so quick we can't even make out who's driving.

As I'm holding both my middle fingers up into the air, hoping with all my heart the driver sees them in his rear-view mirror, Tibo calls out from behind me: "Got a signal."

He pokes at the screen and says, "Okay, we're about fifteen miles from camp." He dials a number, holds the phone to his ear.

"Who… Gideon? Okay listen… no, listen… no, listen… Gideon, stop talking. I'm going to send you a location. There's eight of us out here. You either need to bring the van or… Gideon, shut up. Either bring the van or two cars. Get here as soon as possible. Is everyone else there okay? … Gideon, answer the question. Okay, thank you."

Tibo taps the screen and jams the phone in his pocket.

"Anything from the home front?" I ask.

"Agents tore the place up. Swore they had a warrant but wouldn't show it to anyone. Same deal. No badges, no names."

"Great. Fucking great."

We turn back for the warehouse. I stop and stand there for a second, watch him. Wanting to ask him about Crusty Pete and the deed for the land, because all of this is coming together in an awkward way. He stops and turns and asks, "Coming?"

"Yeah. Sorry."

THE RIDE BACK is nearly as silent as the ride over. Gideon, driving the camp's battered white van, is asking a lot of questions, but I tune him out, so it doesn't count.

Everyone is shaken. Scared. Or in the case of Marx, seething.

I don't know what I am.

Mostly I want to go back to the bus and gather my stuff and get out of here. I have no idea where I'll go. I could rent a motel room, wait out the time it's going to take to get my passport, then head out like planned. But my funds are dwindling. I've got the money I scored in Portland, but I'm going to need to rent an apartment or something when I get to Prague. South Village doesn't exactly pay much. Mostly it's room and board, with fifty bucks a week on top of that. Easy enough to live when your housing and food are covered. Not so great for building up a bank account. I'd rather avoid spending the money.

But I'd also rather avoid getting involved in whatever stupid thing is happening here. At least they don't have my real name. Mister "I'm a human lie detector" isn't really as good as he thinks.

The cool air is blasting but sweat breaks out on my brow. My skin feels itchy. I'm worried it's a signifier of something serious, when I realize it's probably that I haven't had a drink in a little while. I unscrew my flask and take a long pull. Cannabelle, sitting next to me all the way in the back, gives me a sideways glance. I hold the flask toward her. She shakes her head.

Aesop twists around in his seat. His eyes are red, the skin around them a little puffy. "We should get dinner started right away. You good?"

"I'm good."

He nods. Turns back around.

I drink a little more whiskey, get a little more good.

As we pull off the road and into camp, Marx speaks. It's surprising to me it took him so long to speak. I would have expected him to rant the entire ride over. What he says fills the van with a foreboding sense of dread, both for the brevity and because the words are like burning coals.

"I hope you all understand, this was an act of war."

NINE

ONE OF THE two wooden posts marking the entrance to South Village is toppled to the ground, the Tibetan prayer flags strung across them trampled into the dirt.

According to Gideon there were two teams. The first team took us away for questioning. The second stayed behind to search. They focused on the main buildings but also spread out into camp and checked into whatever tree houses they came across. They didn't search the entire property—at 40 acres of woods and swamp, that would take weeks and a few dozen more men. But they covered as much ground as they could and disappeared without saying a word. They didn't hurt anyone here, at least.

As soon as the van stops, Tibo flings the door open and sprints to the Hub. I follow. The office space is trashed. The filing cabinets emptied out, papers strewn on the floor. The chair is thrown to the side. It's hard to tell if anything was taken. I reach into the back of the filing cabinet closest to the desk and find the copy of *The Monkey Wrench Gang* I stashed there. That much feels like a victory. I slide it into my back pocket.

The computer is still here, sitting on the desk, wheezing away. That's a little surprising. Seems a sure bet they would have taken that. There are tracks in the dust around it, like it's been moved. I turn it around and there's a black plastic nub stuck into a USB port. It's nearly flush and I have to use my fingernail to pry it out. I show it to Tibo.

"I imagine this isn't supposed to be here," I tell him.

Gideon is suddenly standing behind us. "What is that?"

"Keylogger or something," Tibo says, taking the nub from me.

"We should hold on to that," Gideon says.

Tibo places the nub on the desk, picks up a stapler, and whacks it. It cracks and shoots off the desk, clattering into some hidden corner on the floor.

"What the hell did you do that for?" Gideon asks.

"It's of no use to us," he says. "And on the off chance it's transmitting off site, I want them to know we found it."

Tibo stands there for a second, surveying the damage, and picks papers off the floor, placing them in a neat stack on the desk next to the computer. Gideon shakes his head and leaves. I ask Tibo, "Need a hand cleaning?"

He doesn't answer. Doesn't look up. Channeling his frustration into the work. Okay then. I step outside and pass Aesop, who's standing on the porch, hands on his hips, staring off into the distance. His eyes glassy and vacant.

"I'm going to make sure my bunk is in order. Then we'll start?"

He doesn't respond. He's staring at a point beyond the trees, at where the world blurs together.

"Aesop?"

He looks at me. "What?"

"Meet at the kitchen in a bit?"

He nods.

I walk to the tree line, climb onto the wooden boardwalk, head toward the bus, pass over a plank that says: *My blood type is Be Positive.*

Fucking hippies.

THE INSIDE OF the bus doesn't look like it was touched. It's easy enough to pass over, maybe even to miss entirely.

I sit down on my cot, put my head in my hands. Take a minute. Breathe deep. Now that I've stopped moving the wave has time to catch up. Before it can hit me I open up my flask and drain it. That helps a little.

The downside of that is I am now whiskey-less, and this is a big problem for me. I've got some stashed at the kitchen and that'll help me get through tonight, but that means I need to make a trip off-campus tomorrow. Which means I need to talk someone into giving me a ride.

There are a lot of things I need to do. Like figure out what a book cipher is. I get the gist. It's a code you crack with a book. It's the finer details I'm not too sure about.

Normally I'd sit on the computer for a little while, but after dinner the computer is off limits—with the power rationing, the lights get priority. Computer sucks up too much juice. And anyway, that bug or whatever the feds planted could have been a decoy. Something they knew we'd find, lull us into a false sense of security, but really there's some programming on the computer that's tracking how it's used. It makes me nervous about my instant-message conversation with Bombay, too. Whether they were able to find it after the fact.

I take a knee next to my duffel and dig out my phone, very thankful that I took a picture of the cipher. I wasn't even sure why I was doing it. Just felt like a good idea at the time.

The phone won't turn on. Battery is probably dead. I shove it along with my charger into my pocket, and figure on skimming a little power out of the main dome. Won't need much.

As I push through the door to leave I ask myself, "What are you doing?"

The way the words spring from my mouth, unexpected but fully formed, leaves me standing there for a minute, confused. Holding the door. Wondering whether I should answer. Ultimately, I decide not to.

AFTER I PLUG in my phone, we get to work. We give Zorg the night off from cooking. Aesop and I have to move quick to get dinner ready and we don't want to eat as late as we did last night. Training someone is going to slow us down.

The time margin is slim so we settle on a big garden salad with oil and vinegar—about as simple as you can get—and a macaroni salad with a tofu dressing. Simple, good, and easily assembled from the flotsam floating around in the chest fridge. We've got some fresh loaves of bread, too, which we can pair with cashew butter and sea salt. Boom. Dinner. I hope nobody was expecting warm food. Or is counting their carbs.

I load some silken tofu and dill and agave and vinegar and salt into the blender, and turn to check on Aesop. He's got his hands on the counter, staring out the window. I turn the blender on and the mechanical roar of it fills the kitchen. Aesop leaps, nearly off his feet. He turns, wild-eyed, looking around like he's trying assess a threat. His eyes settle on me and he closes them.

"You okay?" I ask.

"Fine." He opens his eyes, goes back to work.

"You're lying."

"You're talkative all of a sudden?"

The way he says it is acidic. Not usually his style. I'm about to say something in return when Tibo sticks his head through the door.

"I'd like to get started," he says.

I dump the dressing into the big bowl of cooked macaroni, give it a couple of turns, and wrap some plastic over it. Aesop exits and I take that as an opportunity to grab my stash bottle of whiskey and take a little swig. I'd have preferred a big swig but it's running down. I exit the kitchen in the cooling night air, and everyone is nervously standing around the campfire, which is catching and coming to life.

Aesop walks toward the fire as the group slowly forms into a circle, people reaching out their hands, clasping the hands of their neighbors. I step off to the side, to my usual spot on the picnic table, propping my feet on the bench, and begin my futile attempt to swat away the no-see-ums.

Once everyone is assembled, Tibo nods and bows his head.

When he raises it, it seems like he still hasn't found the words he's looking for. He opens his mouth and Katie clears her throat.

Tibo rolls his eyes. "Trigger warnings… I don't know. We're going to talk about what happened here at camp today. So, I guess, totalitarianism. Overzealous government outreach?" He pauses. "What happened here at camp today. I don't know what happened. None of us do. There's a lot to process. And I fear we're losing our grip on what this place is, and what makes it special. So instead of going off the rails here, I'd like to propose a return to normalcy. So, if everyone could share what they're thankful for, I think that would be a great start."

"Are you fucking kidding?" Marx asks.

Here we go.

"The government stormed in here, took us prisoner, questioned us, and then left us in the middle of nowhere," he says. "No warrant, no nothing. And your response to that is to shrug your shoulders and propose we pretend it didn't happen."

"I never said that we should…"

Marx lets go of the people on either side of him and steps forward into the circle. "That's exactly what you're proposing. What kind of normalcy can we return to? This is all very much not normal."

Some people in the circle nod in agreement. I can understand why. He's not exactly wrong. I expected Tibo's response would be a little more direct, a little less dismissive.

Tibo steps forward. The two of them are standing on either side of the fire, the flames raging between them, painting them both in red and orange. Tibo looks agitated and he never looks agitated. He usually looks down and away from Marx but now he's looking him square in the eye. Most of the circle takes a step or two back, hands unclasping and falling to sides. I don't like the direction this is going so I get off the picnic table, move a little closer.

Marx breaks eye contact with Tibo and walks around the fire.

Not threatening. Orating.

"Those men who came here today had no right," Marx says, pointing into the distance. "Their search and confinement of us was illegal. I wish I could tell you that we do not live in a fascist state. That this isn't Nazi Germany. It's not Putin's Russia or Kim Jong-un's North Korea. But the truth is, we do live in a fascist state. This is the new face of America. This isn't a democratic nation. It's an oligarchy. And it's our own fault. Every single one of us here today. We let it happen. When we surrender, we condone it."

As he speaks, he stops in front of people, scanning their faces. Gauging their reactions? Smiling at some folks, passing by others.

Looking for disciples, maybe?

"Marx, this isn't the time," Tibo says. "It's definitely not the place."

"When is the time?" he asks, spinning around. "When are you going to stop with this lazy leadership? You're nothing but an enabler. It's like you're on their side."

"This isn't what we do here, Marx. You want to go pick a fight, go pick a fight. Do it away from here. Don't bring violence to our doorstep."

Marx shakes his head. "Violence showed up uninvited. Don't be such a damn coward."

Tibo steps forward and says something to Marx, low enough I can't make it out, but the way Marx tenses up, I know what's coming. He reaches his arm back, twisting his body to swing, but Tibo doesn't wait. He throws himself into Marx's midsection. The two of them topple over, barely missing the fire, crashing to the ground, and everyone is so shocked at the display of violence they stand there frozen.

Me and Gideon and Aesop all make it to the scrum at the same time.

Gideon puts his hands up and says, "Guys, guys," thinking that's going to calm the fight. I look at Aesop and point to Tibo, and Aesop gets it, grabs Tibo behind the arms and pulls him away. Marx sees the opening and reaches his fist back, to slam it into Tibo's gut. I lock my arm into his and yank him away. He spins and falls into me. I grab him by the shirt and throw him at a picnic table, climb on top of him, press my body into his.

I raise my arm, ready to drive my fist into his jaw.

See if maybe I can break it. I bet I can.

For a moment, there's a flash of genuine fear in his eyes. I'm about to bring my fist down when I feel the lapping of the wave at my feet, threatening to engulf me, pull me under. I loosen my grip and he sees this moment of weakness, but before he can exploit it Tibo's voice reverberates through the clearing.

"Enough!"

Again, everyone freezes. I drop my hand and Marx jumps up, pushes me away so that there's a little distance between us. His stare is like a drill, boring into my skin. I return it in kind.

Seems we're on a path now, him and I.

Tibo speaks up again, says, "Everyone, that's enough. Temperatures are running high right now. We can schedule an assembly to discuss this as a group. Right now, let's call a pass on this." He looks at me and Aesop. "Can you set out dinner?"

We stand there for a moment. Clothes bunched up, hair tousled. Teetering on the border of something bad. I'm ready to step over the line. Not that I want to, but it's a gravity thing. Aesop looks frightened, which is a little surprising. Then I look down at his hands and see they're clenched so tight they're white and shaking.

"Can you do that," Tibo asks, except it's not a question.

I exhale. Pat Aesop on the shoulder. He jerks out of whatever daze he's in and follows me to the kitchen.

NOT A WHOLE lot of talking goes on during dinner. People split into small groups, little islands spread across the picnic benches, heads down. I sit on a bench and chew my macaroni salad and when I'm done take out my copy of *The Monkey Wrench Gang* and flip through it. I can't concentrate enough on the words to actually read it. I'm curious to see if there are any notes or scribbles in the margins, but it doesn't look like it.

The book is about a bunch of environmentalists sabotaging construction sites, so between this and the Soldiers of Gaia, I'm beginning to sense a theme.

I watch Marx, too. He's talking to people. Hushed tones, mindful of who's around him. I keep a running tally in my head of who he talks to.

Tibo sits down next to me with a plate of food and pokes at the salad, separating the various components into piles on the plate. He eats the carrots first.

"Thanks," he says.

"Welcome. What did you say to him?"

"That if he kept it up I'd make him leave."

I nod my head. "So, what, you figure Marx is fomenting rebellion now?"

"'Fomenting'. That's a good word. SAT word."

"I'm not just a pretty face."

Tibo eats a little more and puts the plate down on the table next to him. "Marx is a dangerous asshole and I need you right now."

"I'm out of here in less than two weeks. Leaving on a jet plane."

"I don't care what you do in two weeks. I need you right now."

I laugh a little bit at that.

"What so funny?" he asks.

"The John McClane Paradox of Bullshit. Why does the same stuff keep happening to the same guy?"

"I don't get that reference."

"Are you fucking kidding me? *Die Hard*."

"Never saw it."

"I don't know why we're friends," I tell him.

Tibo picks his plate back up. Eats his radishes, then the sliced bell peppers. Katashi walks by with his plate, a big pile of macaroni salad on it. He looks at me and smiles and says, "*Arigato*." I nod at him and he wanders off.

"So what's this thing with the deed?" I ask Tibo.

"What do you mean?"

"The deed. The land. Aesop told me about the dispute. Pete was leading the charge and he ends up dead."

"And you think I killed him?"

"I didn't say that."

"You thought it."

"Look, man, I know you didn't kill anyone. Takes a certain type to kill a person. You're not it. So, tell me what the story is."

Tibo sighs, puts the plate down, stretches his arms up over his head. "This is the problem when you encourage people to be part of a community. Sooner or later, the inmates want to run the asylum."

"Community and power structures sound like opposite things," I tell him.

"It can't just be a free for all," he says. "Someone needs to be in charge."

"So why not do what they ask? Give communism a try."

Tibo folds his hands and leans forward. "Communism always sounds better than it works. There needs to be a hand steering the ship. And I don't care if it's selfish, it was my money that bought this place. I want what everyone else wants. For this place to be sustainable and separate. I don't have some nefarious plan to build hotels here. I'm not exploiting anything."

"To ride out the end of the world."

"C'mon. That was mostly drunken ranting."

"No it wasn't. Not completely, anyway."

Tibo pauses, picking through his words. Wanting to choose what he says carefully. "Things aren't going great, anywhere. The world is falling apart. People are making bad decisions, and those decisions are making things worse. Pick up any newspaper on any given day and it's writ large. This…" He puts his hand up, gestures to the surrounding area. "This is the answer. Small, sustainable living. Rediscovering the meaning of community. Backing each other up. Making things."

"Nice speech." I point into the clearing. "You ought to be making it to them."

He nods. "Tomorrow. The ship is listing a little. It hasn't capsized. Tomorrow we'll see if we can stabilize it. Right now I just want everyone to eat and relax and get a good night's sleep." He hops down to his feet and turns. "What kind of person does it take?"

"What kind of what now?" I ask.

"You said it takes a special kind of person to kill someone and I'm not that person. So, what kind of person does it take?"

I can barely see his face, the way he's backlit by the fire. I can't tell how he's looking at me.

"A bad one," I tell him.

He nods, heads back into the mix of people.

I sit for a little while and watch. People talking and laughing. Being friends. Being normal, even after what the camp went through today. It's incredible how people can fall back into normal so quick. It makes me sad. Because there's a part of me that knows I can't be a part of normal.

Because of Wilson, and what I did.

And there it is.

The picnic table disappears out from under me as the wave hits.

Pushing me under. Roaring in my ears, threatening to pull me down into the dark. Filling my eyes and nose and throat. I'm tumbling, can't tell up from down. I reach out, stumble into the dirt, then get to my feet and run to the kitchen, into the pantry, to my stash of whiskey.

The bottle is nearly empty now. If I take one big swig now and one at bed I might be able to make it through until the morning, when I can hit someone up for a ride and get into town.

This can work.

I suck down a big mouthful. The act of pressing the bottle to my lips calms me too, because I know what's next. The bliss of numbness. I pour the rest of the bottle into my flask and jam it into my pocket. Head outside, grab a flashlight, step onto the boardwalk and follow the circle of blue-white light back to the bus. To sleep. With any luck, a deep, empty sleep.

When I'm far enough away from camp that I can't see the fire, I click off the light and stand there in the dark. Feel those two pairs of eyes on me. Consider turning around and confronting them, but that's the problem: The eyes are always behind me, no matter which direction I turn.

I click the light on and walk.

Okay, plan for tomorrow.

Step one, find someone with a car who can drive me to town to buy a shitload of whiskey. As much as I can manage so that I never run out again. Maybe Aesop. He has a car, and seems to have some kind of hard-on for getting me to be social.

Step two, figure out what exactly a book cipher is. That's going to require a visit to Sunny and Moony, which, truthfully, is not such a bad prospect. As long as the feds didn't get into their set-up. Because I'm not touching the group computer again.

Shit. My phone. Left it back in the kitchen. It's plugged into an outlet on a high shelf, out of view, so probably no one's going to find it. I consider going back for it, though, so I can play at figuring out the cipher, when there's a shuffle behind me.

Some giant angry bug stalking me, no doubt.

Or else it's the wave, sneaking back up.

I take out the flask, to help with the walk back. As I near the end of the boardwalk, there's a creak and a rush behind me and something slams into my back, throwing me forward.

The flashlight and flask go flying from my hands into the brush as I slam into the ground and get a mouthful of dirt. I try to get up but someone climbs onto my back, straddling me and pressing me down, going for my pants.

I pull myself forward but I have no leverage. Whoever it is, he's strong.

Something hard hits me in the back of the head. My forehead smashes into the ground. The world gets a little fuzzy and I feel something hot and wet on my face. The weight comes off and I get myself standing and I'm alone, footsteps receding in the dark.

No flashlight. That's bad enough.

But my copy of *The Monkey Wrench Gang* is gone. So is the whiskey. The open bottle flung from my hand, the contents no doubt spilled into the earth.

I don't know which of these things is worse.

TEN

THE ROPE LIGHTS running along the roof of the bus cast everything in a sickly blue glow. Before my light option gets downgraded to candles, I need to make sure the cut on my head isn't too bad, because blood is now dripping into my left eye. I pull out a shaving mirror and get close to the light. It's small, near my hairline. Not so deep it'll need stitches.

There's a first aid kit on the dash, next to the steering wheel. I get that, open it up, pull out some medicated wipes to clean it out, then use adhesive strips to close it. A few minutes and a few stings later, I've got it situated.

I sit on my cot. Consider heading straight back for camp to confront Marx, who I'm going to assume jumped me and took the book. But if I do that I'm definitely going to beat him until his face looks like hamburger meat, and that's not productive for anyone. I wrap my arms around myself, suddenly cold even though it's warm and a little humid. I don't have that security blanket of booze and it's not a nice feeling. I try not to think too hard about it.

Focus on the task at hand. The things I know.

Pete dies. Pete has a secret code. I find the book that's probably maybe the key to the secret code, and someone attacks me and takes it. Means whatever he's planning, he wasn't alone. Given Marx and his dumb fucking outburst, safe bet on at least him being a part of it.

Next: The FBI, or at least we think it's the FBI, comes storming in here, fucks up our shit, takes a bunch of stuff, quizzes us on militant environmentalists. Maybe Pete was with said militant environmentalists. Marx too. Clearly Marx didn't give up anything during the interrogation, though it's a little weird they didn't keep him, and that they sent us back like nothing happened.

Maybe they weren't looking to do anything but scare us. It was all theatrics, meant to let us know they were on to the Soldiers of Gaia, and they were not fucking around. A little shock and awe to keep the hippies docile.

Okay. Next.

And…

Fuck, I need a drink.

There's nothing outside but a huge swath of darkness, and questions I can't answer, or don't want to answer, so I pull my legs up onto the cot and yank the string to kill the rope lights. Close my eyes.

Vow to not let my guard down again.

And to pick up more alcohol tomorrow.

THE AIR SMELLS green. The rain is still falling hard so I'm pretty sure we're in no danger of being found. I toss aside the shovel, climb down into the hole I dug, and it comes up to the middle of my thigh. I figure that'll have to be deep enough. I climb out, my jeans and boots covered in mud, and I go to Wilson. His neck kinked at an odd angle, his eyes glass, unblinking in the rain. The gray fabric of his sweat suit now dark gray, soaked through.

How can a person be sorry and not sorry at the same time?

I push the body into the hole and look at him lying there, water pooling in the crook created by where his arm presses against the muddy brown wall. His head twisted almost all the way around. I take his gun out of my back pocket and toss it in there with him, then begin to fill the hole in.

There's a sound behind me, and I turn.

Chell and my dad are standing in the rain. Shoulder-to-shoulder, hair and clothes soaked. My dad nearly a foot taller than Chell. That's the thing I remember most about him. He always seemed to be the tallest person in any room.

And Chell. Red hair, somewhere between a flame and the fire engine rushing to put it out. Legs like poison darts, arms across her chest like a cage.

They're looking down on me, disappointed beyond repair.

This is me, I tell them. What do you think?

Dad, did you ever expect I would take your sterling example of heroism and twist it around until I turned myself into an agent of destruction?

Chell, all those times you warned me to calm down, be smart—how upset are you now that I've proven myself unable to take your advice?

You have to know I didn't want for this to happen. Both of you. You have to know that. My regret is a mountain I can't see the top of anymore.

They don't move, don't say anything back to me.

When I look down at Wilson, his head is turned back toward me, his eyes alive again, fixed on mine, and no matter how hard I try, I cannot look away.

I'M ALREADY AWAKE when the first light of morning peeks through the bus window. Sweating, exhausted. Wishing I could sleep and terrified at the prospect. I swing my legs out, stand up and stretch the kink out of my lower back.

The dream is always the same. That moment when I buried Wilson in the woods, somewhere near Mount Hood.

I wonder if anyone ever found him.

For a little while I would read the Portland newspapers online, waiting for the day that I'd see an article about the body, and then about me. Because even though I did a decent job covering my tracks, I'm sure it wasn't perfect. It all happened so fast, I must have missed something.

After a little while, I gave up. I figure my mom would tell me if the cops were looking for me in connection with a dead body. She hasn't said anything during our occasional check-ins, so I'm in the clear until I'm not.

I feel like I'm underwater, figure some coffee might set me right. There's enough light I can see, so I change, get my stuff together, check my head in the mirror, and seems I did a pretty good job of closing the wound. I step outside and head for the shower, which is empty. This is early, even by hippie standards. I clean up, head back to the bus, redress the wound, head for the main camp.

Past the yoga clearing, which is empty, and the public painting project, which is also empty. I stop and look at the painting. Try to remember how it looked when Cannabelle was working on it. It looks like maybe it's a little bit different now, but I can't be sure.

I step off the platform and pass Mathilda.

"What's up, darling?" I ask.

She doesn't look up from the thing she's pecking at in the dirt.

"Fine, fuck you too," I tell her.

The clearing in the middle of the domes is clear, but there's movement in the kitchen. I step inside and find Aesop, in flip-flops and a t-shirt and jeans, scrubbing the counter, which has been completely cleared. His hair is tied back in a tight ponytail. The radio is working again. The Skatalites are playing low.

I knock on the doorway and Aesop looks up and nods like he was expecting me.

"Need a favor," I tell him.

He tosses the rag onto the counter and picks up a dry towel to clean his hands, waits for me to speak.

"Got some errands to run in town. Think you could give me a lift?"

He nods, slowly. "I have to pick some stuff up too. Can you help me finish up?"

I climb up into the kitchen and grab my cell phone. Fully charged. Marx may have the book, but he doesn't have the cipher. I pour myself a cup of coffee from the French press—god bless Aesop for having a batch going already—and peel my shirt off so I don't sweat through it and feel compelled to change before I have breakfast.

"Yeah, let's get sexy," Aesop says, pulling his shirt off, too.

"What needs getting done?" I ask.

He tilts his head toward the pantry. "Clear off shelves, wipe off shelves, restock shelves. Easy enough?"

"Easy enough."

He looks at the bandaging on my hairline. "What happened to you?"

"I'll tell you in the car."

That seems to be enough. He goes back to wiping the counter and I get to work clearing out the pantry, keeping on eye out toward the clearing, in case I see Marx and find myself with the opportunity to smash his head in with a can of beans. I know I should be looking for him right now, but getting into town feels more important. Sobriety is uncomfortable.

AESOP'S WHITE DODGE Neon is immaculate, inside and out. The cars in the parking lot are covered with dust, bumper stickers, full of bags and receipts and accumulated life crap. Aesop's looks like it was recently detailed.

He starts the car and presses the Skatalites cassette he swiped from the kitchen into the tape deck, turns the car down the dirt path. We cross the bridge over the creek. I forgot to check that. It feels okay though. Maybe we can stop on the way back.

We get out to the road and Aesop swings the car onto the asphalt.

"Hell of an interesting two days," he says.

"That it is."

"What's your take so far?"

"What do you mean?"

"I mean you've been sniffing around and asking questions. Tibo told me what you used to do. That you were like a private investigator back when you lived in New York."

"That's not exactly true," I tell him. "I wasn't licensed. I didn't have an office. Just, sometimes people asked me to help them with things. I accepted money, or sometimes booze or drugs. I was comfortable operating on a barter system. I can't claim I ever did this in any professional capacity. And I left that all behind."

"And yet, you're still poking around."

I shrug. "No television. Not much to do. Gotta fill the day somehow."

We come up on the white cable bridge leading the road over some wetlands, the earth flat and stretching around us. Green for most of it, with the Atlantic Ocean off on our right. I love driving over this bridge. You live in New York your whole life, you're not used to seeing so far. Something somewhere gets in the way. A building or a hill. The sky feels so much bigger out here.

I turn on my phone. The screen lights up and I give it a second to figure out if I have any missed texts or voicemails. It seems no. It makes me a little sad, even though I'm not sure who would be reaching out, and for what. But turning on an empty phone when you're in a strange place with a person you don't know—it feels sad. I pull up the picture of the cipher and e-mail it to myself.

There are a few e-mails waiting. That makes me feel a little better. My mom checking in. A notification that my passport application is being processed. Nice. Then it's spam and newsletters. I delete as much as I can until the process strikes me as unbearable, then turn off my phone and stick it back in my pocket.

"Something's going on," Aesop says. "I don't know if the feds have anything to do with Pete. I have to assume it does. Too much of a coincidence for this all to be hitting at the same time."

"I figure the same, yeah."

"So what happened to your head? You said you'd tell me in the car."

I look out the window. Think a little bit about it.

"Someone jumped me last night," I tell him. "Out in the woods."

"Who?"

"Didn't see who it was."

"Do you know why?"

"Still trying to figure that out."

I feel bad lying. But I'm not sure how much I can trust Aesop. He seems to be on the level. Doesn't seem to be taking a side here. If anything, he reminds me a little of me: Someone who's happy to make it through to another day intact.

"Given last night, my first guess is Marx," he says.

"Not a bad assumption to make."

"Man, this shit is getting out of control. If it keeps up like this I'm doing the same thing you are. Getting the fuck gone."

Palm trees appear on the side of the road. That means we're getting close. Within a couple of minutes there's a gas station and a chain restaurant, and a church and a strip mall and a supermarket. That's about it. The road is empty, with most of the visible moving cars lined up in or around a Starbucks parking lot.

We pass the liquor store and I nod toward it, tell Aesop, "First stop. Need to fuel up."

"No can go," he says, blowing past it.

"Why not?"

"It's Sunday. Not open today."

"What do you mean it's not open today?"

"Blue laws, baby."

"Yeah, but… I don't recall ever not being able to buy there."

"You must never have went on a Sunday," he says, pulling up to a red light. "Most counties in Georgia, you can buy booze starting at noon-thirty. But there are still a few counties where you can't get it on Sundays. This just happens to be one of them."

"How far until a county where it is legal?"

"Half an hour."

"Let's go."

Aesop turns in his seat and looks me up and down. The light turns green and the person behind us gives a polite little tap on the horn. Aesop starts us rolling and says, "Not going to do that."

"Why the hell not? I'll pay for gas."

"Because of that sound of panic in your voice," he says. "That's no way to live."

"You're a priest all of a sudden?"

"No, but I've been where you are," he says. "Medicating with alcohol. You want to trash your liver and melt your brain into a puddle, that's your right, but I'm not going to be a party to that. And I'm not going to apologize for it, either. What's the next stop?"

I suddenly like Aesop far less.

"Bookstore," I tell him. "Does that meet your high fucking moral standards?"

"It does," he says, cutting the wheel.

THE BOOKSTORE IS less a store and more of a barn, situated on a rural road a little bit down from the church. Aesop parks and his is the only car in the lot. I'm a little worried it might be closed, being so early on a Sunday, but the sign on the door is flipped to 'open.'

We climb into the morning air and it's quiet and clean, the sun shining, already stupid hot. I'm sweating, probably more than I would have been sweating, because I'm too sober. This liquor thing is going to be a problem. Maybe I can reason with him on the way back.

First things first.

We step inside and while it's not exactly cool, it's cooler than outside. We're flooded with the musty smell of books, surrounded by shelves creaking and overflowing with worn volumes. There's an older, curvy blonde woman seated behind a desk, reading a book I can't see the title of. She looks up at us with deep eyes and a soft smile. She's the kind of pretty that makes me feel like a little boy.

She sticks a bookmark in her book and places it down reverently, turns a little and crosses her leg. Her sundress slips, revealing fish scales tattooed from her upper thigh down to her ankle.

"Gentlemen," she says, her voice deep, almost husky.

"Hi," I tell her, trying to sound smooth, failing. "I'm looking for a book. *The Monkey Wrench Gang* by Edward Abbey."

She nods, points a finger past us, down a long row. "Fiction is right down there. Let me know if you have any trouble. I know we've got a few."

She goes back to her book and we head off.

"That's a good one," says Aesop. "Been a long time since I read it."

We get to the fiction section and Abbey is right at eye level. There are two different editions of the book. I pull them both off the shelf. Neither of them are the same as the one I had. One is a hardcover, missing the dust jacket. The other shows four people riding in a Jeep. It's a small paperback. Much smaller than the one I had. I stand there for a couple of minutes, flipping back and forth between the two of them, a little unsure of what it means that the editions are different, but feeling like that could be a problem.

"Okay, don't leave me in the dark on this," Aesop says. "What's going on?"

Maybe talking this out would be helpful. Sometimes I need a sounding board and Bombay isn't here. For as annoyed as I am with Aesop, my gut tells me I can trust him. My gut isn't always so bad at that kind of thing.

"Do you know what a book cipher is?" I ask.

He nods. "I do."

"Oh thank fuck. Can you please tell me?"

He takes the hardcover from my hand, opens to a random page. "It's a way to assemble a code. You have three numbers. First is for the page. Second number is for the line. Third number is how many words in it is on the line." He shows me on the page, then runs his finger across the page. "Here, say we want to start the code with the word 'blue.' We do page number, then line number, then its place in the sentence. On and on and on until you've got a message. You got it?"

I'm happy in one sense, to finally know what the hell I'm dealing with, and upset in another, because I think I am in trouble. I confirm that with the paperback edition. The word 'blue' in the hardcover doesn't line up the same way with the paperback. Given the sizes and layouts and fonts, the whole thing is thrown off. It's not enough to have the book. You need the right edition.

I put them back on the shelf and head to the front, where the woman looks up at us again and smiles. "Find it?"

"Yes and no. I was wondering if you have a storage room or something. Maybe some extra copies floating around? I'm looking for a particular edition of the book."

"Which one?"

"Not sure. All I know is the cover. It's a paperback, with a dead end sign and a winding road. The coloring is like a sepia tone."

"Harper Perennial," she says. "Published around 2000, I think."

"You've got an incredible memory."

She tilts her head. "It helps. And I just happen to really like the book. Sorry to say, what we've got out is what we've got. And this is used books only. We can't order, we just get what comes in. If I find one, I'll put it aside for you."

"Thanks. I don't know how much longer I'll be in town, but thanks."

We head outside and climb into the car. Aesop turns it on and cranks the AC. We sit there for a minute before he asks, "So what does this have to do with Pete?"

"I found something in his tree house. A code, which that FBI asshole referred to as a book cipher. I also found out that Pete had been carrying around a copy of *The Monkey Wrench Gang*. I got the copy he'd been reading. The person who attacked me last night took it. The cipher is gone, too, but I took a picture of it first." I pat my phone. "Still got that."

"So whoever attacked you has one piece, the feds have the

other piece, and neither side knows how those pieces fit together," he says.

"Yup."

"Well, we've got that much on them. I'll tell you, this shit is really starting to line up nicely."

"How so?"

"Look, I don't know anything about these Soldiers of Gaia, but I do know a lot about the Earth Liberation Front. They use book ciphers to communicate. They're easy to move around and nearly impossible to crack unless you have the right book. And books are generally easy to find."

"Well, in this case, not so much."

"It'll be fine. We'll call around to some bookstores. Someone is bound to have it."

"What's with all this 'we'?"

"I'd like to help."

"Not a great idea."

"Why not?"

"Because… when people get involved in the stuff I get involved with, bad shit ends up happening to them. I don't even know why I'm doing this. Just… curious."

"Yeah, curiosity," he says. "That's it."

The way he says it is like he doesn't believe me.

THE SUPERMARKET IS frigid. I am angry at all the shiny happy people. The smiling families giving us side looks. In New York we'd look homeless, or like we were from Williamsburg. Here, though, in our dirty clothes, ragged hair, we may as well be space aliens. In the spice aisle a woman actually goes wide-eyed at the sight of us and hides her toddler behind her.

None of that touches Aesop. He's floating through the aisles, grabbing the occasional thing we can't grow. Boxes of cheap pasta. Turmeric. A few packages of bacon, which we'll have to smuggle in, but will ensure I can fulfill my promise to Alex.

As the cart fills up my anxiety grows. We pass a beer case that's empty. Beer would be okay. I don't put it much higher than water, but enough of anything will do the job. I consider bribing one of the stock boys to meet me out back with a six of something, and then feel ashamed at the fact that I'm planning to buy beer like some junkie would buy heroin.

Once we're done we head out, passing through the parking lot, and four assholes right out of a Hillbilly Identification Guide are lounging around a pickup truck. The second I see them, the way they look at us with leering smiles on their faces, I'm bracing for the comment.

A guy with a shaved head and a big gut and a flannel shirt with the sleeves ripped off snickers as we walk by. "Fucking hippie faggots."

He says it loud enough so he's sure we'll hear it.

I look over my shoulder but don't stop walking. "Fuck you, you redneck fuck."

Aesop groans.

He sticks the key into the trunk of his car, pops it open, and drops the bags inside. As he closes it he says, "You could have said nothing, you know?"

We turn, and the four guys are now coming at us, thrilled that some shit is about to go down. Clearly their idea of a fun Sunday is hanging out in a supermarket parking lot, looking for a fight, and given my mood, I am more than happy to oblige.

"The fuck did you say to me?" asks my new redneck friend.

"I was not in the mood for this today," says Aesop, as he sticks out his thumb and forms a V with his thumb and pointer finger, and jams it into the guy's throat.

ELEVEN

THE FAT GUY goes down hard, hands around his throat, choking. The other three pause. They've still got the advantage, but it suddenly doesn't feel that way. It seems the guy writhing around on the ground was the alpha. The rest of the pack is rudderless without him.

Aesop nods toward the guy on the ground.

"Take him and get the fuck out of here. None of the rest of you need to get hurt."

The way he says it is like he's ordering coffee.

The three guys look between each other, waiting for someone else to make the first move. The guy on the ground makes the decision for them, scrambling forward to grab at Aesop's legs. Aesop sidesteps and throws his knee into the guy's head with an audible 'klunk'.

Unfortunately, this is sufficient to spur the others into action.

A scrawny guy with long gray hair tied back in a bandana comes running at me, reaching around to throw a haymaker. Sloppy. I step to the side, use his momentum to toss him across the lot and onto the ground. Which leaves me free to confront his friend, a baby-faced guy in jeans and a black t-shirt and work boots.

This one looks like he can rumble. Thick shoulders, lots of padding. I set my feet and let him throw a few punches, put my arms up to block, let him wail until there's an opening and jab him in the nose. It opens like a faucet, crimson blood spilling down his face. I follow by throwing my weight through my fist and into his gut. He doubles over, struggling to breathe as the air escapes and he gurgles on blood.

Aesop is standing over two prone figures now. The alpha, and the last of the bunch, a young guy with barbed wire tattoos on his thick arms. He clearly didn't last long.

The August sun beats down on us as Aesop and I stand there looking at each other, seeing each other laid bare for the first time, as the four hillbilly idiots squirm at our feet.

"We should go," I tell Aesop.

He nods. "Yes we should."

We jump into his car and Aesop peels out, swinging us onto the road with a little more tire-crunching zeal than he displayed on the way here. Neither of us speak for the first few blocks. Some sweet 60s Jamaican ska blares out of the speakers, completely counter to the animal energy in the car.

We cross the outskirts of town, onto the lonely road guarded on either side by tall trees. The tension eases now that we've got a little distance, and the adrenaline has some time to wear off.

The pieces come together. The precision with which he attacked those guys, and his loose-bodied confidence around violence. Aesop is trained, not some sloppy brawler. That, plus the general cleanliness, and the level of order he maintains in the kitchen, means I can make at least one educated guess about him.

"You were in the military," I tell him.

"United States Marines Corps, First Lieutenant."

"Where'd you serve?"

"A little Iraq. A little Afghanistan. A little stuff I can't talk about. I know it's probably a little funny, considering."

"Considering what?"

"Gay hippie in the military."

"You're gay?"

He looks at me and furrows an eyebrow. "I don't hide it."

"You don't advertise it. It's a little surprising to hear."

"Because I can handle myself? Or do you think all gays should be flaming queens?"

"I don't mean it like that. It's just…"

"This," Aesop says, "is why it's nice to sometimes talk to people. You learn things about them. You can have conversations with them. Make a play at being part of a community. I promise you, it's not so bad."

"Whatever you say. Good on ya though, with the service."

His voice frosts over. "I wouldn't say that."

"Why not?"

"I know that's what you're supposed to say, thanking people for their service." He shakes his head. Like he's staring into an abyss, contemplating whether he should leap, and ultimately deciding not to. "I'm not looking for sympathy, and I'm not going to pretend to be unique, but that whole thing ended on bad terms. And I'd rather leave it at that."

"Don't worry. I know all about not wanting to talk about shit."

"You mean like with your dad?"

"How'd you know about that?"

"Tibo mentioned it. I forget how it came up. Sort of slipped out, so don't think he was volunteering that. He was a firefighter? Went down with the towers?"

I watch the trees go by for a bit, staring into my own abyss.

"I'm sorry," he says.

"It's fine," I tell him. "He was off duty. Got inside to help evacuate. Never found him."

"You must have been just a little kid then."

"I was."

"Can I ask you something?"

"Sure."

Aesop doesn't immediately follow that with a question. I turn and he's looking at me, trying to catch my eye while not missing too much of the road. A few minutes ago his eyes looked cast out of iron. Now they're gentle. Almost sad.

"What do you think about what we did?" he asks. "Going over there. Fighting that war. That whole thing was supposed to be about you and what you lost. I'm sorry if it's a weird question. I'm just… wondering."

I go back to watching the trees. Unsure of what to say. Not sure if I even want to engage with this. But there's a part of him that needs to hear something. The need is so thick it's palpable.

And he did give me a ride.

So finally I settle on something. Not the whole truth, but enough. "Bunch of rich men sending poor kids to die, I don't see how that solves anything. No offense to you and what you did. I do believe it's a noble thing. But my dad didn't stop being dead."

Aesop looks away when I'm done. He seems satisfied with the answer.

After we've parked the car and unloaded the bags and we're walking down the worn dirt path toward the kitchen, Aesop clears his throat.

"I'm sorry I didn't take you to get your booze," he says. "But I promise you, whatever you're using it to cover up is going to come to the surface. Maybe not soon, but it will. Best to confront it. It won't be easy. But I know where you are right now. If you ever want to talk about things, you let me know."

"Okay."

We walk in silence the rest of the way to the kitchen.

ONCE THE GROCERIES are away and we've hidden the bacon, Aesop leaves to do something else, and I go over the place like I'm looking for forensic evidence. Or, more appropriately, like a boozehound who suddenly finds himself sober.

I figure maybe there's something that got stashed away and forgotten about. A can of beer. A half-finished bottle of wine. Something to chip away at how I feel right now.

I come up empty. Walk to the doorway and sit on the staircase leading into the kitchen with a mason jar full of water. Sit and watch the courtyard. Job is sitting on the far picnic bench strumming an acoustic guitar, Alex sitting next to him and singing, but so low I can't make out the words. Katashi is lying on a picnic table, reading a book that he's holding over his face. Sunlight spills through the leaves, casting shards of gold on the ground. There's a nice breeze drifting through the trees.

Aesop isn't wrong. I think I knew it myself. Keeping afloat on a sea of whiskey isn't healthy. Sooner or later there was going to be a reckoning.

Maybe talking would help. I put up a wall when I first got to Portland. Crystal helped take it down. Far enough I could see myself making a life with her, so in a sense, it was great.

But in another sense it was terrible. Because after I found her kidnapped daughter, after I traced the plot back to her absentee congressman-in-waiting dad, after I accidently killed the guy who did all the heavy lifting—I'd made such a mess of things I had no choice but to leave. To protect the two of them.

That's what I tell myself.

In the few weeks after leaving Portland, I got twelve missed calls from Crystal. Two voicemails where she didn't say anything. Just hovered over the speaker, breathing, and hung up. No texts.

I think a lot about where Crystal and Rose are. What they're doing. If they're safe. I feel like an asshole for not knowing, and an asshole for leaving, and an asshole for so many other reasons. It's hard to keep track anymore.

All of these things happened because I thought I was smarter than I really am. Tougher, faster, stronger. More capable. I have made so many decisions that have made things worse. I did them because they felt right at the time.

The last thing in the world I want to do is talk about what happened with me and Wilson. About the wave that laps at my feet in moments of weakness.

So that means I should probably talk about it.

I look up and Tibo is wearing an open button-down shirt and green khakis, crossing the courtyard.

"Hey," he asks. "Have you seen Marx?"

"No. That reminds me, I've been meaning to beat his ass."

"Well, no one has seen him since last night."

MARX'S TREE HOUSE is on stilts, twenty feet up in the air, a long staircase leading to the door. Tibo and I stand outside, looking up. There's no way to tell from down here whether he's in.

"What do you think?" Tibo asks.

"Let's go up and knock."

"And if he's there?"

"I'm probably going to knock him the fuck out."

"Okay," Tibo says. "I'll go first."

He climbs the steps, which are narrow enough I can't follow next to him, so I go up behind. The wood creaks under our combined weight. Tibo stops at the top and looks in and says, "Huh."

"What?"

He doesn't answer, pushes the screen door and steps inside. I follow and it's empty.

The layout isn't too different from Crusty Pete's tree house. There's a platform for a mattress or a sleeping bag, and a makeshift desk. This one has a bookshelf. But otherwise it's the same naked wood, same sloppy construction, random nails sticking out in stray corners. There's not much to see, but I check under the desk, move the bookcase. Tibo asks, "What are you doing?"

"Searching."

"For what?"

"Won't know unless I find something."

"Should we be doing this?"

I put the bookcase back and stand up. "The dude's a ghost."

"Right, but..."

"You own this tree house. Not him."

"Fair point."

I check along the walls and under the surfaces, to be thorough, but there's nothing. Not even a stray piece of trash. It's like walking into a hotel room before you put your bags down. Untouched. I hop up onto the platform and sit.

"Okay," Tibo says. "He's gone. So where did he go?"

"We should ask around," I tell him. "See if anyone knows anything."

"What are you doing?"

"Trying to figure out..."

"No, I mean, all this," Tibo says, waving a hand toward the outside. "You came here and put your head down like the rest of the world didn't exist. You were clearly hiding from something, and it's something you haven't wanted to talk about, and I respected that. Now you're playing detective again. What is it you want? To go sit alone on your bus? Or do you want to be a part of this community?"

"I never said I wanted to be a part of anything."

"Except you're acting like it. And on top of it, you've reached incredible new levels of dick. You live on a hippie commune, dude. You're going to get hit with stray hacky sacks. It's an environmental hazard. You can't throw them into the woods like you did. Because then those people come to me and complain and wonder why my buddy from back home gets a pass on behavior that would get someone else kicked out."

I shrug at him.

"What happened in Portland?" Tibo asks.

I shrug again.

"Where were you with Aesop all day?" he asks.

I shrug a third time.

"Why do you have so little respect for me?"

"I have plenty of respect for you."

"Then be honest."

"No."

He narrows his eyes, stares at me hard. "You did something bad, didn't you?"

I don't answer him.

"You're hiding. That's why you're here. Is that why you're leaving the country?"

I don't answer that, either.

I'm kind of hoping my tactic of not answering him will work out in my favor. But it doesn't, because the longer he stares at me, the more he can see. The stereogram image comes into focus, until his eyes go wide and his mouth drops open.

"You killed someone, didn't you?"

I don't need to answer that one. It's rhetorical. Instead I get up, push past him. Head down the steps and by the time I make it to the boardwalk I'm running, trying to outrace the waves. I'm running and running and then I trip, and I'm in the air and come down hard on my hands and knees.

The plank under me says: *The past can't be changed, but the future is still in my power.*

Fucking fuck. I hit it with the flat of my fist and a jolt shoots through my arm. I grab the corner and pull. It's nailed down good. I brace myself, putting one foot on the forest floor, and put all my weight into prying it up. It tears free of the base and I pick it up over my head and slam it down once, twice, three times. On the fourth it breaks and splinters. I drop it and there's a splinter of wood embedded in my hand. I pull it out and a thin stream of blood follows.

I sit there for a little bit, to get my bearings.

Try not to think about whiskey.

I should go see the girls. I need to see them anyway. Maybe they have some booze. Maybe I can kill a few birds with less stones than there are birds.

SUNNY AND MOONY live in the most remote tree house in camp. I know I'm within a hundred yards when I pass a wooden sign with words carefully carved into it. "If you don't have an invitation, please turn back."

I've never seen their place before, and I almost miss it. It sits close to the ground, and looks more like one of the domes at the front of camp. It's nearly covered in a creep of ivy so it blends into the surrounding forest. Psychedelic curtains hang in the windows, blocking the view. I climb up the steps and knock on the doorjamb.

"Who goes there?" calls a voice from inside.

"Ash."

"Two minutes."

I sit down on the step, look out at the green expanse of the woods. Run through the stuff I need to do if I successfully talk my way inside, because I'm sure I won't have long. The door opens and Moony steps out wearing a robe she's not doing a great job of holding shut, so I can still see most of her pale, awkward body.

She smiles, brushing her black hair out of her face, her cheeks flushed red. "Sorry, we're in the middle of a session."

"Yeah, about that. I need a favor."

She tilts her head and smiles.

"Did those fed thugs make it out here?" I ask.

"They did not."

"Good. I need some computer time. I don't trust the house computer."

She seems to think about this for a second, but ultimately frowns. "You know we don't let people use our rig."

"That's why it's a favor. I'll owe you one."

It's a big ask. The office computer is a tricycle. The one here is a Ferrari. It would need to be. As I'm to understand things, they used to live in the real world, where they earned some good money and acclaim doing cam shows. They heard about South Village shortly after it opened and decided they wanted to move their operation here. But they wanted to do it on their terms, so they cut a deal with Tibo.

The hut was built custom for them, and they paid to install fiber optic internet and a dedicated feed of electricity. Only to them, not to the rest of the camp. That was Tibo's decision, even though they offered to extend the lines to the main part of camp. He thought more robust internet and electricity were a slippery slope to turning this place into a Best Western.

South Village gets a small cut of their profits, as a form of rent. In exchange they get to live on the land, get access to everything in the camp, and maintain a level of privacy they hadn't been afforded previously. Plus, they don't have to do chores.

Besides the sign warning away visitors, everyone who comes to South Village gets a very stern warning about staying away from here. You normally don't even come up to this place unless you've been invited.

Which makes me feel a little like an asshole even being here.

"A favor, huh." Moony smirks. "What's this I hear about night bacon?"

"Did Alex tell you?"

"She might have let it slip."

"You want in on the bacon?"

"Both of us do. It has to be me and Sunny."

"Is anyone here actually fucking vegan?"

She shrugs. "How long do you need?"

"Hour would be good."

She whistles. "That's a lot. Sunday is a big day for us. A lot of guys sitting at home with nothing better to do than to give us money."

"Look…"

"Actually, maybe there is something else you can help us with."

I nod, slowly. I feel like I know where this is going. Whenever someone gets that tone, it's because they're going to ask me to do something I'm not sure I want to do.

"We think there's been someone outside at night," she says. "The past few nights, we've been hearing stuff. Could be a squirrel, could be a person."

“What do you want me to do? Sit on the porch all night with a shotgun?”

She shakes her head. “Keep an eye out. If you want to wander over here tonight for a few minutes, fine. You don’t have to move in. But, weren’t you, like, a private eye or something?”

“Listen, we’ll do a bacon party soon. Have you talked to Gideon? He’s the security guy.”

“Gideon insists on coming inside.”

“He’s kind of a creep, isn’t he?”

She nods. “He is. Let me grab Sunny. We’ve got an errand to run anyway.”

Moony ducks back inside and I sit down. More tasks to fulfill. This is like playing a video game and I’ve got side quests. But coming over tonight will be an easy thing to do. I figure it’s nothing. Nerves are running high, rustling suddenly sounds like footsteps.

Sunny comes out and as she walks past me, she points and says, “Night bacon.”

“Night bacon,” I tell her. “Got any booze on hand? I could go for a cocktail.”

Moony follows. She sticks one finger up in the air. “No. You have one hour.”

Dammit. “Okay.”

“Also, be careful about what you touch.”

“Double-got it.”

The two of them amble off into the woods and I step inside.

The air is heavy with incense. I can taste it. The room is dim, so it takes a second for my eyes to adjust. When they do, I am surrounded by dildos.

Surrounded.

In every size, every shape, every color of the rainbow. There are cartoon characters—Disney princesses and superheroes and figurines. Some are small and simple, others are large and intricate. A couple scare me deeply. They're carefully arranged, like religious icons, glittering in the dim light on shelves that run the length of the room. There are two doors on the far end. Bedrooms, I figure.

In the middle of the room, there's a massive Oriental carpet, on which there's an assortment of plush, satin pillows. There's a small stack of towels and a couple of bottles of lube off to the side, as well as a stack of board games. On the other side of the carpet is a half-disassembled Jenga tower, and a whiteboard with goofy names written on it—screennames, probably—with numbers scribbled next to them.

This makes me incredibly curious about the peculiar demands of guys who like to watch cam girls. I'll need to revisit this.

At the other end of the room is a Mac, the monitor so big it could be mounted behind a bar playing a football game. It's flanked by some big speakers and a couple of smaller camera rigs that are all wired into the monitor. There's a chair set in front of it—I suspect for my benefit. I sit down, click on the desk lamp next to me.

First up, I open a web browser, drop into incognito mode so the computer won't save anything I do, and get the cipher from my e-mail. I really don't want to write this thing out since it's pretty long, so even though I don't see one, I click the printer button and pray. There's a soft whirr off to my right. These girls are prepared. I take the printout of the photo, fold it up, and stick it in my pocket.

Next up, I confirm which edition of *The Monkey Wrench Gang*

I need. Then I do a search for every bookstore in the area, come up with more than a dozen. Mostly used stores. I click on a website, find an e-mail address, write a quick e-mail with what I'm looking for, then send. Click, paste, repeat. I hit 11 in total. That's a good start.

I do a quick check on Amazon. They're not selling the edition I need on the main site, and I find a re-seller who's got a used copy for three dollars. The shipping information is a little unspecific—two to ten days. I click on it anyway, have it sent to Momma's. A little insurance if the bookstores don't bear out. And if it gets jammed up and arrives after I'm gone, fuck it, they can donate it to the library.

There's a ping, so I click over to my e-mail and see my mom is requesting a video chat. When I left I promised I'd always answer when she called, which hasn't been easy considering how often I don't have a cell signal. I don't get off camp enough to call her. This much, I owe to her.

But as I'm clicking the 'accept' button I realize my mistake.

A window pops up with my panicked face, and there is no mistaking that I am framed by the largest assortment of dildos ever assembled in one place.

There's a small black cloth folded up under the monitor, and I drape it over the top of the computer, where the little green light is showing that the camera is active. My face disappears as my mom's face appears.

She's lit blue, slightly distorted. Her neat hair a little grayer than I remember it. This is the first time I've seen her since I left. There's a tightness in my chest. That feeling of emptiness expanding and pressing itself out.

She looks around like she's searching an empty room. "Honey, are you there?"

"Yeah Ma, I'm here."

"I can't see you."

"I think the camera is busted. I can see you okay though."

She looks so sad. That makes me feel terrible. Not bad enough to remove the cloth.

"So how are things with your friend down in Georgia?" she asks.

"Good. It's hot. Ma, the bugs down here. Spiders the size of kittens."

"It doesn't sound good."

"It's not bad."

"Still planning your big trip to Europe?"

"Got my tickets. Leaving in less than two weeks now."

"Well, that's nice…"

Her voice trails off. Which means she doesn't think it's nice. What she wants is for me to come home. Even a quick stop. She also doesn't want to ask me to do it, and I don't want to offer. Home right now is a big bridge that's been burnt down to embers. The reason she didn't fight me leaving is because she knew I needed it, but I'm sure we've gotten to the point where she regrets it.

"Ma, how are things at the house?"

"They're good. Still getting water in the basement."

"You call one of dad's friends?"

"Yeah. Billy Ryan. You remember him? He does foundations."

"I do, yeah." Firefighting doesn't pay well—tragically—so a lot of guys tend to take side-gigs. Especially in construction fields, because it's good, off-the-books money. I don't think a single job has ever been done in my parents' house that wasn't done by someone on the job.

Thinking about that makes me think about my dad. What he would be doing if he were still alive. He'd still be on the job, I'm sure. For as little as I remember, he didn't seem to be the retiring type. Maybe he'd do electrical work. I seem to remember he was pretty good at that.

It makes me wish I could remember more about him.

Again, I am happy that my mom can't see my face.

I check my watch. I've got about a half hour left. No time to be wistful. "Ma, listen, I'm sorry but I'm on borrowed time here with the computer and I got a few things to finish. Can I call you soon?"

"Maybe you can try and fix the camera for next time? It'd be nice to see you."

My hand reaches up toward the lint cloth. Maybe I can tilt the monitor. Maybe if I click off the desk lamp the background will fade out and she'll only see me. Give her that much.

And then I pull my hand back. Wonder if she'll see that stereogram image. She's good like that. The thought of putting that kind of hurt on her isn't worth it.

"I'll give it a try next time, Ma," I tell her. "I'm sorry about that."

"Okay. Call soon."

"Got it. Love you."

"Love you too."

There's a look on her face as she signs off, in that frozen moment before the screen disappears, somewhere between sadness and disappointment. I'm not sure where on the scale it lands, and even thinking about it stings, so I click out of my e-mail.

Back to work. I search for the Soldiers of Gaia.

And find nothing.

Well, not nothing. I find a song by a weird electronic rave band called Soldiers of Gaia. I knew it sounded like a band. There's also a role playing guild for an online war game. But nothing related to eco-terrorism. Nothing that would spur the feds to storm in here and give us the Guantanamo treatment. I'm clicking over to the second page of search results when I hear a rustle outside.

Sunny and Moony maybe? I check my watch. Still got fifteen minutes.

Could be an animal.

Footsteps come up the porch. There's no mistaking that sound.

What if it's not Sunny and Moony?

What if it's someone who saw Sunny and Moony out and about, and figured this place would be empty?

I close out of the browser and cross to the door, my footsteps echoing in the hollow of the raised floor, and realize too late that it must be audible from outside. I get the door open, my eyes stinging from the sudden blast of sunlight, and I see something crash through the woods.

I follow, running hard, trying to keep from tripping over the stray log or elevation in the earth. I can't even see who or what I'm chasing. I think maybe there's a flash in front of me, but that could be my eyes playing tricks. Once you're in the woods the world looks like a painted backdrop.

There's an open clearing ahead. As I'm about to enter it, passing the trees guarding the perimeter, something hits my face. Heavy, sticky strands wrap around my head, and something hard scratches against my nose.

My insides scream.

There is a spider on my face.

There is a giant monster spider on my fucking *face*.

I fall to the ground and slap at it, trying to get it off me. Spitting, crying in my throat, my mouth clamped shut so hard my teeth ache. The web is keeping it pressed to my face so I pull at it and when I feel like I've got a good grip, fling my arm out so hard it hurts my shoulder.

After I'm sure my face is clear—and only then—I open my eyes. Brush away the rest of the web that's wrapped around my head, shaking, breathing so fast it's making me dizzy. My heart feels like it's going to explode in my chest. I press a hand to my sternum, calm myself.

In front of me there's a loose pile of earth, freshly turned over. I stick my hand in it because of how odd it is. It's like the kind of earth you would dig up out of a hole. Except there are no holes. This is a completely untouched portion of camp. It looks like a cross between forest and jungle. Probably drops off into swamp in another few hundred feet.

The freshly-uncovered earth makes me think of Portland, and the hole I dug, and I feel the waves lapping at my feet, and it gets even worse when I look up and see Cannabelle's body, limbs splayed out, staring up, unblinking into the sun.

TWELVE

I'M STILL RUNNING when I get back to the main part of camp. The clearing between the domes is empty now. Aesop, shirtless in a pair of jeans, is coming out of the kitchen and reads something on my face because he breaks into a run, too.

"Where's Tibo?" I ask.

He shakes his head. I take off toward the office dome, with Aesop following behind. Tibo is inside the bar area, sitting in a chair in the corner, reading a book. I stop to catch my breath as he sticks a scrap of paper into the book and puts it down besides him.

"What happened?" he asks.

I check around to make sure it's the three of us. When I'm sure of that I tell him, "Cannabelle."

"Is she okay?"

"No."

Tibo gets up, his face twisted in panic. "Let's go."

I LOST MY BEARINGS, so we have to go to Sunny and Moony's place to find her again. I follow the path I made through the forest. I'm worried I went the wrong direction but the clearing appears. I was really hoping it was a hallucination. That I was wrong. But no, Cannabelle is still lying there.

Aesop stops and puts his hands on his knees, looks at the ground, breathing long and slow, in through his mouth, out through his nose. He does this a few times and straightens up.

"What happened?" Tibo asks.

"I don't know. Someone tried to sneak up on Sunny and Moony. I chased them. Found this."

"Why were you with Sunny and Moony?"

"I was using the computer. They let me. Let's concentrate on this right now?"

The sun is beating down on Cannabelle so her skin still looks flush, but there's purple creeping around the lips. Her skin is slack, falling away from her. Dead not like dead in the movies. There are flies buzzing around her, a fat black one perched on her lip.

As Tibo inches forward a twig cracks underfoot and he steps back. He looks up and there's a long, heavy branch of a tree overhanging her, casting a shadow across her midsection.

"Maybe she fell," he says.

I squat down. Her neck is broken. It's tilted at an inhuman angle. Just slightly too far. I'm not an expert but her arms and her legs look intact. The canopy above us is high. Three stories, at least. A fall like that would have to fuck up a body more than this.

There's no blood, even. No fallen branches. Almost like she's lying down to take a nap.

Her hands are caked in dirt, too, the whites of her fingernails dark from where it's packed in and caked. She was digging.

"I don't think she fell," I tell them. "I don't think her grow rigs are around here."

"Okay," Tibo says. "Okay. Fuck. Whatever happened, I need to call Ford. We have to keep this quiet. I don't want anyone else knowing right now."

"Are you sure?" Aesop asks.

"If this is a crime scene, then we don't want everyone crowding around here. I don't want another Pete."

"I'm going to retrace my steps," I tell him. "See if the person I chased dropped something, or if there's anything else worth finding."

"You sure those things are connected?"

"If it's the same person, they killed her before they came to see Sunny and Moony. Wouldn't have been enough time to do it while I was chasing them. Worth checking."

Aesop steps toward me. "I'll come."

The way he says it, like a statement, makes me figure I shouldn't refuse him.

Tibo nods and jogs off, crunching through the brush.

And then it's me and Aesop. And Cannabelle.

We stand there for a few moments, baking in the heat. We look at each other, both of us searching for something to hold on to. We recognize that in each other and it's a bit much, so we both look away.

"You want to lead?" he asks.

"Sure."

We set off through the woods. I feel bad leaving Cannabelle alone, and need to remind myself that she's dead.

Aesop and I walk in silence, single file, looking around for things we don't know we're looking for. When the clearing has disappeared behind us and we're surrounded by trees and foliage on all sides, I hear Aesop come to a stop behind me.

"Pete wasn't the first dead body you've seen," he says.

"Can't be your first," I tell him.

I say it like a challenge, hoping he takes the hint and doesn't broach the subject any further. I can feel his eyes on me, like he's trying to figure me out. I'm not a big fan of that, but there's not much I can do.

We walk again for a little bit, until the footsteps behind me cease. This time I turn and Aesop has taken a knee, peering off to the side of our path. I come up next to him.

"What is it?" I ask.

Instead of answering he stalks off through the woods, staying low and quiet, like he's hunting something. I try to see what he's seeing. There's a broken branch. I bend over for a closer look and see the outline of what could be a boot print, heading in the direction Aesop is walking. I go after him, keeping an eye out for spiders and other forest monsters.

The terrain gets rougher, more uneven. The branches come out and brush against us, and then they impede us. The odd one looks broken, like maybe it was trampled. I try to differentiate between what's here and what could have been changed or affected by someone else.

One of the chores here at camp is machete duty. Which is

pretty much what it sounds like. You take a machete and crash through the brush, clearing the footpaths. But only in the parts of camp that are commonly tread. This area hasn't been touched, though we're sort of close to the back road that runs behind camp.

My foot swings out and hits something metal. I bend down and pick up a shovel. The wooden handle is a little worn and there are dots of rust on the blade, but otherwise it's in pretty good shape. I hold it out to Aesop and he takes it.

"Did you see all that fresh earth over by Cannabelle?" he asks.

"You think someone was trying to bury her?"

He looks around, thinking about it. Finally says, "There was no hole near her. I don't know that she's been dead so long. And she didn't seem to have been touched."

"So what do you think?"

"Could be nothing. People are sloppy. I've found the odd piece of equipment lying around in the woods. But all that earth… someone was digging something. Let's use this spot at a starting point. Spread out in a circle, see if we find anything."

A HALF HOUR GOES by and we don't turn up anything. Empty forest. A weird looking bug I don't know the name for that lands on my wrist and bites a little circle into my flesh. Some bones, which I think might be related to the disappearance of Malmon, the chicken who went missing a few weeks back.

I stop when the land drops off into swamp. Nothing that way, I'm sure. The leeches and alligators make sure of that. The alligators never come up out of the water, and the deal seems to be that in return, no one ventures in.

By the time Aesop and I get back to the clearing, Ford and Corey are already there with Tibo, the three of them standing around Cannabelle, looking down at her body.

Ford does not look happy.

He nods toward us. "These boys know what happened?"

"Nothing beyond what I told you," Tibo says. "Ash found her. He was out for a walk."

Tibo's eyes hammer into me on that last bit.

Ford turns toward me. "Well, Ashley, walk me through what you saw."

"Not much to say," I tell him. "I was out, found her, went and got Tibo, here we find ourselves."

He takes his sheriff's hat off to reveal that his short gray hair is soaked in sweat, like he dunked his head in a sink. He wipes his brow with the back of his sleeve and puts the hat back on. "This was the girl always climbing up in the trees, correct?"

Tibo nods.

"Why did she to do that?"

"People are into a lot of different things," Tibo says.

Ford takes a knee next to her body, looking back and forth between her and the canopy. "Well, doesn't look like she fell. I've seen people fall from that kind of height. The ground is kind of soft here, but I don't think that happened."

So at least my suspicion is confirmed.

Ford straightens up and turns to Tibo. "Now we got a real problem here, son. I got to send out a forensics team, again. They won't be too happy. Found nothing worth finding around your friend the other day but one of them got bit up by fire ants pretty bad. I need to interview people. Guests and staffers. And you and I need to sit down and go over a few things. So, I hope you're ready for a long day."

Tibo grimaces. "I want to help."

Ford takes the hat off and gestures toward camp. "After you, then."

FORD WANTS TO set up shop in the office dome. I ask if he wants to sit down and talk with me, but he waves me off. "You think of anything else, you come and find me," he says.

And with that me and Aesop find ourselves outside Eatery.

"What do you think?" I ask. "Should we let the horde fend for themselves?"

"It'd be anarchy," Aesop says. "I won't stand for that in my kitchen. C'mon. We have a responsibility to keep these people fed."

"The timing just sucks. I mean… it'd be nice to take a minute."

"Our job is to make sure the wheels keep turning, because all of them out there," Aesop gestures toward the rest of camp, "they're going to need that minute. Now c'mon. Let's get to work."

We settle on some raw pizza dough we've got stashed in the chest fridge. We'll roll out a few pies, douse them with some sauce and vegan mozzarella—much to my chagrin because it's got the consistency of sawdust and I'd rather leave it off, but some people are sticklers for appearance. We can toss them in the bread oven, put a salad on the side, and call it dinner.

Aesop pulls little plastic bottles of spices off the rack over the sink, popping the tops and giving them a sniff. The labels have long since worn and washed off. Once he's sorted out which ones he wants to use he says, "It'll be nice to get back to cooking for real at some point. I'm getting tired of half-assing this."

"Only so much you can do when shit like this is happening."

"Yeah."

I put an onion on the cutting board and pull out a long chef's knife. Go to cut it but my hand feels funny and it slips, sliding off the onion and just missing the thumb on my left hand before clunking on the board. I put down the knife, hold my hand out. It shakes a little. I must be tired. Anxious. Over stimulated. My heart races again. I take a deep breath to calm down.

Footsteps at the front. Zorg comes in, wearing a tank top and a red floral swimsuit, and says, "Hello Aesop. It is I, Z…"

He sees me and stops himself. I wave my hand. "You want to play your make-believe fucking name game, go ahead. Though, you ought to think about whether you want people to take you seriously. Because you sound fucking ridiculous."

The gravity of the room changes. I turn and Zorg's face has dropped, like he's gotten some very bad news. Aesop, meanwhile, is furious. His ears are red, and the breeze is actually cutting through the kitchen so I know it's not from the heat. He looks about to say something when there are more footsteps and Tibo comes inside.

"What's up?" I ask, very thankful for the distraction.

"Need you all to grab whatever identification you've got and come on by the dome."

"I have my ID on me," Zorg says in a quiet voice. He puts his head down and goes to leave, but Aesop puts his hand on his shoulder.

"Zorg, you can give your ID later," Aesop says. He points toward a bowl of vegetables. "Can you do some chopping? Side salad."

Zorg nods slowly, looking at me with an abundance of caution. He pulls an apron off the wall and slips it overhead, moving like he's trying to not wake a sleeping animal.

Aesop goes to the knife rack. Tibo turns to leave and I catch him outside, out of earshot of the others. "Anything on Marx?"

"Nothing. People are going to bring him up. I can't control the message on this. I have to figure out how to handle it."

Gideon comes up to us, wearing a torn t-shirt and jeans and no shoes. He says, "Everyone needs to get to the dome with their ID."

"Yeah, I know," I tell him.

"Okay. Get a move on then."

"Fuck off, you twat."

He blusters at me as Tibo drops his head into his hands and walks off toward the dome.

"What exactly is your fucking problem?" Gideon asks.

"You are my problem, you lanky fuck," I tell him. "Walk away right now, or I am going to take your fucking teeth out."

He doesn't move, but given the look on his face, that seems to be more out of fear than defiance. I'm wondering if maybe I should give him a quick slap when Aesop comes out of the kitchen. "Ash, I have to grab my license. I'm guessing you need yours too. Want to take a walk?"

"Sure."

Gideon opens his mouth to speak. "Bu…"

"What did I fucking tell you?" I ask. "Don't fucking talk to me."

Aesop nods to Gideon. "You'd do well to listen."

We leave him there with his mouth hanging open, make it a little bit away from camp, onto the boardwalk. I pass over a board that says: *Go where the peace is.*

There's something heavy in the air between us. Aesop is extremely unhappy right now, and I've never seen him like this. After a little bit of walking in silence he says, "You shouldn't be such a dick to Zorg."

"What's the problem?" I ask. "Goofy kid wants to live in his little goofy hippie world, doesn't mean everyone else has to play along."

"You really are an idiot," he says. "So much more of your bullshit makes sense to me now."

I stop, turn to face him, the two of us close on the boardwalk, standing so near each other I can smell his sweat. "The fuck is that supposed to mean?"

"You think that kid's doing it for a laugh? You can't see that he's carrying something? Not everyone handles shit by drinking themselves stupid. I don't know what it is he's carrying, but it's what he needs to do. It's a defense mechanism. And it's way less shitty than yours. Who the fuck are you to say otherwise?"

The words splash and burn my skin. The realization makes me feel a few inches shorter.

I was being a bully.

The hollow in my chest aches.

"I'll apologize to him," I say.

Aesop nods, face still downcast but accepting that I understand. "C'mon. My home is up first."

He leads me off the boardwalk, through a bundle of brush, down a path I've never walked before. I probably wouldn't have noticed it if he wasn't showing me the way. The dirt path under us is smooth and narrow and we're on it for a little while, until we reach another boardwalk, older than the main artery that connects the various parts of the camp. The wood is darker, the shape different. It leads over a small green pond where the sun bounces off the water, through a clearing in the canopy. Insects flit through the air and a duck drifts across the glass surface of the water.

Across the way is an open-air dwelling. A roof and posts but no walls, like a gazebo. It's screened in and raised off the ground, the area underneath it blocked by wooden lattice. There's a long line of Tibetan prayer flags—dozens, maybe a hundred—strung around and around the roof, hanging down and gently swaying in the wind.

At the foot of the bridge over the creek Aesop pauses.

"Can you stay here?" he asks.

He's not being unkind. He looks genuinely uncomfortable at me being this close. Which, given the nature of the place, hidden away like a secret, that makes sense. I nod at him, take a step back for good measure.

He crosses the bridge, goes inside the gazebo, the door slamming shut behind him on a strong spring. Once he's inside it's too dim for me to see what he's doing. I look around, kick the dirt, step off to the side and take a quick piss against a tree, which is long enough for a bunch of fire ants to climb up my ankle, so I finish up and brush them away and Aesop is coming back across the boardwalk, slipping something into his pocket with one hand, carrying something in the other hand.

It's a bottle of wine.

He steps off the boardwalk and holds it up to me, sunlight reflecting off the bottle. I want to take it even though I think maybe it's not as simple as a straight offering.

"I get it," he says. "You've seen some shit. You're having a hard time with it. But that doesn't give you the right to be an asshole to other people. If anything, you should be sympathetic. You were a prick when you were drinking and I was hoping that not having booze would mellow you out, but that doesn't seem to be the case. So how about this? Take this and keep on medicating."

His hand drops an inch.

"Or make the decision to be better," he says.

He holds up the bottle of wine to me again. Closer this time. It's a white. I hate white. White is boring. But right now anything with ethanol looks good to me. I can feel a tug, somewhere on the inside of me. Someplace primal. I want it, very very bad.

Which is a compelling reason to choose the second option.

I take the bottle from his hand, and his face gets soft and sad. I heft it, feel the weight of it. Close my eyes. Take a deep breath. Think about the comfort it would provide.

Think about the empty black hole this will bring, instead of that wet, muddy hole I'm destined to spend tonight in, burying Wilson while Chell and my dad stare at me.

Think about having to do that every night for the rest of my life.

And I hurl the bottle into the pond. It flips through the air and splashes down, sending up a spray of water that glitters in the sun, scaring the shit out of the duck, which is now flapping its wings and puttering to shore.

"What the fuck did you do that for?" Aesop asks.

"I… thought the point of this was you wanted me to reject the bottle."

"I didn't want you to fucking throw it!"

"I thought it was symbolic."

"No, it's my bottle of wine. I was still going to drink it!"

The bottle bobs in the water not too far from us. I have no idea how deep the pond is and I'm not entirely excited to find out. But Aesop is now even more annoyed, so I go looking for a long stick.

ONCE WE'RE BACK on the pathway to the bus, I tell Aesop, "I'm sorry. And thank you."

"You're welcome. Maybe next time try not to be so dramatic."

"Relying on props to make a point is pretty dramatic."

He doesn't say anything to that.

We get to the bus and Aesop asks, "Can I come in? Can we sit and talk for a minute?"

I lead him inside and shut the door behind us. I dig my ID out of my bag so I don't forget it. Sit on the platform bed and he pulls up the chair, says, "I overheard something."

I lean forward. "Okay."

"There's a meeting tomorrow night. Magda was talking to Gideon about it. Like she was feeling him out. It was over by the showers. I don't think they knew I was there. But, you know, I was in the Marines. I know what recruiting sounds like."

"Okay. Why has no one recruited us?"

"I don't have a taste for Kool-Aid, and I think most people know that," he says. "You're just an asshole."

"Hey."

"Am I wrong?"

"… No."

He smiles. "Plus you've got a tenuous connection to Tibo, so that puts you on the other side of the debate."

"So where's the meeting?" I ask.

"No idea."

"We could follow Gideon and Magda."

"Risky. I'm betting it's off site. Far off site. Especially if Marx is involved."

"How do we find out where it is without arousing suspicion?"

"I've been thinking about that," Aesop says. "Thinking about how the people here break down. Who might be Team Tibo and who might be Team Marx. And the problem is, I can't figure out who might be loyal enough to one side that they wouldn't go tell the other."

"Maybe Katashi?"

Aesop runs his hands through his hair, undoes the elastic band holding his hair in a ponytail, shakes it out, and puts the ponytail back together. "I've tried to talk to him a couple of times. He knows a few basic words in English and doesn't seem interested in learning any more. They might not have tried. Even if they did, we might not be able to get it out of him. Unless you know some Japanese."

"I do not. What about some of the new guests?"

"Too hard to call where they might land on it."

"We need someone who hasn't been swayed yet," I tell him. "Someone who's new enough to the camp but doesn't seem interested in the team aspect of it. Who's the newest arrival?"

Aesop smiles.

ZORG IS WASHING the knives and laying them out on a tea towel as we get into the kitchen. The vegetables we gave him to chop are in small, neat piles, everything diced to nearly identical proportions. He looks up at us with wide eyes, looking for approval, but also a little worried about what I might say.

I stand at the counter next to him. He eyes me like a small animal would eye a predator, which just about breaks my heart.

"I'm sorry," I tell him. "That wasn't cool, the way I acted before. There was no reason to be unkind."

He seems at peace with me now. "I understand."

"No, say it like you want to say it."

He smiles. "Zorg understands."

"Good." I pat him on the back, send his slight frame nearly flying into the counter. I pat him again, softer.

Aesop walks to the kitchen and hangs himself out the door, looking around, and pulls himself back in. I check the pantry, because you never know. Once we're in the clear Aesop turns on the radio. Rage Against the Machine plays, which seems oddly fitting.

"Do we need a soundtrack for this?" I ask him.

He spins a finger in the air. "Bugs."

That's a fair point. I didn't think the feds might have left behind some listening devices. It makes me suddenly very nervous about what I might have said up until this point.

"We need to ask you something," Aesop says to Zorg.

Zorg nods, very cautious.

"There's some stuff going down," Aesop says. "Stuff that might be bad. We're not sure what yet. But we think there's a meeting tomorrow night. We're trying to find out where that meeting is.

Has anyone approached you? Tried to feel you out for something?"

Zorg nods. "Magda."

"Does it make you uncomfortable to talk to us about this?" he asks. "Like you might be betraying her confidence?"

Zorg shakes his head.

"We would like it if this stayed between us," Aesop says. "Can you do that?"

Zorg nods.

"Where's the meeting?" I ask.

"The beach," Zorg says.

"Oh, fuck," Aesop says. "That makes sense."

THIRTEEN

AFTER LETTING FORD take down my information, and setting out a subdued dinner for the camp, I call it a night. Head back to my bus, whiskey-less, and settle in. I figure I'm worrying too much about it, like maybe it won't be too bad. I can make it through the night unscathed.

I am wrong.

I'm exhausted but sleep sits a couple of inches outside my grasp. Time feels faulty, like it's skipping around. Mostly I stare at the roof of the bus but sometimes I find myself standing at the edge of the pit, looking down at Wilson. I alternate between sweating and freezing as my heart revs. I must be coming down with a fever or something. This is not a great time for that.

As the sun comes up I'm in a damp, sweaty fog. Stuck in some weird twilight zone between asleep and awake. And I've still got the whole day to run out the clock until tonight's secret beach rendezvous.

On the way to the shower I pass a cop I don't recognize. A black guy with a swimmer build and a face like an ancient statue, walking from one place to another. He nods at me and I look away from him. There have been cops in and out, talking to people, checking on the area where Cannabelle died.

Every new face is an opportunity for someone to recognize me.

Even though I've been sober more than a full day now, I feel like I'm hung over. It's not too hot, the clouds holding back the sun. I stand under the shower for a bit, naked and soaked in the breeze, and it helps, but only a little.

After I'm dressed, my brain feeling like it's full of gravel and wet leaves, I head over to Hospice, the medical dome.

A rainbow curtain hangs from the door. I push it aside and get hit with the thick smell of herbs and incense. The far wall is honeycombed with cubbies that are filled mostly with glass jars, those jars holding variations of leaves or liquids or roots.

To the left is an exam table and a cabinet full of first-aid supplies, everything meticulously gleaming. To the right is an old metal desk covered with stickers. Alex is wearing a floral skirt and a black tank top, her bare feet up on the desk, reading a graphic novel. She was a nurse in a previous life, I think.

Alex looks up and extends one slim finger to me.

"You still owe me night bacon," she says.

"Soon. I'm feeling feverish. Got anything that might help?"

She places down the graphic novel, swings her legs onto the floor, and folds her hands, suddenly all business. "Symptoms?"

"Sweating, chills, headache. Can't sleep."

"Have you lost the will to live? Do you feel the pull of eternal darkness?"

"What the fuck are you talking about?"

"Just making sure it's not nihilism."

"No, it's not fucking nihilism."

"Okay, because it's been going around." She sits back in the chair. "Any cough, sore throat, congestion?"

"Not that I noticed."

"Do you prefer the hippie dippie stuff, or something that's actually going to work?"

"Real stuff, please."

She opens a drawer in the desk and pulls out a bottle of ibuprofen and tosses it my way. "Take two. Eat some food. Drink a lot of water. I mean a lot. You might be dehydrated. Even if you're not, you will be soon."

I open the bottle, shake two into my palm, throw them back, and place the bottle down. "Thanks, doc."

"And do not forget about my night bacon."

"Ten-four."

I head to Eatery, drink a whole bunch of water, some coffee, some more water, until I'm stepping out into the tree line every ten minutes to pee. I feel a little better. Working helps, too. Something to keep my hands occupied. Zorg and Aesop are doing most of the work of cleaning and prepping for the rest of the day, so I take a break every now and again to sit outside in the breeze. Sometimes I doze off. Mostly I stare into the canopy.

After a little while I get bored and head inside to see if there's something I can do. The dishes from last night are sitting in the drying rack. I go about putting them away, and get most of the glasses away before my hand jerks and I drop one. It shatters across the floor, glass spreading like a wave.

Sigh. I must be more tired than I thought. I grab a broom and get to work cleaning.

AFTER DINNER SERVICE, after part of the camp seems to up and vanish, I stop in the main dome to get a flashlight. Sitting next to the flashlight bin is the lost and found bin. It's usually full but tonight there's nothing inside but a hat. It's a green baseball hat, but with a flat top instead of a rounded top, military style. I take it out and find it fits nicely and I am happy to have a new hat.

When I'm sure the coast is clear I head for the back of camp, to meet Aesop on the service road. It takes me a little while to get there, crossing the boardwalk, then dirt paths, and finally the brush. Trying to use my flashlight as little as possible.

The forest is so quiet. All encompassing, like a void I'm falling into.

Aesop is sitting in the car, the engine off, and when he sees the beam of my flashlight cut through the window he starts the engine, but he doesn't turn on the headlights. I climb in and the radio is off. We drive slowly down the narrow pathway, illuminated barely by the night sky, enough that we can see a few feet in front of us.

Once we get to the road, Aesop clicks on the headlights and slams on the gas.

I have heard of the beach. I've never been there, because the beach is a group activity, and I'm not usually down for those. It's not far from South Village, but far enough you have to drive. We cross marshlands, guardrails on either side to keep cars from falling into the swamps, neither of us speaking, both of us vibrating with anticipation. Things are getting heavy now, and I think we both know we're taking it to the next level.

We could have told Tibo. We could have told the cops.

We didn't.

I wonder why he's doing it. He doesn't have a horse in this race. No reason to be out looking for trouble. Though, technically, neither do I. Maybe it's something to make the time go by.

That reminds me: I pull out my phone, turn it on, check my e-mail. Three bookstores wrote back. Two said they don't have the edition of *The Monkey Wrench Gang* that I'm looking for. The third, a couple of towns over, says that yes, they do.

"Found the book," I tell Aesop.

"Good. That's tomorrow's task, then."

"Speaking of tomorrow, we're going to need an alibi," I tell him. "Someone might notice we're gone tonight. So if someone asks we should come up with an excuse about where we were. Just to be safe."

"Okay," Aesop says. "We have time to come up with something."

We cut down a wide street, big houses set back across lawns that slope up and away from us. Along the right it's dunes, reeds and vegetation sticking out like unruly hair.

"We can stash the car down here and walk along the beach," Aesop says. "Usually when people come to the beach they use another entrance. This way no one will come across us."

Aesop finds a little stretch in the dunes to put the car, pushed in far enough from the road that if you were driving, you'd have to turn to get a good look at it, and in the dark you might miss it entirely.

We get out and the air is warm and smells like salt. I'm still a little sweaty, and now a little achy on top of it. My head spinning a bit, probably from the anticipation, which is weird, because I usually don't get this way. I wish I had more ibuprofen. It sucks but I'm not about to complain in front of a former Marine.

We're both in dark jeans and dark t-shirts, which I now realize means we'll stand out against the sand. Should have thought about that. We climb to the top of the dunes and Aesop continues down the other side but I come to a full stop.

In either direction, it looks like the skeletons of a hundred massive beasts have washed up on shore after some apocalyptic event. It takes me a moment to realize they're trees. They stick out of the sand at severe angles, half-buried. Branches poking out like rib cages, trunks like spines.

I climb down the dune and onto the smooth surface of the sand and I touch the branch of the nearest tree. It's bleached and worn smooth. The moon is half full and it washes the beach in blue light.

And when I look up, I can see the stars.

Ever since I was a kid I would look at the night sky and wonder what they looked like. You can never really see more than two dozen at a time, with all the light generated by the city, bouncing off the atmosphere and wrapping the sky in a sickly veil of yellow. Which is the trade-off, I guess. Give up something beautiful to live someplace beautiful.

I remember the first time I saw the stars, up in Bear Mountain, camping with my dad. Like someone filled a bucket with diamonds and kicked it across the sky. It was a wide universe of questions and possibility.

Here, now, it brings me back to that moment of serenity. Back before my father's death poisoned me. Because that was it, wasn't it? He died and I raged at the entropy of the universe.

Aesop is standing next to me, looking into the tableau.

"This is incredible," I tell him.

"Isn't it though?"

I look for a minute longer. This same sky covering Crystal and Rose, and my mother and Bombay, and New York and Portland, and the places I've loved and the things that I've seen. For a moment, it allows me to believe those things aren't gone from me.

"Which way?" I ask.

Aesop points down the beach, back in the direction of the way we came. "Thataway."

The trees loom ahead of us in the darkness, scattered randomly, so we have to walk a winding path. One thick jumble of branches forces us to walk closer to the water, into the surf. It comes up around my feet, colder than I would have expected given the August we've had. The wave pulls the sand out from under my feet and I sink down into it a little.

I look up and Aesop is standing there.

"What is it?" he asks.

"It's nothing."

He takes a step toward me and puts his hand on my shoulder. "What is it?"

Normally I'm no great fan of touching. Personal space is a nice thing. And I want to move away from him, but I've got this feeling, completely irrational, that if I move I'm going to slip down into a bottomless pool of water. So I let him leave his hand there. "Just…

I have a thing about the water."

"Tell me about it."

"Nothing to tell."

He takes his hand back, waves for me to follow. "Tell me about the water. That's it. If you don't feel a little better after getting it off your chest I will never ask you to share anything ever again."

We walk in silence for a few minutes.

Then I tell him.

A MONTH BEFORE MY dad died I nearly drowned.

Every summer, the first week of August, my dad's firehouse would host a day trip to Lido Beach, out on Long Island. Barbecue and volleyball. Beer for the adults, Italian ices for the kids. It ranked up near Christmas on my list of cool shit that happened on an annual basis.

I don't remember much about Lido. I do remember domes that looked like giant mushrooms, painted teal and maroon. There were picnic tables underneath them. The walking paths were beige stone, nearly the same color as the sand. There was a playground that looked like a pirate ship. The horizon was a hill of sand dunes, red fence posts and thin blades of tall green grass.

There was a footbridge over the dunes that led down to the beach, which was always crowded, but not too crowded, because you had to pay to park there. The sand between the end of the bridge and the water was white hot and I had to run across it as fast as I could to get to the surf.

The year my dad died was the first year my parents thought I was old enough to go down to the water by myself. This was an important milestone. To be old enough to do a thing where they weren't watching me.

I've never been a big fan of the ocean. I don't like that you can't see what's underneath. I don't like that things live in there. I wouldn't want someone fucking around in my home in the pursuit of leisure. But some of the bigger kids were wading out and bodysurfing back toward shore. It looked like fun and I wanted to revel in my newfound freedom. I splashed out, up to my waist, then my chest. The deepest I'd ever gone, even with my parents watching.

A big wave came up, like the lip of a giant mouth, and I got ready to leap and ride it to shore. But it smashed into me and I lost my bearing. I tumbled, got spun in a circle, the water roaring over my head, the force of it dragging me under. Saltwater in my mouth and ears and eyes, filling me up and choking me.

I kicked my feet out, trying to find the bottom, but there was nothing. I couldn't tell which way was the beach and which way was the rest of the ocean. Which way the sand and which the sky.

Another wave hit.

That's when the fear gripped me like a hand, dragging me deeper. At this point I was sure I'd been swept out to sea, the shoreline disappeared, the ocean floor forever beneath me. I was kicking at the darkness, my eyes stinging, my throat raw and my sinuses full of water. Every time I sputtered or cried out, more water rushed in.

It was the worst thing I ever felt. The deepest, most primal bout I've ever had with fear. I was sure I was drowning and I'd be dead soon.

Somebody pulled me out. I don't remember who, somebody

else who was in the water. Not a lifeguard, which thinking back on it now, makes me think I wasn't in there too long. I probably wasn't in all that much trouble. It was panic warping the experience.

When I got to the sand I was crying. I fell to my hands and knees, coughing the sea out of my lungs. I bumped into someone's leg and looked up and it was my dad.

It's been so long, I'm starting to forget what he looked like. I have pictures, and I remember what the pictures look like. But how he sat in the kitchen, or drove the car, or worked in the yard. It's like he's drifting off into a fog. I can see him, but the finer details are slipping away.

I remember how he looked that day. Graying hair slicked back, Hawaiian shirt open, red bathing suit, leather sandals. Aviator sunglasses and a cigar clenched between his teeth.

I remember suddenly being less afraid of the water and more afraid of him. He'd granted me this freedom and I'd ruined it. He whipped off his glasses and looked down at me. I had no idea what he was going to do, but I was bracing for the worst. Formulating an apology. Before I could speak he said, "C'mon kid, after that you need a cherry ice."

He reached his hand out to me and pulled me to my feet, and we walked back across the hot sand, up to the bridge. I looked back, at the wide expanse of the Atlantic Ocean, thinking that it had almost killed me.

I've done my best to stay out of the water since.

THERE'S A FLICKER of orange light in the distance. Aesop crosses over to the dunes and climbs to the other side. I follow.

We make our way along the road for a little, with the dunes on our left and trees on the right, until we get to where we can smell the smoke.

Aesop stops and holds his hand out flat and lowers it toward the ground, then drops onto his stomach. I follow and we crawl through the brush until we're overlooking the fire. The road has gone up and the beach has dipped down so we're pretty high up at this point, and the steep sand looks treacherous. I stay far from the edge.

There's a clearing in the middle of the skeleton trees, lit harshly in orange. The fire is given life by a pile of driftwood, and Marx is standing next to it, wearing jeans, an open tuxedo vest, and combat boots. Still wearing that stupid bowler hat, too.

There are people sitting in a circle around him. I can see some of their faces, but not all, with the way the light is moving around, and the people who are facing away from me. I see Magda and Gideon. Doesn't look like Sunny or Moony or Alex or Katashi are there. No Job either, which is surprising, because I thought he and Marx were tight. Katie the Trigger Warning Girl is here. Some of the guests, too. People whose names I don't know. I'm glad Aesop is here. He'll know them. I count nine people in total.

With Marx that's ten. Ten troublesome dickbags.

Marx is stalking around the fire, using his fist to punctuate his words. Looks like we came in a little late.

"Petitions don't change anything," he says. "Do you know why? No one cares. Who the fuck cares about signatures on a piece of paper? Give it to your local politician, and what does he think? He already carved up his district. He picked his voters. Someone else gave him the money he needed to get elected. You may as well be handing him toilet paper."

There are nods from the audience.

"The time for peaceful engagement is over," he says. "What has that ever solved? These projects go through. They rape the planet. The earth's temperature rises two more degrees, and we are fucked. We'll be killing each other for fresh water. And we don't have a Plan B. There's no place else to go. But it doesn't matter to the coal company. They got rich. They can't see beyond their next Lexus. It doesn't matter to the worker. They have a job, and they've been bred to believe they ought to be thankful for that, even if it's back-breaking, shit-paying labor. It doesn't matter to the local government because somewhere, somehow, they're getting something out of it. Campaign contributions. Poll workers. Fuck, a nice dinner. The government is already protecting them."

Feels like something is crawling up my leg. I shake it out, try not to think about whatever horrible thing is trying to eat me.

"You saw that when the FBI stormed into our camp and pulled us out," Marx tells the crowd. "We were taken to a remote location. We were beaten. Interrogated for hours. And then left there, like nothing happened. No recourse. They did it because they wanted to scare us. Because they think we're weak. Because they've been bought and paid for, the same as everyone else."

He's embellishing a little. And damn he's a good speaker. Even despite everything I know, it's the kind of speech that makes me want to sign up for whatever he's got planned. I'm still steamed up about Tim and his friends pushing us around like they did.

The fervor dies down. Marx puts his hands on his hips and sighs.

"Some of you may know this," he says, his voice softer now.

"Some of you, maybe not. But I lost both of my parents. These guys were working for a logging company, clearing out forest. They were throwing their cigarettes into the brush. It started a fire. I lost my parents to a company destroying the planet, and the employees who were not only complicit in that action, but careless. Not a day goes by that I don't think of them. That I don't wish they were here, and I didn't have to do these things. But I owe it to them. I owe it to future generations who will be deprived of a peaceful life because of recklessness and malice."

Christ. How different are we, really? Both of us are carrying the loss of parents. Should I be sympathetic?

Marx says, "We can stand outside with our signs and hope that they listen to us, but really, they're going to be laughing. That's all we are to them. A joke. It's all a big game that they win in the end because it's rigged. It's time to do something. Hit them where it hurts. The Soldiers of Gaia are going to strike."

Trigger Warning Katie raises her hand.

"When is this going down?" she asks.

Marx's shoulders drop.

"That's the problem," he says. "Pete was in contact with the Soldiers. He had the cipher with the time, date, and location. We're ready to translate it. I just have to get it. That asshole Ash has it."

"Am I really that much of an asshole?" I whisper to Aesop.

"Yes," he says. "Shut up."

"How do we get it from him?" Katie asks.

"I'm working on that," Marx says. "But as for right now, the thing I need to know is, who's in? Who's ready to strike a blow against corporate and government oppressors? Who's ready to show them that we will not sit down and bear this? We will not accept our world being summarily destroyed to make a quick buck? Who's with me?"

The girl raises her hand again. Marx smiles, but she says, "What exactly are we talking about here?"

My arm is itchy, like something is crawling on it. I reach up to scratch.

"The time for peace is over," Marx says. "The time for pretending like we can politely make a difference is over. The Earth Liberation Front failed. They set fire to some Hummers. But people are still buying Hummers. We're going to make people stop laughing and pay attention. We're going to use their own tactics against them. Desperate times, my friends. We're going to..."

Something moves on the edge of my vision. Long and shiny. For second I think it's another bug, but when I slide back I'm looking into the black glass eyes of a snake.

I jump up and yelp, completely involuntary, and I fall backward, push myself away, hitting Aesop. As I fall back toward the roadway I catch a glimpse of the faces around the fire, turned up and looking at us.

FOURTEEN

MY HEART SLAMS against the inside of my rib cage. I turn and there are more snakes, five or six, blacker than black, slithering down the sand toward us. They seem to be moving toward me, specifically.

Aesop grabs my shirt and yanks at me. "C'mon!"

He takes off running, up a large slope of grass, perpendicular to the roadway, toward a big beautiful house with no lights on. I follow, feeling nauseous and dizzy. Aesop gets to the house and cuts around it, into the back yard.

He keeps running, off in the general direction of the car, using the yards as cover, sticking to the shadows. The houses mostly seem empty. The yards are all connected, long strips of grass with the occasional change in landscaping or short fences that are easy to hop.

Aesop is faster than me, in better shape, so I pump my legs, try to keep up, struggling to breathe. I'm glad I quit smoking. My lungs have healed up enough I don't want to immediately die. But every house we pass makes me feel like someone is building more houses, and I'll never stop running past houses.

I turn and check behind me, expect to see something on my heels chasing me. For a moment I forget why I'm running. My brain feels like a CD that's skipping. The song starts again. Aesop stops, looks back at me.

"We have to keep moving," he says.

"They saw us," I manage to get out between gulps of air.

"It was too dark up on the dune. They were all looking into the fire. They wouldn't have seen anything but shapes."

"Do you think they were poisonous?" I ask.

Aesop arches an eyebrow at me. "Were what poisonous? Listen, we have to get going. If they find our footprints they'll get back to the car. We need to get out of here before that."

I stand, bend back a little to stretch, and jog after Aesop, struggling to keep up.

"Should have walked in the surf," Aesop says, barely breathing hard. "There'd be no footprints then. Stupid mistake."

My muscles are on fire when we get to the car. I run into it, fall forward and splay out onto the trunk. I fling my arms over my head, giving my lungs room to expand, and take deep breaths. Aesop climbs into the driver's seat and I don't even bother walking around to the other side, I open the door behind him and crawl across the back seat. Try not to puke.

Before I've got the door all the way closed Aesop is tearing out of the spot, popping a U-turn, and we're speeding down the road, not back the way we came. Someone is in the front seat with Aesop, talking to him. I sit up and check but find it's only him. He's navigating by the moonlight. The road is a straight shot and there's enough light to see that things are clear, but it's not doing great things for my nerves. My hands are shaking and I can't seem to get them to stop. I lay back down, look at the ceiling of the car.

"You okay back there?" he asks.

"I don't believe in jogging. Jogging is bullshit."

It's not just my hands. Even though it's warm in the car I'm shivering.

"What were you talking about before?" he asks. "What was poisonous?"

I go to answer and suddenly can't think of his name.

Bombay?

No, Aesop.

Christ, I must be tired. When did I sleep last?

"The snakes," I tell him. "That's why I yelled. I'm sorry. I've never seen snakes out in the wild before and it was a little scary. I mean, I don't know shit about snakes…"

"Ash. I didn't see any snakes."

"Really? There were a whole bunch of them."

"Oh fuck."

"What?"

"Ash, how much did you used to drink?"

"A lot?"

"Lie back and get comfortable, okay? Try to relax."

AESOP STOPS THE car on the road behind camp. Probably too risky to go through the main entrance. That makes sense. He turns off the engine and the ceiling of the car disappears and it's black. I sit up and look out the window, see shadows moving around us, the outline of faces peeking into the car window. I blink hard, thinking they'll go away, and they don't.

Aesop turns to me and says, "We need to go."

"We can't get out here," I tell him. "There are people outside."

"Fuck," he mutters under his breath.

He gets out of the car and clicks on a flashlight. The shapes retreat behind him. I can still see them. I don't understand it. Who they are, or why they're waiting out there in the dark. Aesop opens the door and drops down into a crouch, so he's looking me in the eyes.

"Do you know what delirium tremens is?" he asks.

"Alcohol withdrawal."

He nods, slowly. A finger curls out of the darkness, brushes his face, retreats. He doesn't move, like he didn't feel it, but I see the hand coming again so I slide across the seat, away from him. From it.

"You have to trust me," he says. "Can you come with me?"

There's a flash of movement at the corner of my vision. Shiny black bugs crawl up from the floor onto the seat, and I figure now is a good time to go. I scramble out and stand in the clearing next to the car.

There are whispers out in the forest. Asking me questions I don't want to answer. Something grabs my hand. I try to get away, sure that it's the mouth of some terrible insect latching on, but it's Aesop, his fingers entwined in mine. He points his flashlight into the woods, the circle of blue light like a path of safety we can follow.

"You're seeing things," he says. "Hallucinating. I promise you, it's safe."

I know it is. I know it's safe. I've walked these woods in the dark, never been stalked, never had bugs crawl up in great waves. There are no people out there. I know that intellectually. But I see them. I hear them.

Aesop walks, holding my hand tight, pulling me after him. I follow the tunnel of light, the world around me coming unglued, dripping down around us. The voices grow louder. Some of them sound familiar, some of them new. Children and men. Songs and poems. Threats and promises.

The two voices I don't hear are the ones I want to hear. The two faces I don't see are the ones I always feel watching me. I wish Chell and my dad were here, even if they were judging me. Even if they were upset with me. I need them right now. Maybe they finally got tired of me.

Aesop clicks off the flashlight and I feel myself floating in the black. He leads me through something, a giant spider web that wraps around my body. No, fabric, drawing itself across me like a hand.

A light clicks on. White-blue rope light, wrapped around the room at the tops of the walls. We're someplace familiar, someplace I feel like I was not too long ago. There are things crawling on the walls. I try to back out and Aesop grabs me, shakes his head.

He pulls my shirt over my head and douses me with water. The water feels good, and then it doesn't and I'm shivering. Aesop pushes me down on a chair. Something crunches underneath me.

"Do you trust me?" he asks.

I nod at him, because I think that's what I'm supposed to do right now.

He hands me a coffee mug full of water. I cradle it in both hands.

"Drink that," he says. "Slow."

I hear the word slow and I know what it means but I throw it back in one big gulp anyway, immediately retch it all onto the ground. He takes the mug from my hands, refills it from a pitcher, gives it back. There are things moving under the surface of the water so I offer it back to him.

"I can't drink this," I tell him.

"What do you see?" he asks.

"Bugs."

"Are there more bugs in the room?"

I nod toward the wall next to us, where shiny black roaches are crawling from some unseen crack. Aesop slams his hand against the wall. Nothing happens to the bugs. His hand goes through them.

"You're seeing things," he says. "There's no one in here but the two of us. Do you understand that? Can you concentrate on my hand?"

I look back down at the water and it's clear. Up at the wall, and it's clear, too. I take a tentative sip, focus on keeping it down. Breathe in and out. My vision is clear for the moment but I can still hear the voices, like there's a group of people crowded around the dome, whispering at me through the walls.

Aesop is rooting around, doing things with his hands I can't see because his back is turned to me. I want to ask him about the void. Maybe I have caught the nihilism that's been going around. I thought it was a fever.

He turns with another mug. I think he's taken the mug out of my hands but I'm still holding the mug that I was holding. It's a different mug, clay and painted, like a kid would make in kindergarten class. There are curls of black smoke coming off the top of it.

He pulls a chair until it's sitting across from me and sits on the praying mantis that had been sitting on the chair and holds the mug out to me. The black surface of the liquid bubbles.

"If you can get this down I won't have to take you to the hospital," he says.

That sounds like a challenge.

He hands me the mug and it's hot. His hands are still on the mug with mine and our fingers touch. He helps me press it to my lips and it smells like feet. That makes me think too much about feet—Crusty Pete liked feet—so the hot liquid dribbles off my mouth and down my face.

"Ash, you need to drink this. Please."

I hear his voice but I don't see him. Aesop has disappeared into the void, my vision swallowed up by black liquid that bubbles up from every surface of the room.

Sip a little.

And a little more.

The world gets hazy, disappearing into tufts of black smoke.

A SLIVER OF SUNLIGHT hits me in the face. I wake up fast, like coming out from a nightmare, but I can't remember what the nightmare was. My stomach feels like someone is pushing their fist from the other side, trying to turn it inside out. I stumble toward the door of the bus, push through, fall to my hands and knees in the dirt.

A little liquid comes up. Not much, but I keep heaving. I arch my back, look up at the canopy, sunlight pouring through the leaves into the clearing. Beautiful, all the pain and existential dread aside.

My stomach feels raked, my throat raw, my head three sizes too small. My skin is sticky with dried sweat, my shirt gone but my pants damp. I press my hand to the crotch and I think I might have pissed myself. I'm not even sure. I don't know how I got to the bus.

There's a crunch behind me. I turn and it's Aesop, bleary-eyed, shirtless, holding a bottle of water. He comes around to the front of me and sits in the dirt, unspins the cap, puts it down. I come off my knees and sit in the dirt across from him and pick it up.

"Small sips," he says. "You need to get that down. You're dehydrated. I can't believe you even have any sweat left in you, given how much leaked out of you last night."

"How do you know…"

"I stayed. Made sure you didn't have a seizure."

"You…"

His name escapes me for a second.

Then I remember, "Aesop."

He nods. "Good. What's your name?"

"Ashley. Ash."

"Where are we?"

"Georgia. South Village."

"Who was the lead singer of Guns and Roses?"

"Axl Rose."

"Who was the ninth president of the United States?"

"I wouldn't know that even if I had my shit together."

Aesop sighs. "William Henry Harrison. Who was the first president?"

"George Washington."

"Okay. We're on the right track."

I take a small sip of water. My stomach revolts. I close my eyes, lean forward, hold it down.

"You gave me something last night," I tell him. "What did you give me?"

"Valerian root tea," he says. "It's a holistic alternative to benzodiazepines, which are generally used to treat DTs. Best we had handy."

"What now?"

"DTs affects everyone differently," he says. "The fact that you didn't have a seizure last night and you're mostly lucid right now is a very good sign. How do you feel? Are you still hallucinating?"

I look at Aesop. At the forest around us. I think I see the world as it is. In the bright light, it all looks laid out bare. Quiet, no voices but ours. Occasionally something shimmers on the edge of my vision. Or on his chest, the jumble of tattoos shuddering, like they're struggling to take on life but failing.

"A little," I tell him. "My vision is wonky. But no bugs, no snakes. And I feel tired. Like you know how your brain feels when you've been up for two straight days? Like that."

"To be expected. But all good signs."

"So I'm past it?"

He laughs. "Fuck no. The next couple of days, you're going to feel muddy. You'll definitely hear some weird shit, maybe still have the stray hallucination. Hopefully nothing as bad as last night. But it tends to be worse at night, anyway."

I take another look at the bus. There's a string of prayer flags hanging over the door. I nod over toward them. "Those are new."

"I put them up last night," he says. "There were some extra in the medical dome. There are always extra lying around. Figured it would give me something to do, and anyway, you could use it."

"What do they mean?"

Aesop looks up at them, like he's studying each one in turn. "The five colors represent the five elements. Blue for sky, white for clouds, red for fire, green for water, yellow for earth. Tibetan medicine promotes the balance of those five elements. And as the wind travels over them, the air is purified by the mantras written on them."

"Do you really believe that?" I ask.

"Better to believe in something than nothing. And they certainly aren't going to make you feel any worse." He stands up and reaches out his hand. I take it and he pulls me to my feet. "I'll show you how to make the tea. It'll help. Sipping on it during the day should help mellow you out, and have some before bed, to help you sleep. Couple of days, you should be a little better."

"Given last night, I don't think we have a couple of days."

"We'll get to that. Let's take it slow today. Tea and food first."

He turns and leads me toward camp. We step up on the boardwalk and I pass over a board that says: *I am improving each day.*

A little beetle comes up through the slats in the wood. I don't know if it's real or not, and it scuttles back down between the boards before I can check with the toe of my shoe.

The yoga clearing and the public art project are empty. Like the camp has suddenly been abandoned. Aesop leads me into the clearing between the domes, where Katashi is reading a book, and Alex is nestled on Job's lap in an Adirondack chair. Aesop brings me to the steps leading up into the kitchen.

"Can you hang around a bit?" he asks. "I'll go get more valerian root."

"Sure. I'll be fine."

Truthfully I don't want him to leave because I don't want to feel like I can't function without him around. And of course, as soon as he's out of sight, I have that little kid feeling, like I'm lost at the mall without my parents.

"Drink some water," I hear a voice say.

Could be Aesop calling back. Maybe not. Either way, good advice.

I step inside and stand at the sink, turn on the filtered faucet. There's a slow trickle of water, slower than normal, which can happen, so I put a mason jar under the stream and then poke around the kitchen.

Someone calls my name from outside. I step to the door and there's no one there. Katashi is still reading, Job and Alex still sitting in their chair, none of them looking at me.

Okay. This is going to be a fun few days.

I check behind the cleaning supplies underneath the sink, and then in the back of the pantry, not even sure what I'm looking for. I go back to the sink and check behind the cleaning supplies again. It takes three more trips between the pantry and the sink to realize I'm looking for my stashes of alcohol, which I know are gone.

I need something to do with my hands. Something to distract

me. I turn on the oven and pull over the bowl of mushrooms by the sink that Aesop has foraged and cleaned. Little white guys this time. I pull out a couple, cut them into strips, douse them with oil and salt, lay them on some foil, and pop them in the oven. I want something savory. Something salty and comforting. I'd prefer bacon. This will have to do for now.

Forgot about the water. The mason jar in the sink is overflowing. I turn off the faucet and take a sip. It stays down. I close my eyes, take another sip. Hear my name again, figure it's another hallucination. I put the mug down and someone is slamming into me from behind, pressing me into the counter. The mason jar shatters on the floor.

I spin around and Gideon is holding my shirt in his balled up fists, pushing me so hard I'm bending back over the counter a little.

"Where were you last night?" he asks.

"What?"

I try to push him off me but he's got good leverage and my circuitry is fried. There's something about this that feels very familiar and I ought to be able to handle it but I can't. It's too much. I want to puke. I'm about do it, right on his face, when Gideon goes flying across the kitchen and hits the doorjamb. Aesop is standing between us now, on his toes, his shoulders tense and his hands up.

"What the fuck is wrong with you?" he asks.

Gideon scrambles to his feet. "I need to ask you the same thing. Where the fuck were you last night? Huh?"

Aesop pulls something out of his pocket and slams it on the counter, wraps his hand around the back of Gideon's neck, and pushes his face down until it's shy of slamming into whatever it was he put down.

"The theater in town was showing *Apocalypse Now* last night and we went to go see it, fuckface," Aesop says through gritted teeth. "Today Ash is not feeling well. He ate too much popcorn. You put your hands on him again and we're going to have a problem."

Gideon pushes away, picks up the tickets, inspects them, places them back down on the counter.

"Okay," he says. "Your car was out all night and I found it on the back road. There's a… we have to keep an accounting of all our people. After what happened to Cannabelle."

"Yeah, well, I hate driving over the bridge at night so I went the back way."

"Okay…"

Gideon lingers, like he wants to say something else. Now I remember what it was I should do. I should punch him in the face. I ball up my first, ready to throw it into his jaw and see what comes loose, but he ducks out of the kitchen before I can.

Aesop turns to me. "Are you okay?"

"Yeah. But, what's with the alibi? That was convenient."

Aesop throws some wood into the stove and places the kettle down on top, then grabs the broom and pushes the shards of the broken mason jar into a neat pile. "You said we needed an alibi, remember? Last night, on the way back, I took the long way around, through town, so we wouldn't run into anyone. We passed the movie theater so I stopped and fished these out of the trash out front. Figured, just in case."

"I don't even remember that."

"You were talking about the void by that point," he says. "I never knew you to be so interested in nihilism."

"I think Alex planted that seed. Anyway. Good work."

It's not long before the kettle is spitting steam. Aesop pushes the glass into a dustpan, dumps it into the trash, and takes the kettle off the heat. He places it down on a folded tea towel on the counter.

"You have to let it cool for a few minutes," he says. "Straight boiling water will kill off some of the lighter oils in the root."

He takes a tea strainer, a little metal ball on a clip, fills it with the small chopped brown roots from a plastic bag, and places it in a mug. "Pack this strainer about halfway during the day. Don't have more than three or four mugs. Before you go to bed, pack it full. Let it steep about ten minutes when you put it together. That should help. It'll keep you nice and chilled out."

"Thank you," I tell him. "For all of this. I don't know what I've done to deserve it."

"Nothing," he says. "It's the right thing to do."

"No, really. I don't know why I deserve anything nice. Not with the way I've acted here. Not with the way I treat people. But you're good to me. Cannabelle was kind. And I'm just… I am an asshole."

"You're a New Yorker, so that's your default setting," he says. "Truth is, you're not nearly as bad as you think you are. Most people here feel pretty bad for you. That's why we're all so nice."

I think he thinks I'm going to find that comforting, but it's not. It's actually pretty fucking sad.

He dips a pinkie into the top of the tea kettle, quick. He makes a face when he pulls it out, and pours some water into the coffee mug. As he's doing this I remember the mushrooms because I can smell them now, so I pull the tray out and put it on a tea towel on the counter to cool.

"C'mon," he says. "Let's go sit out in the sun. Give this all a few minutes."

The clearing is empty now. We sit on a bench together, leaning back against the table. He's close to me, and it feels good, him being close.

"So… what do we know?" he asks.

"Last night, there was a meeting. Some people from camp. The Soldiers of Gaia are planning to hit something, but we don't know what."

"That's right. They're not based here. Looks like Marx is trying to get in on the action. He's a soldier, not a general. That's good. He's using this place to recruit. That's not good. Seems you're the key to all this."

"Why me?"

"They know you have the cipher. Or at least, they're assuming you have the cipher."

"Right. The book, god what was the name of the fucking book?" This is so goddamn frustrating. The words are all there, encased in a block of ice, and I feel like I'm using a dull spoon to chip it away so I can reach them.

"*The Monkey Wrench Gang*," Aesop says.

"Right. I found it. I know where it is. It's at a store. A store got back to me. We can go and get it."

"Good," he says. "If we find it, we have a chance of stopping them."

"We?"

"Well, after the FBI came in and fucked up our shit, I'm not going to them," Aesop says. "Tibo seems to think Ford is trustworthy, but I'm still trying to figure out if Tibo is trustworthy."

"He is," I tell him. "I think he is. I've known him for so long."

"Leadership changes people."

"Well, whatever. The important thing is, we can decode the fucking cipher. We can get the book. We can do that, and decide what to do next."

"Good. Let's get your tea and something to eat and we'll go. I'd rather not be here anyway. This place is starting to make me nervous."

We step into the kitchen and Aesop walks over to the tray of mushrooms on the oven. He pops a couple into his mouth, chews, and makes a face.

"Ash, where did you get these?"

I nod toward the sink. "Your bowl."

Aesop pulls the bowl toward him, looks down into it, and goes white. He puts his hand over his mouth.

"Destroying angels," he says.

"What?"

He doesn't answer. Doesn't even indicate that he heard me. He moves quickly, putting some fresh and cooked mushrooms into a sandwich bag, then dumps the remaining mushrooms into the trash. He pours the contents of my mug into a battered blue thermos, which he hands to me.

"We have to go to the hospital," he says.

He steps to the trashcan, sticks his fingers down his throat, and heaves. Coughs and spits chunks until his mouth is clear, and looks up at me.

"Right fucking now," he says.

FIFTEEN

WE'RE AT THE car before he finally slows down enough that I can ask him, "What the hell is going on?"

He climbs into the driver's seat so I circle around to the passenger side. "I'm okay to drive but if I need you to, you might have to take over. Can you handle that?"

"Yes, but tell me what's happening."

He starts the engine, slams the pedal down, sending up a spray of gravel and dust.

"Amanita bisporigera," he says. "Those mushrooms. They're called destroying angels. It'll be hours before the symptoms hit, and by then it'll be too late."

"Fuck."

"Fuck is right," he says. "Someone left them there for us."

"Who…"

"That's not important right now," he says. "Focus. Do you think you're okay to handle the car? How do you feel?"

I look out the window, at the world passing by. My vision is wavy on the edges, things flitting in and out, but the adrenaline is helping to keep me focused.

"Ash!"

"I'll be okay. Are you going to be okay?"

"As long as I get treatment quickly, I should be." He pauses. "I should be."

He sounds far less sure the second time he says it.

We drive some more. I open the top of the thermos and sip at the tea. It's hot and tastes terrible. My hand shakes a little. I turn the cap closed so I don't spill any of it.

"I want to tell you something," he says. "I don't know a lot about amatoxin poisoning. I know it's very, very bad. If I'm going to die, I can't die holding onto this. I need to tell someone this."

"Okay," I tell him.

Aesop swings onto the road at the same time that he reaches across and slams his fist on the glove box. It pops open to reveal a crumpled pack of cigarettes. He opens it up, takes one cigarette and a pink lighter out. Crumples it and tosses it into the back seat. He fires up, and the car fills with cigarette smoke. He opens the window and the smoke gets sucked out. He takes a deep drag with his entire body, blows it out.

"There were two guys in my unit," he says, his voice drifting to someplace distant. "Sick bastards. They stuck together 'cause you could tell no one else would want to stick with them. And… it's a whole big story I could get into, I guess, but I kind of don't want to get into particulars."

He takes a drag of his cigarette. Contemplates it between his fingers.

"They were hunters," he says. "Little kids, specifically."

He glances my way, to gauge my reaction. I don't know how to react to that.

"The way they figured it, Iraqi kids were expendable," he said. "We were killing enough innocent civilians by accident. What were a few more? Apparently it went on for a while. The brass found out about it. They covered it up. If word got out it would be a recruiting tool for al-Qaeda. So I killed them both."

He takes a drag, lets the smoke pour out of his lungs.

"That's… terrible," I tell him.

He shakes his head. "The reason I killed them is, I caught them. They were… there was a boy. Couldn't have been more than ten. When I found them he was dead. And the mother… her husband had been killed and now her boy was dead. And she begged me. She begged. Do you understand that?"

He looks at me, back at the road. His voice cracks, tears forming in the corner of his eyes.

"She begged me," he says. "She said she couldn't go on like that."

He looks back and forth, between me and the road. Crying full now, and I don't know what he's looking for. Consolation. Forgiveness. I don't know what I can give him other than listening. My emotional core feels like it's been tossed into a blender, and now this.

A deathbed confession.

At least, that's what it feels like to Aesop.

He doesn't talk for a little while, just drives like he knows where he's going. I have no idea. I don't know where the closest hospital is. At this point, I feel as useless as a doorknob drilled into a brick wall.

Aesop takes one last drag of the cigarette, down to the filter, and tosses it out the window. The tears are gone. The composure is back. His voice is level again.

"I killed twenty-nine people over there," he says. "And for some fucking reason, I don't regret her. I saw it in her eyes. The second I stepped out of there she was going to open her wrists. What I did was a kindness. It's those two assholes I regret killing."

"Because they got off easy," I tell him.

He looks at me, kind of surprised, and nods.

"What happened after that?" I ask.

"I got what's called an Other Than Honorable Conditions Discharge," he says. "They didn't want to give me an Honorable Discharge, and they didn't want to run the risk of burning me so bad with a Dishonorable Discharge that I'd go to the press."

"Why not go to the press? Why not report it?"

"Because… they weren't wrong. Can you imagine anything worse than that? It sets the cycle anew. They weren't going to stop, so I made them stop. The only safe thing to do was live with it."

We come up on a red light. Aesop weaves around the car waiting at it, almost gets creamed by a car coming the other way, speeds on.

"I killed a man," I tell him, the words jumping out of my mouth. Quiet, like I'm hiding from them. Aesop doesn't say anything. Just leaves me room to speak.

"I didn't mean to kill him. I was protecting someone and… it happened. And ever since then I've had this feeling like I'm drowning. That's the thing. The wave. The thing pulling me down. It's why I was drinking. Drinking was the only thing that got me through the day. It was the only thing that helped me sleep at night."

We pull up on the hospital, a massive sandstone building with glass and metal accents, a red cross at the top, glittering in the sunlight. Aesop doesn't even bother finding a spot, pulls the car into the ambulance bay. He turns off the car and twists in his seat so he's looking at me, but I'm already drowning. It's the first I've said it aloud to another person.

He puts his hand on the back of my neck and looks me in the eyes.

"Now you know you can die," he says. "Now you know how fragile all of this is. When you realize that, it's a lot."

And he lets me go.

The wave recedes.

Just like that. The roaring stops. I can feel the sand under my feet. I can stand tall and lift myself above the waterline.

"Do you understand what I mean?" he asks.

I nod, breathe in, and throw myself around him. Press my face into his neck and sob. I can't help myself. My body feels light. Like I've been carrying something heavy up a hill and set it down.

He pulls away from me, crying a little too, and kisses me on the cheek, squeezing the back of my neck again. I feel naked. It's the only way I can put it that makes sense. We linger in it, neither of us wanting to leave the car, for fear of what lies outside.

Except we have to go, because Aesop is dying.

"Now, c'mon," he says. "If we can manage it, I'd like to live to see this whole mess through."

SOUTH VILLAGE

THE WAITING ROOM in the ER is nearly empty. Long rows of green leather chairs, a few dotted with people dozing off or watching a baseball game on a flatscreen television mounted on the wall.

A black woman in pink scrubs is sitting behind the counter, the only employee in sight. She's talking on the phone, curling a loop of her long black hair around a finger tipped by a long orange nail. She barely looks up at us as Aesop puts the plastic bag containing the mushrooms on the counter.

The woman's nametag says "Brenda" in white lettering on black plastic.

Brenda slides a clipboard overflowing with forms across the counter at us without breaking the flow of her conversation. Which is basically her offering positive affirmations like "really" and "oh sure" and "I believe so."

"Excuse me," Aesop says.

Brenda sticks an orange nail into the air, indicating she needs a minute.

Aesop reaches across the counter and presses his finger on the black plastic tab, hanging up the call. Her eyes go wide with rage and I am pretty sure she is going to tear his trachea out.

"You may have a minute, but I don't," he says. "I've ingested extremely poisonous mushrooms."

She purses her lips and looks at us like we're both dummies.

"Well why didn't you say so?" she asks.

"I was trying to..."

She nods toward the hallway. "Triage. First door." She picks up the ringing phone and speaks into it, but I can't hear what she says because we're already turning the corner, Aesop balancing the bag of mushrooms on top of the clipboard.

The triage room is small, with two chairs and some machines and cabinets. There's a young nurse in green scrubs, her light brown hair twisted into short dreads. She says something into a phone and starts taking Aesop's vitals, moving around him efficiently as he scribbles at the forms.

I linger in the hallway. I can feel the buzzing of the fluorescent light on my skin. It feels like ants. Ghosts dance at the edge of my vision, moving back and forth at the end of the long hallway. When I turn to look at them they're gone. I don't feel safe in the hall so I step into the room. Another nurse arrives, a kid with acne and a bad bowl cut. He's wearing bright blue scrubs and looks barely out of high school. He hands Aesop a cup of thick, black liquid, which Aesop drinks, grimacing as he holds it to his lips. He pulls it away from his mouth and his teeth are black.

I think I'm hallucinating again. The male nurse looks at my face and says, "Activated charcoal."

"This does not taste good," Aesop says. And he drinks some more.

The male nurse turns to me. "We have to get him inside. Are you family?"

"No, just… a friend."

"I'm going to have to ask you to sit in the waiting room."

Aesop gets up, tosses me the keys to the car. I don't put my hand up in time and they fly into the hallway, where they hit the floor and skid into the wall. He rolls his eyes. "Take care of my car. You're going to be okay. Keep up on the tea."

The two nurses lead Aesop through another door.

And I'm alone.

I WATCH THE BRAVES beat on the Mets for four innings. I should feel bad because the Mets are my home team, but I was always partial to the Yankees. I sip at the tea, which is cooling off, which makes it taste worse. The ER stays mostly empty. A guy comes in with a blood-soaked towel wrapped around his hand. He sits for five minutes and goes in. There's another guy here who was asleep when I came in and he hasn't woken up yet.

I don't know what to do. Driving back to camp doesn't sound like fun. Mostly because of the hallucinations but also because of the people there who apparently want to kill us. But I have to get that book. Something bad is about to happen, and the book is the key.

I don't want to leave Aesop. In part, because leaving a man behind isn't how I roll. But also because I feel like I need him. Not just that in my fucked-up, DTing state, I need a shoulder to lean on.

It's because of what he said.

It's like he flicked a light switch. This emptiness inside me is suddenly filled up. Not fixed, not healed. But there's enough light for me to see what I'm doing. To maybe get working on feeling like a human again.

The game ends. I want to stay here in the air conditioning and the comfy leather seat and melt into a puddle of myself and think about all the fun new things I've been given to consider, but I know I have to get moving.

Brenda is at the counter, still on the phone. I approach, stand off to the side. Enough so she can see me, but not enough that I'm intruding. She sticks her finger in the air, and this time I abide. After another three or four minutes of affirmations, she hangs up and turns to me.

"Can I help you, darling?" she asks.

"My friend," I tell her. "I was hoping to find out how he was doing. Maybe I can see him."

She nods. "What was his name again?"

"It's..."

I realize that Aesop is more than likely not his real name.

"This is going to sound ridiculous but I only know him by his nickname," I tell her.

"You're right, that is ridiculous. Without a name, there's not much I can do."

I look around the waiting room. "It's pretty empty. It's not like there's a whole bunch of other people who came in with severe mushroom poisoning, right?"

She huffs, picks up the phone, asks, "Davea, can you come here?"

She puts down the phone and points to a nearby chair. "Just wait."

After a few moments the triage nurse from earlier comes out. She goes up to Brenda and the two of them chat for a minute, throwing glances my way. I probably look half homeless and half crazy. Unkempt hair and beard, sweat-stained clothes. I wouldn't blame them if they just called a security guard to deal with me.

Luck is on my side. Davea comes up to me and says, "You came in with Mr. Stack."

"I did. Is he okay?"

"He's gone..."

I jump to my feet. "What?"

Her eyes go wide. "Oh god, no, I'm so sorry, no, I didn't mean it like that, oh fuck…" She looks around, and Brenda is shaking her head. "I mean he was transferred. In cases of amatoxin poisoning the patient has to be taken to a hospital with an active liver transplant unit."

I sit on the edge of the seat, my hand on my chest, trying to will my heart to stop screaming.

"I'm so sorry," she says. "Really. I'm new. I'm getting used to some of this stuff. I should have..."

"No, no, it's fine," I tell her. "Just, okay. Can you tell me where he was taken?"

She goes to the desk, takes a sticky note, scribbles on it, and hands it to me. "It's a few towns over. They took him by ambulance. It's a precaution."

I stand up, turn nearly in a full circle, not sure what to do next.

She looks at me with a little more caution. "Do you need me to call someone?"

"No, I'm good."

It's a lie, but she seems to accept it.

I START THE CAR, turn on the radio. "You Learn" by Alanis Morissette. That's a good one. I call up the bookstore on my phone, pull up the map app, and it's about twenty minutes away. Click on the GPS button and a robotic female voice tells me to turn left out of the hospital.

I hope the battery lasts because once this is gone I have no fucking idea where I'm going. I don't even know where South Village is in relation to here.

I take it slow, turning out, giving a wide berth to the cars that are approaching. After a few minutes I feel confident enough to pick up speed. My vision is still a little wonky, but no snakes, no bugs. No ghosts throwing themselves in my path.

It's good to have a purpose.

Having a purpose makes everything a little bit clearer.

I SIT OUTSIDE THE address for a few minutes, wondering if I got it wrong, or the information is out of date. It's an old house. A house that time and landscapers forgot. There are weeds growing up around the base of it, the lawn wild and overgrown. The siding around the upper windows is falling apart and the stairs leading up to the porch are crumbling.

Then I see the cracked and faded sign next to the door. I squint and can make out: SONNY'S BOOKS.

I step out into the heat, feel something crawling on the back of my neck, slap it and come back with a clean hand. Blink a few times. Climb the steps. The door is open and inside there's a staircase, and darkened rooms to either side. It's immaculate, a stark contrast to the outside. The only light is what's streaming through the windows. There are shelves on every wall, close to buckling but arranged neatly, almost reverently, with books.

No one seems to be around. I start in the room to my right, scanning the shelves, wondering if there's anyone here to help. I circle half the room before I realize all these books are non-fiction, which means the book I'm looking for isn't in here.

"Can I help you?"

Standing in the doorway, like he materialized out of shadows, is an older, stooped man. Snowy white hair and beard. His body is caving in around the stomach region. He's in a blue polo and khakis and nice shoes. The sight of him makes me miss the insanely beautiful woman at the other bookstore.

"I sent an e-mail," I tell him. "I was looking for a book. *The Monkey Wrench Gang*."

He disappears into the darkness of a hallway. There's a chair in the corner so I sit.

After a few minutes, footsteps approach and the man reappears, holding the book. He presents it like a QVC model and it's the same edition I had in the library dome. I stand up, relieved, and he tucks it under his arm.

"How much?" I ask.

He shrugs. "How much do you have on you?"

I pull out my wallet. I keep all my money in a coffee can buried ten paces from the bus. I only keep a little on me. There's never any reason to exchange cash at South Village. I've got a ten-dollar bill, folded neatly and tucked behind my driver's license, for emergencies. I take it out and unfold it.

"That works," he says, taking the bill and handing me the book.

"Well then, thanks," I tell him. I place it under my arm and turn to leave, but he clears his throat.

"You're from that place with all the hippies, aren't you?" he asks.

That makes me laugh. I must really have gone native. "That I am, sir."

"Well, listen, I got something that might be of interest to you and your friends," he says. "Will you hold on a minute?"

"I'm in a bit of a rush…"

"Please," he says. "It's important."

"Okay."

He disappears into another room. I scan the shelves and it's not long before he comes back. He holds out a flier. There's a protest scheduled in two weeks, to oppose a new fracking operation in the town between this one and South Village.

I may not be an expert on fracking but I've absorbed some stuff through osmosis. It's a popular topic right now amongst the environmentally-conscious at camp. Liquid gets shot into the ground at high pressure to break up shale rock and free the natural gas inside. It's a little like solving a problem by hitting the earth really, really hard. Which is how I like to solve problems, so right off the bat, I figure it's not a good thing.

Fracking comes with risks. Contamination to ground and surface water, air pollution, the possibility of triggering earthquakes. There was a guy at camp a month or so ago, said he was traveling the country to spread the word about it. He would show people a video on his phone, of a man leaning over his kitchen sink, the water running into the basin, and holding a match to it.

The water caught fire.

Water isn't supposed to catch fire.

Apparently the groundwater feeding his town got contaminated by methane freed up by a nearby fracking operation. Guy notified the Environmental Protection Agency, but the company doing the fracking said there was no way to prove a connection. So the guy sued them. The company won, then countersued for damages. They won again. The guy lost his home. Six months later the EPA proved the methane came from the fracking.

I don't usually get sucked into political causes, but this one pissed me off.

"Do you think you and your friends could join?" he asks.

"I'm a little surprised we haven't heard about this," I tell him.

"Local city council manipulated the rules to push it through without a public hearing," he says. "They didn't want us to know about it. There's a group of people getting together to explore legal options, but we're going to try some good old-fashioned protesting, too."

"I'll put up the flier, make sure people know," I tell him.

"Will you?" he asks. "We need to fight this thing. We can't let some rich sons of bitches put our town at risk just so they can afford a third vacation home."

"I will," I tell him. "I promise."

He smiles, hands me back the ten-dollar bill I just gave him. "You know what? The book is on the house. You just make sure to get some people out there."

I fold up the flier and the bill, put them in my pocket. "Thank you."

As I head out, I figure he'll be getting his wish, probably sooner than he expects. I can't be sure until I sit down with the cipher and the book, but this seems like the kind of thing the Soldiers of Gaia would want to hit.

MY PHONE IS nearly dead by the time I get back to South Village. I park on the back road again, because I'm worried about who might see me coming in the front, and anyway, it's closer to the bus.

I trudge through the forest, going slow. It's bright and hot and the forest is filled with the sound of insects, a slight breeze rustling the greenery. As I approach the bus I see movement inside.

I stop, crouch down into the brush.

Maybe I'm seeing things.

No, there's definitely someone in there.

I push aside some dry earth, stick the cipher inside the book, and put the book into the ground. Cover it up with dirt and leaves at the base of a tree I'll know to look for. So I can find the right spot quickly, I use a stick to make a light gouge in the bark. Then I stay low, creep up on the bus, putting my feet down carefully in spots where it looks like I'm not going to crunch anything. I manage to get up alongside the door. The windows are down so I can hear the person inside.

It's a conversation, but one-sided, like the person is talking on a phone. Which is weird, because this is a dead zone for cell service. Some carriers get a weak signal by the main dome. This far out, there's nothing.

I listen. Male. Don't recognize the voice.

"He hasn't been here all day… I'm sure of it… Do I wait and find out or do I blow my cover? … No, his name keeps coming up… He has to know something… Okay, let me get out of here before he comes back."

I stand up, push my way through the doors, and climb onto the bus.

Holding up his hands, one of which is clutching a big chunky device that looks like a cell phone, is Katashi.

SIXTEEN

"*KON'NICHIWA*," KATASHI SAYS, his face breaking into a wide, confused smile.

"Shut the fuck up," I tell him. "I heard you."

"Okay," he says, his voice neutral, completely unaccented. It takes on a chilly quality. He looks around the bus. Thinking. Probably about what he said, and how much I heard, and how much I could have surmised from it.

"There's an explanation for this…" he starts.

"You're with the FBI, aren't you? Are you an informant, or an actual agent?"

He doesn't say anything.

"So, agent then," I tell him. "That kind of sucked that they maced you too when they dragged us all out of here."

"It's important to keep up appearances."

"Look," I tell him. "Why don't you make both of our days easier and tell me what the fuck you're looking for. I'm willing to bet whatever it is, I don't have it."

"Bullshit," he says. "You and Aesop are hiding something."

The whole English-as-a-second-language thing was smart. The sheer frustration of not being able to communicate with him made a lot of people pass him over until he was wallpaper. He leaned into that, smiling a lot, being polite and considerate, enough that he never got on your nerves, but you didn't appreciate him so much you wondered how he spent his time.

Now that the truth is in the open, he looks like a different person. Coiled. The fingers of his left fist are curling inward, like he's getting ready to use it, in case I decide to do something silly. A southpaw, then. That makes me think this isn't the first time he's been on my bus.

I'm nearly twice his size and he doesn't seem too concerned. I'm sure he has actual combat training. I'm not currently playing with a full deck. This isn't a fight I want to have.

"Aesop and I aren't hiding anything," I tell him. "We drive around, pick up chicks, trade beard-grooming tips. Guys doing guy stuff. Like Vikings."

He squints, not thinking my Viking joke is funny. "What's with the sudden interest in books, then?"

"What do you mean?"

"The trip out to the bookstore yesterday. Did you find what you were looking for?"

Motherfucker. They're tracking the car, or my cell.

"I've got a thing for the Hardy Boys and the library here didn't have *The Secret of the Old Mill*," I tell him.

"Bullshit," he says. "You're looking for the key to the cipher. And I think you have it. You can end this whole thing by handing it over."

Okay. He can't be the one who rushed me in the woods. His asshole buddies took the cipher off me back at the black site, so if he did have the book, he wouldn't need me. Which means it probably was Marx who has the book.

Maybe this is me being petulant, but I'd rather bring this to Ford, rather than the FBI. Ford will have our backs. At least, I think he will. I don't trust the FBI to not tear this place to the ground, or assume we're all conspirators just because we're in close proximity to what's happening.

"I have no idea what you're talking about," I tell him.

"If you could be reasonable here, I can protect you," he says, dropping the tough guy act, thinking he'll reach me another way. "I promise."

"Protect me? You're going to protect me? I'm supposed to trust you, after you and your friends dragged us out to the middle of nowhere for an interrogation that shit on, what, two or three constitutional amendments?"

"That wasn't my idea," he says.

"Why even do that? What did you hope to achieve? All it seemed to do was piss off Marx even more."

"That was kinda the point, yeah," he says. "The Japanese thing, we thought it was a good idea. Help me keep a low profile. But I wasn't getting the intel I needed fast enough. Someone got the bright idea that if we made some noise it'd move things along. And it did."

"You assholes. You thought the best way to handle a powder

keg was to put a match to it?"

He shrugs. "Like I said, not my idea."

"If you were following me and Aesop, how did you miss the beach meeting?"

"We got there after everyone left."

"God, you suck at your job."

"Listen. You don't understand what we're up against, okay?"

"Enlighten me."

"How much do you know about industrial farming?"

"Are you kidding? Nothing."

He points to my bed as he sits in the chair in the corner. I want to stay standing, because I don't want him to feel comfortable, but my whole body aches.

"Here's the thing about farming pigs," Katashi says. "Pigs shit. A lot. Tons and tons of it. And it all has to go somewhere. So you've got these things called concentrated animal feeding operations. CAFOs. So at CAFOs, they pump the pig shit into lagoons. They're pretty frightening to look at. Because they turn bright pink. It has something to do with the interaction of bacteria and antibiotics. So there was one up in North Carolina, people in a nearby town start getting sick. Seems it was seeping into the groundwater."

"That sounds bad."

"So you know what the Soldiers of Gaia did? These people you're protecting? They marched the guy in charge to the edge of the lagoon and pushed him in. He drowned in toxic pig shit. Then they tried to burn the place down, but ended up killing half the pigs in the process."

"So… some asshole was doing some shitty thing to the environment and they killed him. Look, I'm not going to say he deserved to die for that. But you have to acknowledge that this whole thing is a little more complicated than the way you're presenting it."

"Bullshit. We know they're hitting something soon. We just don't know where, or when. There are a dozen potential targets within a hundred miles of here. We don't have enough to move on. These are not good people, Ash. Why are you protecting them?"

"So you're the *good* guys?"

"Yes, we're the good guys," he says, smiling, thinking he's reached me.

"You don't act like it."

"Now isn't the time to debate tactics. This is about saving lives."

I know the responsible thing to do here would be to help them.

I know that.

But Tibo's words are ringing in my head. Marx's, too, for as much as I hate that.

The Soldiers of Gaia are terrorists. And I don't give a damn about color or creed or geography or end goal. Terrorism is the thing that took my dad. Just thinking about it lights a blue flame at the center of me that unless I hold it in check, threatens to consume me.

But the game is rigged. The more of these stories I hear, the more I realize that the winner is always going to be the guy with the gun, or the guy with the money, or the guy with the badge.

No one's doing this for the guy who ends up sick from toxic pig shit.

Or the guy whose sink catches fire.

I'm going to figure this out and take it to Sheriff Ford. He strikes me as an honorable guy. He's given us and this place far more credit and respect than these assholes, who thought the best way to achieve their goals was through shock, awe, and liberal doses of pepper spray.

"You can fuck yourself," I tell him. "I don't know about any book. That's all I've got to say."

Katashi nods, like he's weighing his options. I don't know what those options are, so I turn to leave. Figure at this point, what do I have to lose?

"Hey," he calls after me. "About your passport application."

That stops me cold at the door.

"You think we haven't run checks on every single person who's come through here?" he asks. "I know you applied. Fleeing the country?"

"Taking a vacation."

"Either way, all it'll take is a phone call and the application gets held up. I imagine you're leaving soon, given the expedited processing. So I'll make you a deal."

Bastard. "Go ahead."

"Whether you have the book or you don't, that's irrelevant. You're going to get it for me. I'm going to knock on this door first thing tomorrow morning, and you better have it. If not, the passport goes bye-bye."

He stands up and takes a couple of steps toward me, gets in my face, his nose nearly touching mine.

"That's not all, either," he says. "I can make your life very hard. I'm talking full weight of the FBI hard. If you have so much as a speck of bone dust in your closet, we will find it, and use it, and exploit it until you never see natural sunlight again. So it's in your best interest to keep this conversation between us, and get that fucking book for me. You got me?"

A year ago that threat wouldn't have worked.

Now I have a literal skeleton in my closet.

By closet, I mean at the base of a tree off a hiking trail in Portland.

"Yeah," he says. "That's what I thought. I'm going to give you a chance to come around. Think real hard about where you're going to land on this. Because you're with us, or you're with them. You have to choose. I'll see you in the morning."

"I'm not much for team sports," I tell him, exiting the bus.

There's nothing on it for me to protect. Whatever he wants to have seen, he'll have dug up. He has my name and my address back home and everything. I consider going back for the book and the cipher, but he could follow, so I head back to camp. Make sure he sees me do it.

I need to have a talk with Tibo, anyway.

As I climb onto the boardwalk I cross a plank of wood that says: *If we all had a bong we'd all get along.*

THE SWEDISH COUPLE that's been visiting for the past couple of days come out the back of the main dome, carrying roller cases behind them, heading toward the front of camp. They were supposed to be here another week. But with two people dead and the FBI sniffing around, it was only a matter of time before people began to clear out.

Tibo comes out of the main dome, sees me, and runs up to me, Zorg keeping pace next to him.

"There you are," Tibo says. "What the hell happened? And

where's Aesop?"

As soon as I stop jogging, it hits. The nausea. That fuzzy, exhausted feeling. I need food. I need caffeine. I need more of that tea.

"Can we talk in the kitchen?" I ask Tibo. "Alone?"

"First, is Aesop okay?"

"He accidently ingested poisonous mushrooms. But we went straight to the hospital. They transferred him. He should be fine."

Tibo shakes his head. I climb into the kitchen and open the coffee maker, dump in some grounds and some water, feel a bug crawling up my arm, so I stop and itch and the itching won't stop so I really dig in. I mutter curses under my breath.

"Fucking monster fucking bugs in this stupid fucking forest," I say. "I fucking hate it."

Tibo gets closer. "Ash, what bugs?"

The frustration that's been pending all day explodes at the base of my spine. I swing my foot out and kick a cupboard, splitting the wood.

My brain feels like it's trying to crawl out my ear.

A moment's peace. That's all I want.

I sit on the floor of the kitchen, put my head in my hands.

Breathe deep. Concentrate on where I am. Filter out the noise and the bad feelings.

Tibo sits next to me.

"What's the matter?" he asks.

"Detoxing."

"Shit man. DTs?"

"Yeah."

"Ash… what the fuck is going on? You've been on your own

planet the last few days. More than usual."

I drop my head back against the cabinet, stare at the point where the dome meets its apex. At the dark, heavy wood keeping it aloft over us. Stained and darker than the rest, from smoke and heat and moisture.

"Tell me what's going on," Tibo says.

"Turn on the radio," I tell him.

"Why?"

"Just turn it on."

He stands and goes to the ancient stereo and clicks it on. Rage Against the Machine again. I stand, pour myself a mug of coffee, drop in a little cool water to even it out, and put the kettle on so I can whip up some valerian tea. I grab a handful of granola out of the stash and wash it down with the coffee. Get to where I feel a little bit settled.

And I tell Tibo everything.

About not trusting him. About the cipher, and the book, and someone stealing it from me. About the trip with Aesop, and how he made me stop drinking. About who I saw at the bonfire, and my suspicions about the fracking site, and about Katashi, because fuck that fucking asshole.

I tell him about all of it and he listens silently, nodding at points, his face never changing. Serene and calm. He pours himself a cup of coffee halfway through, keeping an eye on the door, making sure no one is close enough to hear.

He takes this all very well.

"Magda, Gideon," Tibo says. "That sucks. I would have thought better of them. Well, Magda definitely."

"They're playing for the Soldiers. And they're planning

something."

"This place is nearly empty," Tibo says. "So whatever is happening, it's probably happening soon. What happens tomorrow when you don't give Katashi the book?"

"How do you know I'm not going to give it to him?"

"Because it's you. You are incapable of doing things the easy way."

"I don't know. He's going to fuck shit up for me and for the camp. I need to buy some time. He can't hold the passport up once it hits the mail. If I can squeak out another day or two, I might be okay."

"Well, you know what the answer to that is," Tibo says, like it's obvious.

"What?"

"How could you not realize that?"

"My brain feels like pulped newspaper. Fucking tell me."

"Give him a different book. Make one up. How would he know the difference?"

"And maybe they realize I'm fucking with them."

"You want time? That's time."

"Okay, that makes some sense. So that's step one. Step two is, what do we do about the Soldiers?"

Tibo opens a cupboard and takes out a bag of pecans, shakes some out into his hand, chews them, staring out the window, at the green expanse of the forest. I take this contemplative moment to pull the kettle off the stove, dose out some water into a mug, and load up the tea strainer with some valerian root, my hands shaking and spilling chopped brown stems onto the counter.

"Here, let me do that," Tibo says.

He places the stems in the filter, tamps them down, closes it, and places it in the mug. Turns to me.

"I'm happy to see that you're not drinking anymore."

"Well, it was an expensive habit."

"Don't joke. I know you were doing it to cover something up. That's not good. I didn't say anything because I figured you'd tire yourself on it and come around. You fall into funks and come out of them. But this one was bad. And, honestly, I was getting a little frustrated with you."

"Let's call it even," I tell him. "I'm sorry I kept all this from you. I should have come straight to you."

He nods.

"So all of this, you investigating this—is it because you thought I might be responsible for Crusty Pete's death?" he asks.

"No, I don't think you're capable of that."

"Why?"

"You're not a killer."

"Are you sure?"

"What do you mean?"

The level of his voice doesn't change. "Ash. I cut the rope. I killed Pete."

SEVENTEEN

TIBO LOOKS AT me, unblinking, like he told me the weather report. I don't know what to say and I'm digging for some words when Zorg pokes his head into the kitchen.

"Zorg doesn't mean to interrupt, but we're getting close to dinner..."

Tibo nods. "Sure. Why don't you two get started?"

"We need to talk about this," I tell him.

"And we need to get the people who haven't abandoned us yet fed. Get started and we'll talk about this later."

"Are you serious?" I ask.

"Not a debate," he says.

I hold his eyes for a second. He doesn't seem at all bothered by what happened and I wonder how he pulled that off.

People handle killing in different ways, I guess.

Tibo leaves and Zorg comes in, hovering by the doorway, in an open vest over his bare, small chest. In the center is a red cartoon heart, the size of a silver dollar, tattooed into his skin. Sloppy, like a stick-and-poke job. He looks at me like a puppy.

"So..." he says.

"Let's get to work. Asian stir-fry. We can bang that out quick."

Hanging from the ceiling is a wok that's more than two feet across at the top. I pull it down from the hook and place it on the stovetop, get it fired up. Line up a big pile of vegetables—mushrooms, peppers, onions, garlic, broccoli, snow peas. Then I grab a few blocks of tofu out of the chest fridge.

"Chop chop," I tell Zorg, pulling a knife out of the block and holding the handle out to him. He takes it and attacks the vegetation with confidence.

I rush through the prep, thinking about what Tibo said. It tracks, sort of, that he killed Pete, in the sense that he's been distant and vague, on top of there being some kind of strife between the two of them. But I can't make the connections. The 'why' of it. Every time I get on a train of thought for too long, it derails, crashes, and burns, and I have to start at the beginning. It's hard to focus, especially with the temperature in here climbing. I pour myself a big mason jar of water, down the entire thing in a few gulps, and pour another.

Zorg senses that something is off because he keeps throwing me sideways glances, until finally he dives in.

"Are you okay?" he asks. "You look like you're not feeling well."

"I've been better."

"Want to talk about it?"

My gut response is to say: Not really.

But Aesop was right. Talking about things has helped. Versus what I've been doing for so long, hiding a part of myself so no one could see it. Staying away from the circle, sitting on the bus, drinking myself into oblivion, until there was nothing left but a void.

So I try something new.

Because something new has to be better than where I am.

"Delirium tremens," I tell Zorg. "The price you pay for self-medicating with alcohol."

"That's what the valerian root is for, then?"

"It is. Aesop hooked me up."

"How are you feeling today?"

"Not as bad as yesterday. Still not great."

"Some people it's a day or two. Others it's weeks. It can get much more extreme than this. You should be okay."

"How do you know that?"

"My dad."

The period on the end of that sentence is a fine point that brooks no further conversation.

When the stir fry is done I dump it into a big bowl, check on the rice. It needs another few minutes. I slam the lid back on.

"I'm sorry again I was such a dick to you," I tell Zorg.

He shrugs. "I've heard worse."

"Seriously though. Everyone here is so goddamn nice and I haven't done much to deserve it."

Zorg shrugs again. "Community is all we have."

I remember those words from someplace, like hearing a bell off in the distance. It takes me a second, and then I'm standing on a street in Portland. Someone helped me who didn't have any business helping me, but he did it anyway, because, according to him, community was all we had.

Something I never really thanked him for, either.

I'm a little sad it took hearing that a second time to properly recognize it. But Hood was right, and so is Zorg. Community is all we have. This is a big bad world full of assholes, and if there's an opportunity for a few like-minded folks to buckle down and do the right thing for each other, it's worth taking.

For the first time since I got here, I realize I'm going to miss South Village when I leave. I still think it's a good thing to go. I've never been to Europe, and tickets to Prague are expensive. I probably can't get a refund at this point.

Anyway, I've got a bone church to visit.

But this is a place I'd be happy to come back to.

Monster bugs and scary toilets and heat like I'm sitting in an oven. Everything.

I check the rice again and it's done, so I dump it into a bowl. Zorg carries it out and I ring the dinner bell, then head down to the chalkboard to list all the ingredients.

The circle assembles slowly as Tibo stokes the flames in the center of the clearing. It catches as the sun approaches the horizon, washing the woods in golden light. The no-see-ums are out, buzzing about my skin. Real bugs being slightly more comforting than imagined ones.

There's an odd hesitancy to the proceedings. I take my spot on the bench and Tibo nods at me as the circle closes. Half the size of what it was two days ago. Sunny and Moony are here. So are Alex and Job. That makes me happy. Makes me feel like they're still on our side. Everyone else is scared off or plotting destruction or, in the case of Katashi, found out.

Tibo bows his head and thinks for a minute.

"South Village is a very special place to me," he says. "Some of you may not know this, but the reason I picked the name was to pay tribute to the East Village in Manhattan. It's where I grew up. It used to be a thriving artistic community. Now it's a commodity, where artists are pushed out to make way for people with money. The things we have aren't supposed to last forever. Sometimes you have to accept fate and move on. This was my next thing. This was my answer to a world where art and community have been devalued. I truly believe these are the things that will save us."

He sighs. "I've made mistakes. Some of those mistakes are coming to bear on the camp right now. I have done things that are rash, and irresponsible, and thoughtless. I'm still learning. Through that, I want to thank you all for being here. Given what's happened, you would have left if you didn't believe in it."

I know Tibo isn't talking to me, but it feels like he's talking to me.

Without even realizing I'm doing it at first, I hop down off the bench. The leap taken, I'm able to step toward the circle. No one notices me.

"I love this place, and I will fight like hell to ensure that it survives," he says, eyes still downcast. "But I want you to know that I am thankful for each and every one of you. I am thankful for your contributions, and your compassion, and your understanding. Even though there are things I've done that maybe I don't deserve it. Thank you for believing what I believe in…"

He looks up. Stops mid-sentence, locking eyes with me as I step between Zorg and Moony. They sense someone is coming and part to allow me in. When they see it's me they're both taken aback. But then they stretch their hands out to me. I take them. Zorg's is small and warm, sweaty from being in the kitchen. Moony's is rough and bony. Her long fingers wrap around my hand and seem to meet on the back of it.

The two of them smile at me.

I turn to Tibo and he's smiling too. His eyes gone soft. I feel like an alien. So out of place, and worse, so vulnerable. And yet at the same time, welcome. It's a feeling I haven't had since I was home, and maybe not even then.

"That's what I'm thankful for," Tibo says. "Who's next?"

He looks at me.

I shake my head a little at him.

Baby steps.

He seems to understand.

"Moony?" he asks.

ONCE EVERYONE HAS had their fill and I'm sure there's enough food to go around, I fill up a bowl and see Tibo sitting off at the far end of the circle, on the last picnic bench before the forest drops off into shadow. That's where I usually sit. I figure he's waiting for me.

As I approach, he scoots aside so there's room for me to sit. I step onto the bench and sit on the tabletop, take a few bites. A little salty but not a bad effort for a rush job. It feels good to have some hot food. I look into the darkness around us and it feels like we're in a bubble, the rest of the world dropped away.

There are shapes out in the shadows. Things moving. Not as

pronounced as yesterday. I really have to be looking to notice. That, at least, makes me feel like maybe I'm on the mend.

"What happened?" I ask.

Tibo puts his empty bowl aside and folds his hands. "A few weeks ago Pete came to me with a proposition. He wanted to turn this into an outpost for the Soldiers of Gaia. He didn't volunteer a lot of information. Enough for me to know it was bad news. What they want is completely contrary to what I want. We're all here, each and every one of us, because we feel like the world has failed us in some way. But that doesn't mean I want to destroy it."

"Skip to the good part."

He looks at me, raises an eyebrow. "You were right. Of course you were right. I cut the rope halfway. Figured he'd walk across the bridge and fall and break an ankle or an arm or something. Enough to slow him down. Make him look someplace else. I had no idea it was going to break his neck. It was… it was so stupid."

I remember what Tibo said as we stood there over Pete's body. That it was his fault.

"Why not go to the cops?"

"And tell them what? I didn't even really know what the Soldiers of Gaia were at that point. And having a bunch of cops crawling around here… that's not ideal."

"And you're okay with the fact that you killed someone?" I ask.

Truthfully, I want to know. Because since Tibo told me I keep looking at him, expecting to see it. That stereogram image. Instead he looks like a person, living his life. No outward signs of rot.

"Of course I'm not okay with it," Tibo says. "I didn't intend for that to happen. But at the end of the day, Pete wanted to hurt people. He wanted to burn the world down because of a philosophy.

So yes, I feel terrible. But I won't let it drag me down."

"I wish it were that easy."

"Why?"

"I killed someone too."

Tibo pauses, laughs a little. "So now you admit it."

"Was it really that obvious?"

"The way you've been acting. Trying harder to push people away. I knew it was something big. And it had to be real big, because after everything that happened with Chell, you still set yourself right. And with this, you just kept spiraling down and down and down. So what happened?"

"Back in Portland, I met this girl," I tell him. "Her ex-boyfriend took their daughter from daycare. We didn't go to the cops. She didn't want to. Thought maybe an ex-junkie stripper was going to have a hard time once child services got involved."

Tibo sticks his finger in the air. "Ex-junkie stripper? That is a fair and accurate point."

"Well, I tried to handle it myself. It's a whole thing, but in the end… you know I found the guy who killed Chell, right?"

"I figured as much."

"I didn't kill him."

"No one would have blamed you if you did."

"I wanted to break the cycle of violence," I tell him. "The thing he did to Chell, it wasn't going to get fixed by killing him. I had to believe that there was a path to redemption. Less for him and more for me. So I sicced the cops on him. And the whole time I was in Portland, falling into old habits, I swore to myself, I wasn't going to be that guy. But when it came down to high noon, me and this guy, I hit him a little harder than I should have."

"Look at the two of us," Tibo says, patting my shoulder. "Accidental killers."

"Well, yours was an accident," I tell him. "I think a bad part of me got loose for a second. The vicious part of me. The part of me that likes to hurt people." I look down at my hands. I can feel blood on them, thick and wet, even though they're clean. "Maybe that's the thing. Why it's affecting me so hard and not you. You're not a killer. You made a mistake."

The next words are hard to say, and as I'm saying them my vision goes blurry, hot tears forming in the corners of my eyes. "I think there's something rotten at the core of me."

Tibo huffs. "You're not a bad person. Because for all your bullshit, at the end of the day, you do the right thing. Even when it means putting yourself on the line. That's a lot more than other people can say. And second, man, this whole thing, it's not a contest. You are the sum of all your parts. You are the end result of a long line of decisions. But you can be whatever the hell you want."

"I want to be free of this feeling."

"Then be free. Accept what you did and move on. Make up for it if you have to. But there's no trick or secret to this. I have to live with the fact that I killed Pete. I'll manage. Because otherwise it means shutting down. And this place and these people—they rely on me. So I'm not going to do that to them."

I look out into the clearing, at the people who are still here. Working through the pain and confusion of the last few days. Eating and smiling and laughing. I feel apart from them, and maybe I always will be.

"People rely on you too, Ash," Tibo says. "You do things other people can't. The things you do… they're not rotten. They're special."

"Killing someone isn't special."

"Protecting people is," he says. "That's what you do. It's what you gravitate toward. You knew something was wrong. You couldn't help yourself. You needed to fix it. Not everyone can do that. But you have the capacity for it."

Capacity. Temperament. It makes me think about Bill and his horses. The job that may not sound glamorous but needs to get done.

Everything we have is so fragile.

"So, what's the plan?" Tibo asks.

"Get the cipher, figure it out, and then get Ford," I tell him. "I think we've both learned a couple of times now that boxing out the authorities isn't the best way to handle these things. I think we can trust Ford."

"We can," he says. "I trust him."

"Okay. We do that then."

WE WALK IN silence, twin beams of light slicing the dark, showing us the safe paths to take. We climb through the woods and it's quiet all around us. Every few hundred feet I stop and put my hand on Tibo's chest to get him to stay still.

The third time I do it, he asks, "Why?"

"Listen. In case someone is following us. Do you hear anything?"

"No."

"Good."

I need him to listen. I can still hear whispers out in the dark.

We get to the bus and check around it, make sure Katashi or Marx isn't lying in wait. After we're sure the area is clear I search for the tree. It takes a little while to find in the darkness, but finally I do. Run my finger through the gouge I made in the bark.

I dig a little.

Then a little more.

Come up with nothing but dirt.

Tibo asks, "What?"

"It's gone."

"Are you sure this is the right tree?"

I touch my finger to the mark again. "Positive."

"That's not good," Tibo says.

I fall back into the dirt and sit, staring up at the canopy. "No, it's not."

Maybe Katashi poked around after I left. Maybe someone else was following me. Regardless, it's gone. The cipher is still safely tucked in my e-mail and my phone, but I've got nothing to pair it with. The code is useless without the book. The last I checked my phone, none of the other bookstores had gotten back to me in the affirmative.

We are back to zero.

EIGHTEEN

I SHINE THE FLASHLIGHT on the boardwalk, regret not asking Tibo to come with me, because the whispers are freaking me, even though I know they're not real. I stop a few times and try to listen but can't make out what they're saying. It's a jumble. And if I stand for too long I get that feeling of climbing up the basement steps as I turn out the lights, and something is coming up behind me so I have to outrace it.

First, I stop in the library dome. After making sure it's empty I grab the first book in arm's reach. *I Am Legend* by Richard Matheson. There's my fake cipher. Let Katashi have fun with that. Then it's off to the kitchen, which is clean and spotless. Zorg does good work. I put on the kettle and prep an extra strong dose of valerian root. Something to get me through the night. I can't say this for sure, but I feel like if I make it through tonight, I'm going to be in the clear. I have this feeling, like dawn breaking over the horizon.

I won't be cheesy enough to call it hope. But it definitely feels optimistic.

Once the tea is done I dump it in a thermos, head back to the bus, which is empty. I give it a quick sweep with the flashlight, turn on the rope light and have a look around. I'm so tired, and within moments, I feel the drag, pulling me under the surface of the water, but this time, it's far less terrifying.

If anything, it feels comforting.

THE DREAM IS different.

It's not raining, which is the first big difference. The sun is out. A rare sight in Portland. I'm still digging the hole, still covered in mud. But Wilson isn't here. I turn and Chell and my dad are standing over me, arms crossed. They're soaking wet but the sun behind them is bright and shining strong.

We stand there like that, them looking at me.

Something about their demeanor has softened. It used to be, when they looked at me like this, it was an emotion somewhere on the scale from anger to frustration. Now, I can't put my finger on it, exactly, but I would say it's more like pity.

Which is better, actually.

They both open their mouths to speak and I wake up.

I PHASE IN AND out of sleep. Sometimes I hear a crack outside the bus and it could be something or nothing. Real or imagined. Voices drift in through the windows. I'm getting used to the feeling now. It's less terror-inducing.

I think maybe I've been asleep for eight or nine hours but it's still dark, so I click on my phone and the blinding white light tells me it's 2 a.m., which does not bode well. I see someone in the corner of the bus, but when I hold up the phone to illuminate the area, there's no one there.

The phone goes off and plunges us back into darkness and I think I see someone sitting in the corner again. Scratch at my arms to get the bugs off but don't feel any bugs. What I would give to be in a hotel. Around people. With a television I could leave on. Just the electric hum, making me feel like I'm not alone. Out here, it's alone alone. I consider going to Tibo's bunk, or checking in with the cam girls, to have someone to spend the night with.

Truthfully, I wish Aesop were here.

THE SUN IS out. I lift my head off the cot, look around. Katashi is sitting at the wheel of the bus, facing me. He's flipping through the copy of *I Am Legend*.

"I'm glad to see you came around," he says.

I get up, walk past him and off the bus. The sky is washed gray and it's raining softly. Still hot, but nice nonetheless. I piss against a tree and get back on the bus, open the thermos, take a sniff. Christ this stuff is nasty cold, but I take a little sip, something to even me out. I will be happy to leave this behind. No more treating problems with substances. After this, it's clean living.

"Did you decode it?" Katashi asks. "Do you want to save me the trouble?"

"Nah, that's the beginning and end of the favors I'll be doing for you," I tell him.

"You think because you handed this over, this makes you square?"

"Nope. But, and I would like to point this out again for posterity, I do not like you. I do not like your organization. I do not like how you handled things here. So go, do what you have to do. I gave you what you wanted. I don't want to be involved anymore."

He gets up and offers me his hand.

"You saved a lot of lives," he tells me.

I look down at his hand until he retracts it and gives me a withering look.

"Have fun," I tell him. "Tell Marx I said hi."

"Oh we're going to nail that motherfucker," he says, smiling.

"He is a dick, but part of me doesn't blame him."

"What do you mean?"

"With his parents. The way they died. The fire."

Katashi laughs. "You bought that shit?"

"What do you mean?"

"Marx's name is Bryon Turner. He's some trust fund kid from LA. His parents are alive. Who do you think pays for him to travel around the country and live like a hippie? Don't get me wrong, he's dangerous, but no, his whole backstory is a myth. Honestly, I think he uses it to get laid."

Huh. That certainly changes things. And now I dislike him even more.

"And, look, one last thing," he says. "I'm sorry for jumping you in the woods. That was bad form. But I had to get the book and didn't want to blow my cover."

"Wait… that was you?"

Oh shit.

That doesn't make sense. I thought it was Marx or Gideon.

Katashi gets a funny look on his face and for a second I think he's piecing together that there's something wrong, but after a moment he says, "Like I said, I'm sorry. I thought you had the book on you. I didn't realize it was the wrong book."

He thinks I'm really angry. That's good. I mean, I am. But this means I was wrong about the book. He had *The Monkey Wrench Gang*. And they got the cipher at the black site.

"You are an asshole," I tell him.

"Well, here's a little payback. I would get far away from this place if I were you."

"What do you mean?"

"It means you're about to have some company."

He smiles his snake smile at me and leaves the bus, disappearing into the woods.

I don't like the way that sounds. I step out into the morning air. The rain seems to be picking up, but besides the sound of it tapping the leaves, the forest is quiet. The air is stagnant. Like all the animals up and left, anticipating something was about to go down.

I step into the bus, put all my belongings into a backpack, and cinch it tight to my back. Leave behind a few items of clothing that I feel like I can live without because I don't want to be weighed down. Go outside and count off the paces to my coffee can stuffed with cash. It takes a minute of digging to get down to it, and that, at least, is untouched. I take the money and stuff it in my bag. Wonder if I'll be coming back.

I run back to the main part of camp, get to the clearing as the rain is picking up and people are diving for cover. Tibo steps out of the kitchen and says, "I was looking for you. I called Ford..."

"It was the wrong book."

"What?"

"Katashi. He jumped me. They had the book and the cipher, but they still couldn't translate it, which means I had the wrong book."

"So... how do we find the right book?"

I nod toward the library, figuring that's as good a place as any to start. We step inside, the rain now nearly torrential outside. It's empty, so I pull off my backpack, stash it in a dark corner where it can't be easily seen—better that than it getting soaked—and walk the spiral stack reaching up to the ceiling.

"Let's work this out," I tell him. "First thing first. Why use a book cipher in the first place?"

"Easy to move around," Tibo says. "You can send it over e-mail or by the mail, and even if the wrong person sees it, it doesn't matter. You can't translate it unless you have the right book."

"Correct. Now, the Soldiers of Gaia are a terrorist group, right? Cells that aren't connected to each other. Clearly, because Pete was the only one here connected to them. Marx wasn't able to contact them, or else why need the cipher? So, think about that for a second. You've got a lot of people spread out like that..."

It hits me. Something I should have realized sooner. And maybe I would have, if I wasn't either drunk or withdrawing.

"What's the point of picking a book that's so damn hard to

find?" I ask.

"So you think it's something easier to track down," Tibo says.

"Maybe."

"How did you even settle on *The Monkey Wrench Gang* in the first place?"

"Cannabelle. She said she saw Pete carrying it around. I figured that was the book he had before he died. I found it in the library. I thought…"

"That's not precise at all. That's required reading for environmental activists."

I think back. The scene of Pete's death. There's something there. Something scratching at me. Something I saw that stood out as weird.

And then I remember.

WHOEVER SEARCHED MY bus seems to have searched Pete's tree house, too. Everything is put back in its place but still feels slightly off. Sitting out, like before, is *The Kiss of the Rose*. Seems I'm not the only person stupid enough to overlook it.

"That's it?" Tibo asks as I pick it up.

The cover says it's a *New York Times* best seller. I flip through to the copyright page, and find it came out last year. "This is new. And popular. Way easier to find."

"So whoever took the stuff you hid has bad information."

"Right. And it couldn't have been Katashi, or else he wouldn't have shown up this morning. So figure it's someone on Marx's team. Either way—I think we might be the only ones who actually have everything we need."

I pick up the book and pull out my phone. Still enough juice to see the cipher.

"Do you have a pen?" I ask.

"No."

"Let's go see the girls. They're close. Might help to have the computer, too."

We make our way out of the tree house, climbing down the branches, careful not to slip on the wet bark. I hop onto the boardwalk and jog for the camgirl house, which isn't too far away, Tibo right behind me. We get there and I knock. There's some shuffling inside and Sunny peeks her head out. I can't see anything past her collarbone, but she doesn't seem to be wearing any clothes.

"We need light and a computer and various other things," I tell her, stumbling over my words.

"Ash, we're broadcasting right now..."

Tibo pokes his head around. "Sunny, it's important. I'll hold you harmless on the camp's cut for the next two months if you stop the show and let us in."

Sunny thinks about it for a second and says, "Three months."

"Deal."

She disappears. There's murmuring inside. After a few moments Sunny opens the door in a flower-print robe. Moony is standing behind her, barefoot in a too-long t-shirt, face flushed, looking a little annoyed. I think there's a third person in the room with them, lying on the pillows at the center of the room, but then realize it's a blow-up sex doll with "NIK" written across the stomach.

We step inside and the bright light makes us both squint. Tibo looks around at the shelves, and the glittering rainbows of sex aids, and says, "That's an awful lot of dildos."

Moony smiles and shrugs.

Sunny sees the book in my hand and says, "Why do you have that piece of trash?"

"Hey, that wasn't a bad book," Moony says.

"Here we go again. She writes like a grade-schooler."

"Yeah, and she's also a multi-millionaire," Moony says. "Clearly she understands something about the world that you don't, smarty pants."

"Fine," says Sunny, rolling her eyes before she turns to us. "What's going on?"

I cross to the desk, grab a pen and a piece of paper out of the printer, sit on the chair next to the computer. Get to working on the cipher while Tibo explains to them, in broad strokes, what's happening.

I'm halfway through when Tibo finishes his story. He lets it settle and Moony says, "We think someone's been trying to get in here to use our rig. Like I mentioned to you the other night, Ash."

"I'm sorry I couldn't come by. There's a lot going on."

"You still owe us from the first time you used the computer."

"Yes, I know. Night bacon. We'll settle up. Right now we've got to settle this."

I finish the cipher.

It's numbers. A lot of numbers.

I don't know what to make of them. It's a long string. I tap the pen against the page. The three of them crowd around me, looking at the paper.

"What do you think?" Tibo asks.

"No idea."

Sunny kneels on the pillow next to me, adjusts her robe

to protect her modesty, and takes the pen and paper out of my hand. She looks at the cipher on my phone, starts counting off and putting slashes through at various points.

"What are you doing?" I ask.

"You did it as one long string," she says. "But look at the way the code is split onto different lines. Like new paragraphs. I think that means the numbers split up, too."

Once she's got the slashes through, she rewrites them in long rows.

After the first two, Tibo says, "Those look like coordinates."

The third row is much smaller.

"I think that's a date," Sunny says.

I take the paper and open an internet browser. I enter the coordinates into Google Maps and it pinpoints a spot about twenty miles away from here. A little fucking around on Google reveals that's the site for the fracking operation. Okay, that much I guessed already.

It's easy to lose track of time in the woods. Sometimes I'd be hard pressed to tell you what month it is, and that has less to do with drinking as much as I did, and more with the fact that time sort of comes untethered when you're not hooked into the grid.

So I have to look up at the top of the screen to verify the date.

It's today.

NINETEEN

THE RAIN IS really coming down now. We sprint for the front of the camp. Tibo yells over his shoulder, "We'll get a car. Get to the road. Call Ford."

But as we make it to the main part of camp, on the other side of the office dome, there's a roar, like a car engine, and a flash of movement. Something dark hurtling through the trees. The FBI van is back.

Katashi did say we were going to have visitors. That kind of slipped my mind.

"Where we found Cannabelle," I tell Tibo.

I run the other way, diving off the path and into some brush. Tibo breaks in the other direction. The place where we found Cannabelle is remote, overgrown and treacherous. The FBI is going to concentrate on the domes and tree houses, not empty stretches of woods. And it's close enough to the back road that I can get to Aesop's car.

I climb onto the boardwalk and run for a little bit, jump off, back into the brush, careful to aim for level ground, watching for things like small creeks and fallen logs and giant spiders in webs spun across trees.

The shitty feeling catches up with me. I try to keep myself steady, but stumble as the ground tilts up, fall to my hands and knees, scraping my palms on the ground.

Get back up and go.

I see the sign warning off visitors to Sunny and Moony. Come up on a creek and leap across, cut it a little close and end up splashing down into the cool water, soaking my shoes. Check around me so that I'm sure I'm not being followed. I stand for a second, breathe in deep, get myself centered.

It's quiet now, all around.

More running. More jumping. I get to the clearing where we found Cannabelle.

A branch appears out of nowhere, hitting me across the chest. I slam into it at full speed, nearly come off my feet, and hit the ground. My head comes down pretty hard. My vision goes wonky as the branch falls to the ground next to me.

There are hands on me, turning me over. Someone pulls my hands behind my back and wraps something hard around my wrists, digging into my skin. Pulls me up into a kneeling position.

I expect to see some asshole in an FBI getup, and instead find Gideon.

He's in a black t-shirt and black jeans and an actual fucking black beret, which if I wasn't zip tied right now I would smack him in his stupid face for wearing.

"Where you running off to?" Gideon asks.

My chest aches. I breathe through the pain. "I'm off to stop whatever tomfuckery you and Marx are up to. And since the FBI is raiding camp I figured it was as good a time as any to go."

He looks into the woods, his face strained with concern.

"I don't see anyone," he says.

"Well, they're there. I figure we have a little time before they show up here and fuck stuff up, but probably not long. How about you untie me so we can get through with me kicking your ass. Otherwise we're just delaying the inevitable."

He reaches behind his back, presents a small handgun and pulls back the slide. It makes a chik-chik sound, and a bullet flips into the air and lands in the grass next to us. He looks down at it, confused.

"Do you even know how guns work, you asshole?" I ask. "Cocking it is stupid movie bullshit. You wasted a bullet trying to look like a tough guy."

He purses his lips, reaches the gun back, and cracks me across the face.

Pain bolts through my skull and I fall to my side. I run my tongue along my teeth and taste blood. He pulls me back up and presses the gun to my head.

"I know how the trigger works," he says. "I figure that's all that matters."

For a second I am pretty sure he's going to pull said trigger, and it reminds me of the last time I was on my knees, surrounded by trees, with a gun to my head. I am not a fan of this trend. I tense my shoulders, say a prayer, and prepare for the lights to go out, when there's a crashing sound in the woods.

We turn and Tibo comes out of the tangle, sees us both, and puts his hands up.

Gideon takes a step back and raises the gun at Tibo. He's far enough away from me I can't dive at his legs. He waves. "Come over, turn around."

"Gideon, let's talk about this…"

"Get over here and turn around!" He screams it so loud his face goes red. Which makes me hope that one of our FBI friends heard it. I wasn't really excited to see them before, but this is the kind of party they're more than welcome to crash.

Tibo walks over and turns, puts his hands behind his back. Gideon zip ties them together, then kicks him behind the knees and drops him to the ground, the two of us now lined up next to each other.

That's thrown him off. He seemed happy to kill me a second ago. Now that he's got two people to handle, it's making things a little more complicated. I figure to lean into what I do best, which is make things worse.

"Nice fucking hat," I tell him. "What kind of look are you going for? Che Guevara's special needs brother?"

"Shut the fuck up, tough guy. Not so tough now, are you?"

"Matter of fact, I am. Because I don't need to hide behind a gun to threaten you. Take these zip ties off, let's have a fair fight. See how long you last. I bet you're on the ground before I get my fucking hands up."

"Shut up," he says.

He swings the gun across my face again. My head snaps back

and I go down. It hurts more the second time. I land on my side and stay there a bit. The rain, at least, feels nice.

"You fire that gun, you're going to bring the FBI over here pretty quick," Tibo says. "They're going to hear that."

Gideon looks down at the gun, and then at the both of us. I climb back into a kneeling position, push my tongue against my teeth to make sure none of them are loose. They don't seem to be, which is luckier than I deserve.

"Fine, then you're coming with me," he says. "Both of you, get up, now."

We climb to our feet and he gets behind us. Tibo is leading, with me in between them.

"Single file, let's go," Gideon says.

"Which way do we go?" Tibo asks.

"Back road."

We walk, Tibo leading the way. Gideon is behind me, but not so close that I can turn around quick and knock the gun away. Not that I even really want to do that, but it at least would have given us a chance. I listen hard, wonder if it's worth calling out for help, but that might piss him off enough that he shoots us.

Tibo glances over his shoulder. "So what's the plan, Gideon? Taking us to Marx?"

"No, I'm taking you someplace quiet, so I can kill you both and get this done with. This would have been a whole lot easier if you'd just eaten the damn mushrooms."

Well, that explains that.

"Fuck you very much," I tell him. "What does it matter anyway? You don't have the cipher. I bet you don't even have the right book."

"Neither did you," he says. "I found your stash. Lucky for us,

Marx sorted it out. The fracking site. It's a little last minute, but we've been getting ready for the past couple of days. Time to get to work."

"Well, good for him."

"Shut up."

We walk a little more. I run through scenarios in my head, try to come up with something that involves us not getting shot. Can't really come up with one.

"This is insane. You know that, Gideon?" Tibo asks.

"No, insanity is signing petitions and going to rallies and expecting things to change," he says. "The only way to get people to listen is to make them listen. That means hitting them where it hurts. That means not showing mercy. We have to show strength."

"Sounds like Marx has got his hand up your ass, working your mouth," I tell him.

"You think I'm wrong?" he asks. "Go ahead, tell me what peaceful protest has ever accomplished. Give me an example."

"How about you give me an example of a stupid fucking plan like this working?"

"We're revolutionaries. The tree of liberty must be refreshed from time to time with the blood of patriots and tyrants. Thomas Jefferson said that."

I laugh at that. "Thomas Jefferson was smart. You're a fucking moron. The thing is, you actually *are* a terrorist."

"Terrorists fight for outdated ideologies. We're fighting for the future. For the greater good."

"You know what the problem with people like you is?" I ask. "It's people who think their good is greater than everyone else's. You're all the fucking same."

"Don't make me hit you again," he says.

"So what are you going to do, exactly?" Tibo asks.

"Shut up," Gideon says.

"C'mon, you're going to kill us anyway."

The way Tibo says this is very cavalier.

"We're going to fuck them up good," Gideon says. "Destroy their operation so that they can't get back on track. At least, not without dropping a ton of money. That's the definition of hitting them where it hurts."

"And how is that some next level shit?" I ask.

"The security guards," Gideon says.

"What about them?" I ask.

"Work got suspended for a couple of days to resolve a permitting issue. There are two guards on site. And they're going to be dead men pretty soon."

Tibo stops and turns. So do I.

"Are you kidding?" Tibo asks.

"They're working for the enemy," Gideon says. "Ignorance is not an excuse."

That's the next level shit. That's the message they plan to send. They're going to kill innocent people to make a fucking point. That guy they drowned in pig shit, it wasn't an accident. It was a statement.

"You really are terrorists," I say.

"History will absolve us," Gideon says.

We're close to the road now.

And I find myself with a choice.

Let him kill me, or make a go of trying to stop him.

I might still get shot in the face anyway, but at least I'll have tried. There are innocent lives on the line now. It would be selfish to not at least make the effort. I slow down a little, thinking maybe that'll get him closer to me, and I can drop low, turn, and throw myself into him. Hopefully knock the gun clear, and he won't accidently fire at Tibo's back.

If this is how I die, I think it'll be worth it.

That brings me a nice little slice of serenity. Nothing will probably ever completely erase all the bad I've done, but it doesn't hurt to try.

Breathe deep.

Just as I'm about to launch, there's a grunt and crashing sound behind me. I turn to see Gideon falling into a heap, Aesop standing behind him, holding Gideon's gun, his hair and beard soaked and plastered to his face by the rain.

TWENTY

"YOU'RE ALIVE!" I yell, rushing forward and trying to throw my arms around him, before realizing they're still behind my back. I turn toward him. "Little help?"

He pulls a small knife from his belt, flicks out the blade, and cuts the zip ties. I turn and give him a proper hug. His eyes look sunken, his skin waxy, but he's all there.

"Guys," Tibo says, pushing us apart. "We kinda have to go. Right now."

Aesop frees Tibo, takes the gun, and puts it into the belt loop of his pants while I pull some zip ties out of Gideon's pants and bind his hands behind his back, then his ankles together. He fights against it but he's not going anywhere.

"You fucking assholes have no idea who you're fucking with," he says, spitting.

I kneel down to him and smile. "You are very lucky I wouldn't hit a guy who's tied up. Because, frankly, you deserve it."

"Help!" he screams. "Help!"

Well. That'll serve to draw the FBI. We make for the back road and there's a car parked behind Aesop's. Presumably the one Gideon was using. The trunk is popped open and inside are two handguns, a shotgun, a hunting rifle, a pile of zip ties, and three canisters of gasoline. There's also a duffel bag covered in dirt.

The dirt. Cannabelle's hands. They must have had this stuff buried out in the woods. She saw it, went rooting around, ended up dead. Good money is on Marx. Me and him are definitely going to have this one out.

"Should we take some guns?" Tibo asks.

"None for me, thanks," I tell them. "I don't like guns."

Tibo shrugs and picks up the shotgun. "Never hurts to be prepared."

He cocks it and a shell ejects, tumbles through the air, and hits the ground.

"Does no one here know how guns work?" I ask.

Aesop takes the shotgun out of Tibo's hands, cocks it until all the shells have been ejected, and hands it back. "Use it like a bat if you need to. But I'm not getting shot because you don't know how to use a gun. I'm going to hold on to Gideon's."

I hand him his keys and we climb into his car. As he turns over the engine, I tell him, "Stop." Jump out of the car and run my hand under the wheel wells. On the right passenger side is a small black box, connected magnetically to the underside of the car. I toss it out into the woods.

"FBI was tracking you," I tell him.

"Fuckers!" Aesop yells.

He slams on the gas, spins the car around, and guns it in the other direction. Within moments we're tearing ass down the road, away from the main road. I haven't been this way before. We drive for a little bit until we're on another service road, and he cuts a hard left.

"So what happened to you?" I ask him.

"Since I only ate a little and puked it up, I was pretty much fine," Aesop says. "Lots of charcoal and fluid and tests. They wanted to keep me in observation but I told them to fuck off. We talked it down to some follow-up tests in a week to make sure my liver function and electrolyte levels are good. I feel run down but I think that's more from not sleeping well in the hospital."

"Glad you're back in it. Especially given the timing."

"What about you? How are you doing?"

"Been better, but I'm not seeing snakes and bugs everywhere I look, so that much is nice."

"Hello? Hello." I turn, thinking Tibo is talking to me, but he's on his cell phone. "Ford, it's Tibo. Listen, we have a problem. That thing we were talking about before? We found them. You need to come meet us."

He gives the town and road we're headed to, and clicks off.

"So, what now?" Aesop asks.

"We keep going," I tell him.

"You mean we try to stop them."

"We're already on the road," I tell him. "We might beat Ford. They're aiming to hurt innocent people. We can't sit by and let that happen."

Aesop smiles. "That works for me."

WE STOP AT the end of a long dirt road leading up a hill. There's a sign for the project at the foot of the road. METCO ENERGY, with a bunch of laminated permits stuck up underneath that. To the right, there's a wide expanse of nothing, just flat land stretching to the horizon. To the left, a long line of trees.

Aesop pulls the car into the trees, until we're well off the road and out of sight. We don't speak.

It feels good to be with Tibo and Aesop for this.

Even if it's a stupid fucking thing to be doing.

But until Ford gets here, it's up to us.

The ground is flat, and we walk in deep enough that we can still see the open field to our right. We march single file, Aesop in the lead, since he's the one who actually has real-life experience with stuff like this.

After a little while he stops and puts his fist up.

I look off into the distance, but it's more trees and forest and open space. He flattens his hand and lowers it, then folds to the ground. We follow suit, and he crawls forward. I follow behind. The canopy is thick enough to keep most of the rain off us, so the ground is wet but not saturated. Tibo struggles a little, dragging the empty shotgun along with him.

Aesop cuts a path to the right, going slow now. As we get closer to where the forest turns into open field, I can make out shapes. Then, trailers, and finally the full construction site. The tree line circles around a little, like a hook, bounding us in.

There are three trailers in total, all of them close to us. Over by the road, there's a bulldozer and a backhoe, sitting quietly as they're pelted by the rain. They're dwarfed by something that looks like an oil rig, but I guess is for fracking. A giant erector set of steel, sticking a few stories into the air. It looks half-finished. There's a crane next to it, and big neat piles of thick steel rods, and sheets of metal, and a cement mixer.

The place looks abandoned. But then someone comes around the trailer. Someone I haven't seen before. Tall guy, broad shoulders, blond beard and dreadlocks wrapped in a rainbow bandana. He's got a hunting rifle held tight to his chest. Given the way he's dressed I peg him as a Soldier rather than a proper security guard.

There's more movement around the tower. I tap Aesop and point. Trigger Warning Katie is hauling a propane tank, which she places at the base of the fracking thing.

We watch the sentry for a little bit. He's walking a clear path. Once he makes his fourth circuit Aesop gets up without warning and runs to the trailer, staying low, waiting at the point where the sentry is going to pop into view next.

My heart slams in my chest. I fight to keep my breathing steady. I've seen some shit but I've never been in a situation like this before. Thank Christ for Aesop. He moves with complete confidence, like this is what he does all day.

With him on our side, I feel like we actually have a shot.

The sentry comes around the bend and Aesop moves so fast it's hard to keep track. He grabs the rifle, jabs the barrel into the guy's face. The sentry's nose erupts and he goes down as Aesop waves us over. Tibo and I get up and follow, running to the spot where Aesop chose, out of view of the fracker and the windows of the trailers. Aesop has the guy on the ground, wrapping him up in the zip ties we took off Gideon, the rainbow bandana already shoved into his mouth.

Aesop presses his gun against the guy's head.

"I'm going to take this out of your mouth and you're going to tell me how many of you there are, and where you're holding the security guards. Understand that you would not be the first person I've killed. So no fucking around on me, okay?"

Aesop pulls the bandana out. "Where are the guards?" he asks.

"Second trailer. The one next to this one."

"You understand what's going to happen if you lie to me?"

"Yes."

"You understand that you're a bunch of stupid fucking kids and I'm a Marine, correct?"

Pause. Then he nods. "Yes."

"Good."

Aesop shoves the bandana back in his mouth. We go to the edge of the trailer and peek around. There are now a couple of people at the fracker. Magda and another guest, a stocky, bald-headed guy in jean shorts and a tank top. I think he's from Ohio but I don't remember his name. They've each got propane tanks, which they're loading around the base of the tower.

"Here's the play…" Aesop says.

He's cut off by the roar of an engine. For a second I'm thankful, thinking maybe it's Ford come to the rescue. But it's a ragged black pickup truck, no lights or sirens, and it comes to a stop next to the far trailer. Out climbs Marx. He's annoyed, looking around like he expects to see something but doesn't. He pulls out his phone, dials it, holds it to his head. Waits a minute and shoves it back in his pocket. Probably waiting for Gideon.

Marx pulls two gas cans out of the back and proceeds to the trailer with the hostages and pours gasoline around the base of it. There's a gun tucked into the back of his pants.

“What now?” Tibo asks.

“We stall until Ford gets here.” Aesop turns to me. “You and Tibo, head over to the tower. I’ve got Marx.”

“Why do you get Marx?” I ask.

“I understand that we all want to kick his ass, but we can’t be greedy now.”

“Fine.”

Tibo and I wait until the coast is clear and Marx has turned completely away from us, and we take off at a run toward the fracking tower, dive for cover behind a pile of steel beams. We look over and Aesop is moving quietly behind Marx, who now has an unlit road flare in his hand.

I take the gun from Tibo.

“What the fuck are you doing?” he asks.

“I’m way more threatening than you are.”

“Fair point.”

We come out on the other side of the construction equipment. I don’t like holding the shotgun but I feel better about it not being loaded. It makes me miss the umbrella I used to carry. The steel rod with a Kevlar top. It felt far less aggressive. And it would be way more useful right now, given the rain.

We find Magda, in a green sundress and green shawl and green ceramic jewelry that clacks as she gestures to points around the derrick, instructing Katie and the other guest to place bags of fertilizer.

The sound of the rain covers the sound of our footsteps, so we get pretty close to them and they still haven’t noticed we’re here. I clack the shotgun, not that it makes a difference at this point, and they turn.

"Ash," Magda says.

"That's me."

"What are you doing?"

"What are *you* doing?" I ask.

"What's going on?" Katie asks.

"Shut up," I tell her, swinging the gun in her direction. None of them seem to be armed, which is good. I nod to Tibo. "Tie them up."

Tibo goes to each one of them in turn and zip ties their arms behind their backs, then says, "Get on the ground." They follow his order, and he lashes their ankles together, too.

"You're just tools of the fucking patriarchy," Katie says. "You know that, right?"

"Don't use words unless you know what they mean," Tibo says. "If anything, we're fascists."

"You know we're not actually fascists, right?" I ask him.

"You are fascists," Katie says. "Defending a system that's killing you. Do you know what this is going to do to the surrounding environment? You're going to wake up one day and find the water at South Village isn't drinkable. What then?"

Tibo pauses. Thinks that over. I can see the wheels turning. He shakes his head. "Doesn't mean you kill innocent people."

She smirks. "No one is innocent."

"Oh, shut the fuck up," I tell her, then turn to Tibo. "Now let's check on Marx and Aesop."

We book it back over to the trailer. We round into the clearing between them and find Aesop is on his knees, Marx holding a gun on him. Another guy, tall and lanky and balding, is holding a rifle on him. The sentry is here too, untied and back in the game. It's raining hard now, getting in my eyes and mouth, turning the earth around us into giant pools of mud.

"Well, that went to shit quick," I say, and point the shotgun at Marx.

He points the gun up at me. The sentry points his gun at me, too. The third guy, Lanky, keeps his gun trained on Aesop.

"Sorry, guys," Aesop says, hands in the air, glancing down at the road, hoping for the same thing I am: That Ford will come tearing up here with backup.

"It's fine," I tell him "I'm not going to let you live this down, though. This fucking dickhead with his stupid fucking hat getting the drop on you."

"My hat isn't dumb," Marx says.

"Yes it is," I tell him. As I say this I inch closer to him, thinking maybe I'll get close enough that I can swing the gun. Something. Anything. Because it's not like I can shoot him. At least he doesn't know that.

"You know the cops are on the way, right?" Tibo asks. "I called the sheriff."

Lanky and Sentry look at each other, suddenly nervous.

"I'll tell you what," I say to the two of them. "If you get going now, you'll have a head start. You might even get gone before they get here. Wouldn't that be nice? Live to save a whale another day."

Sentry shakes his head. "Fuck this. I'm done."

He throws down his gun and runs for the trees.

Lanky grips his gun tighter and points it at me.

Well, I evened it up a little.

"What exactly do you think you're going to accomplish?" Tibo asks. "You're not going to change anyone's minds. You'll end up in prison if you're lucky, and dead if you're not, and the world will hate you. Nothing will change."

"We have to try," Marx says.

"So terrorism is the answer?" I ask.

"It's not terrorism if it's done for the right reasons."

"You are so full of shit," I tell him. "You and your fucking fantasy about your parents. The FBI knows all about you, and the lies you've told. It's kind of pathetic."

This makes Lanky pause and narrow his eyes. And it really pisses off Marx, to be found out.

"The only thing that matters is results," he says, nearly spitting. "And we're about to get some. We'll sacrifice ourselves for the greater good if we have to."

We stand there in the rain. Aesop on his knees, looking for an opening. Tibo behind me, with no idea what to do. Lanky with his gun on Aesop, Marx with his gun on me.

And my gun empty.

This whole thing sucks.

Then I get an idea. It's a ridiculous idea, but that's better than no idea.

"Oh hey look it's the cops," I say, looking at a blank point down the road, beyond Marx and Lanky.

The two of them turn to look.

Dummies.

Aesop follows my lead. He launches himself into Marx at the same time I dive forward and swing the shotgun like a bat, catching Lanky across the face. He goes cross-eyed and hits the mud. I pull the gun away from him as he falls. Tibo is on him quick with the zip ties. I turn to Aesop. The gun got thrown wide, and he and

Marx are untangling from each other.

Marx and Aesop get standing across from each other, both of them covered in thick patches of mud. I slide in next to Aesop.

"I can't believe that actually worked," he says.

"Sometimes you have to keep it simple," I tell him. "Now, should we shoot rock-paper-scissors on this?"

"Why don't you take it," he says.

"How generous." I turn to Marx. "Before we start I need to know. Did you kill Cannabelle?"

"I had no choice."

My body fills with rage like water rushing to fill an empty space. The image of Cannabelle lying on the ground comes back to me. Dead like dead doesn't look in the movies. Sweet to me when she had no reason to be.

"There is always a choice," I tell him.

He growls and comes at me fast. I move to the side and drive my fist into his stomach as hard as I can. He doubles over, hits his knees, falls on his hands. Pukes on the ground. I kick him in the stomach to flip him over, take a knee on the ground, and drive my fist into his face as hard as I can.

Seems he's not as tough as he presented himself.

I've gone against sloppy drunks with more fight in them. But I shouldn't have expected much from a pampered rich kid pretending to be a freedom fighter.

I reach my fist back, ready to hit him again.

Remember what happened the last time I let this feeling take over.

"There is always a choice," I tell him.

I get up, turn him over, press his face into the mud. Tibo binds his hands. I step out to the road and see the vague form of a van coming our way.

"Finally, the fucking cavalry," I say.

Aesop says, "I'm going to check and see what they did to the tower. You see about the hostages."

He takes off at a run and I duck my head into the trailer, see a black guy and a white guy in gray uniforms, tied up to chairs and blindfolded, with heavy headphones stuck over their ears. The kind construction guys wear when they're jackhammering. They don't look to be in pain or distress. I'm about to go inside and free them when the sheriff's van pulls up. Ford jumps out of the driver's seat, gun in his hand, pointed at the ground. Corey climbs out of the passenger's seat, cradling a shotgun.

"What the hell happened here?" Ford asks.

Aesop comes back up to us, leading the three people we tied up at the derrick, all of whom step underneath an awning of a trailer to get out of the rain.

"None of these fucking idiots know how to blow anything up," Aesop says. "They stacked propane tanks and bags of fertilizer up and they were going to light it on fire. That's not how bombs work. They didn't even pick the right kind of fertilizer."

"Will someone please explain to me what in the fresh fuck is going on?" Ford asks.

We take turns, each of us filling in parts of the story. The FBI raid. The Soldiers of Gaia. The plot to overthrow the camp. The stash of weapons and Cannabelle's death.

No one says anything about Pete.

I think we're going to chalk that up to being an accident.

Technically, it was.

When we get through it Ford nods, walks around the tied up folks.

"Really wish you kids had clued me into this sooner," he says. "Y'all cut it a little close. Especially wish you told me about those FBI assholes. It's nice to know when they're fucking things up in my backyard."

"Speaking of, why hasn't the FBI stormed in here?" I ask.

"I didn't call them," Ford says.

"Why not?" Tibo asks.

"Because this is a win for the home team. I don't want them taking the credit," he says, gazing up at the fracking derrick. "You boys, come with me."

"What about the guards?" I ask.

"If they're safe then they can sit another minute or two."

When we're out of earshot of the Soldiers, he asks, "What are we going to do about this?"

"What do you mean?" Tibo asks.

"I mean these fucking things are bad news, son," he says, nodding toward the derrick. "I don't want my sink turned into a fucking flamethrower."

"That's a whole other battle," Aesop says.

"Right," Ford says, adjusting his cap against the rain. "What I'm saying is that the community is really upset about this. And they should be. There is a very good chance people are going to suffer because of this thing. It'd been better if it didn't go up in the first place. Almost makes me feel bad. Like maybe if we didn't arrive in time, they would have taken it down."

"Not with the gear they were using," Aesop says.

"Do you not get what I'm saying, son?" Ford asks, smiling.

"How about I put it in terms you'll understand." He nods toward the pickup truck that Marx drove up in. "That car belongs to them? It'd do a fair bit of damage if it crashed into that. Set these assholes back real good. Best part is, no one gets hurt and the community comes out of it with their land intact. It's too bad we didn't get here in time to stop it. Right, Assistant Sheriff Corey?"

"Flame thrower sinks, you say?" Corey asks.

"Yes, son. That's not the kind of thing I want to wake up to in the morning." Ford looks at the derrick again. "Listen to me carefully, boys. There's nothing around that monstrosity over there, nothing with your prints on it? Any people there?"

Aesop shakes his head.

"Good. Now, I'm glad we brought the van. I'm going to load these people into the back. We're going to radio someone to meet us at the bottom of the road to pick us up. Since you say the guards aren't in distress, we'll just come back for them. What happens between now and then, I can't right say. That thing was a flaming wreck when I got here. You catch me?"

"Got it," Tibo says.

He shakes our hands each in turn.

"I'm not saying these dumb kids were right," Ford says. "I don't want to endorse their plan. But sometimes a man has to step up and take the shot that's been afforded him, know what I mean?"

"Yes, sir," I tell him.

He tips his cap at me and heads back, loads everyone into the van, all of them shooting us dirty looks. Magda says, "Tools of fascism."

"Oh shut up," Ford says. "If anything we're the tools of a totalitarian government, and even that's hyperbole at best."

Ford gets into the car with Corey and they drive off. I walk toward the pickup truck with Tibo and Aesop and ask, "Which one of us is going to do the honors."

"C'mon," Aesop says to Tibo. "Find a cinder block or something."

Aesop goes to the car, turns it on, and puts it in neutral. Then he lashes his belt to the steering wheel. Tibo waddles over carrying a cinder block, which he hands to Aesop, who drops it onto the gas pedal. The engine races.

"Stand back," he says.

He climbs into the car and shifts it into drive. It leaps forward, headed for the tower. After twenty or thirty feet, after it seems it's going to stay straight, he dives out, hits the ground hard, and rolls. Tibo and I run over to him, to make sure he's okay, just as the truck smashes into the concrete base, crumbling the wall, the front flattening.

Aesop gets up, shaking it out.

We watch the wreck for a second, a little disappointed that it didn't do more damage. The car is still running, wheels spinning in the mud, wisps of black smoke coming out of the engine.

"Well that's too bad," Aesop says.

And then the car explodes.

That leads to three or four bigger explosions. I can feel the pulse of them pushing through my body, the heat washing across us like a wave. It throws thick plumes of smoke into the air and we watch it burn for a few minutes. The part of me raised by my dad goes into alarm mode, wanting to pull out my phone and call emergency services.

But I don't have to. We did this.

"You know what this means?" Aesop asks. "We're technically terrorists."

"No, we're not," I tell him. "This is how you do a good thing a bad way. I hope the Soldiers aren't able to claim credit for this."

"I suspect Ford will work something out," Aesop says.

"Guys. Why the fuck are we still here?" Tibo asks.

"Good point," I say.

And we take off for the tree line.

TWENTY-ONE

THE SUN COMES out. None of us speak. There's not much to say. I think we're all carrying the explosion of the fracking derrick in our chests. It was something I don't think any of us were really ready for.

And afterward, we're shocked at the efficiency with which we just did something like several hundred thousand dollars' worth of damage.

A little bit down the road, we pass a long line of black, shiny cars, like beetles gliding down the road. Hopefully the FBI is off to the crime scene and away from South Village for good.

Aesop pulls into the front entrance and over the bridge, and once we're parked, Tibo jumps out of the car, off no doubt to see where he's needed and start moving pieces back into place. Aesop says to me, "We really ought to go check on Gideon."

"Do we have to?" I ask.

"You can slap him around a little if he's still there."

"That works."

We walk in silence, climbing onto the boardwalk and cutting through the woods. I stop at a board that says: *Go where the peace is.* Tap it with my toe. Keep walking.

After we pass the sign for Sunny and Moony's place, he says, "I'm happy to see that you're feeling better."

I stop. After a moment he senses this and he stops too, turning around to face me. The two of us, standing in the middle of the woods, alone and quiet.

"What you said," I tell him. "About knowing you can die. About all this being fragile. It helped. I don't know why. It just did. And I want to thank you for that."

He smiles. It's an easy, comfortable smile.

"I'm glad to hear that," he says. "Truthfully, sometimes I think it's less about the message and more about knowing you're not carrying shit by yourself. You know what I mean?"

"Yeah, I think I do. I just… I guess I wasn't used to people being nice to me. But you, and Cannabelle, and even Tibo, even though he got frustrated with me."

"I know you think you're a bad person," Aesop says. "But you're not. You could have done anything when you got here. You could have taken permanent machete duty and been by yourself all day. But you chose to cook. You chose to feed people. Even at your darkest, you picked a task that would mean giving comfort and nourishment to other people."

Aesop looks up into the canopy, then down at the ground. Kicks at a board.

"Do you know why I cook?" he asks. "It's not because I have any particular affinity for it. It's just… I told you I saw some shit. I had a hard time when I came home. And cooking was something I picked up that covered up all those bad feelings. It gave me a sense of purpose. Across all cultures, across all demographics, food and hospitality are a shared bond. You sit down and break bread with strangers, it's a way of communicating ourselves. After what I did, it feels important to use my hands to create something. To feed people. Do you understand what I mean?"

I sniff and look down, and he's about to say something else when I dive forward, put my arms around him. I'm afraid that after I leave I will never see him again but this has been important to me, and I want him to know that, but I don't know how to say it.

So I hold him, and hide my face so he can't see that I'm close to crying. He hugs me back and we stay like that until finally he pulls back a little and says, "C'mon dude, lay off the theatrics. All you have to do is buy me a drink."

I laugh and we disengage. Walk some more. Get to the spot where we left Gideon, and he's gone. Check the back road, and the car with the weapons in the trunk is gone, too.

We head back toward the main camp and Aesop says, "C'mon, I want to show you something."

He leads me to the artist hut, and the painting that's hanging, untouched by the raid, safe from the elements. He opens up a beer cooler and takes out jars of paint, arranging them carefully on an open table. I step to the painting. Cannabelle was the last person I saw working on it.

A swirl of colors, like a wave curling up, one side of the wave a treescape, the other side of the wave a starscape. They come together like they're part of the same scene, but encroaching on each other in small measures. Trying to find a middle ground between two different stories.

Aesop hands me a jar of paint that's white with a tiny bit of blue mixed in so it's tinted. He nods toward the starscape.

"Go ahead," he says. "The sky could use a couple more stars."

"Are you sure? This was Cannabelle's."

"This is everybody's. Do you know how long this has been here?"

"How long?"

"Years," he says. "It's kind of incredible that it's still standing."

He unscrews the top of the jar of green paint he's holding, dips in a brush, and lays the wet point of it against a dry leaf on the forest side of the painting.

"It changes and it grows," he says. "The original images are still there. I could probably take a knife and pull off bits and show you the layers of color. Point is, nothing ever has to be the way you think it has to be. Cannabelle knew that. I don't think we're going to get a chance to memorialize her. Body got shipped off to the family. So we do this. This is our memorial for her. And one day someone will come along and put something over it, and that'll be okay, too. She'll still be there underneath it."

"Okay," I tell him.

And I lay the brush over the black, bring a little light to the universe.

I PACK MY STUFF. This time in far less of a rush. I check my passport again. I've never had a passport before. Showed up yesterday, and my flight leaves tomorrow. Glad to see Katashi, or whatever the fuck his name was, didn't follow through and have the document pulled.

I check my phone, the harsh white light filling the bus. It's 2 in the morning. A few hours to go before Aesop and I need to be on the road, if I'm going to make it to the airport in time.

The last few days have been busy. Cleaning up camp. Restoring order. Lots of talking to cops and investigators, but luckily their gaze is on the folks they captured, and they're not too worried about us. Ford came through. The official story is that Marx and his crew planned to set off an explosion but messed up. The truck crashing into the tower was an accident. They come out of it looking like buffoons. And they were credited as the Earth Liberation Front, not the Soldiers of Gaia. They can't even make a name off it.

The fracking operation is permanently suspended, too. No kitchen sink flamethrowers.

I'm still a little conflicted over this. It was pretty awesome to blow something up, and I know what we did was for the greater good of the community. I've done a lot of illegal things in my life. This is pretty much way up at the top.

But at night, I sleep, and that gives me comfort.

Sometimes I dream about my dad and Chell.

But not about the hole. That's gone.

I step off the now-empty bus, close the door. Climb onto the boardwalk and head toward the back of camp. It's a nice night. A little cool, finally. The air turning to fall and the brutal summer behind us. The world is changing. I wonder what this place is like when it gets cooler. Less bugs, probably. The fires are probably more welcoming. I'm sad that I'll miss it.

I reach the clearing toward the back of camp, where a fire is already going. Alex and Job are sitting on a log, Job is plucking away at an acoustic guitar while Alex hums the tune to "Redemption Song." A little clichéd and yet so completely perfect. Zorg is here too, and Sunny and Moony, and Aesop and Tibo. And Robert and Ginger, making out like teenagers.

Aesop takes a canvas bag and pulls out three packages of bacon while Zorg sets up a cast iron skillet on a grill grate, which Tibo is feeding with kindling. Getting it nice and hot and ready so I can fulfill the promises I made.

This is my goodbye party.

It makes me think back to home. The night I left New York. There was a goodbye party there, too. Apocalypse Lounge was closing, and it was snowing, and there was a great big party, mostly to send the bar off, but some people there to see me off, and the thought of picking through the crowd, trying to say goodbye to every person, it was too much. So I pulled an Irish goodbye. Up and left before anyone realized I was gone.

Thinking back on that now, I regret it. Here, now, I'm happy to get a farewell.

And I could not think of anything more perfect than night bacon.

Aesop is about to cut open a package when I stop him and say, "We didn't do the circle."

Everyone stops and looks at me, like they don't understand how those words could have come out of my mouth. And then smiles break out across the clearing, faces turning up in the dancing orange light.

Tibo's is the biggest.

We take our spots around the fire, hands reaching out to each other. I end up with Aesop on my left and Zorg on my right, Tibo directly across from me.

"Would you like to start?" Tibo asks me.

"Yes," I tell him. "Community. I'm thankful for community."

"I'm thankful for community, too," Aesop says.

Everyone answers with 'community.' And when we're done we stand there, looking at each other in the glow of the fire. Really looking at each other.

After a few moments, we let go.

Aesop throws the bacon onto the skillet. The scent of it fills the forest and we sit and talk. People ask me questions about my life, how I got there, and I tell them honestly, even the parts that hurt. They share the things that hurt them, and their paths that brought them to the Georgia woods in the middle of the night, sharing fistfuls of bacon in secret.

As we're cleaning up, as the sky is cycling shades of blue, I realize Chell and my dad, they're still there, out in the darkness. But it doesn't feel like they're accusing me of anything.

It just feels like they're with me.

ACKNOWLEDGMENTS

Thank you to Bree Ogden and Jason Pinter for their continued support of both me and this series. Thank you Rayne, for your intel on the inner workings of camgirls. Huge thanks to the booksellers who've carried my books, including Seattle Mystery, Powell's, Poisoned Pen, MysteryPeople, The Astoria Bookshop, Murder by the Book, Barnes & Noble, and The Mysterious Bookshop. Plus all the bookstores I don't know about. Support bookstores! Thank you to my wife, Amanda, for giving me the space to do this. You are the best of wives and best of women. And most of all, thanks to everyone reading this book.

ABOUT THE AUTHOR

Rob Hart is the publisher at MysteriousPress.com and the class director at LitReactor. Previously, he has been a political reporter, the communications director for a politician, and a commissioner for the city of New York. He is the author of two previous Ash McKenna novels: *New Yorked*, which was nominated for the Anthony Award for Best First Novel, and *City of Rose*. He is also the author of *The Last Safe Place: A Zombie Novella*. His short stories have appeared in publications like *Thuglit*, *Needle*, *Shotgun Honey*, *All Due Respect*, *Joyland*, and *Helix Literary Magazine*. He's received both a Derringer Award nomination and honorable mention in *Best American Mystery Stories 2015*, edited by James Patterson.

He lives in New York City.

Find more on the web at
www.robwhart.com and on
Twitter at @robwhart.